"What the hell did you just do?"

"Hope came here asking for a job, Parker, and I gave her one. Okay?" Lydia raised her brows. "We owe her that much, don't you think?"

He scrubbed a hand over his face. "We might owe her," he said. "But I'm pretty sure we can't afford to give her anything."

"You're overreacting, Parker. She's only going to work here. That doesn't mean anything. We don't even know how long she's going to stay."

"It means I'll have to see her every day."

"So will I."

"She could destroy The Birth Place—destroy you."

"I know."

"She could take Dalton away from me," he said, his voice gruff with emotion.

"She's not going to take Dalton away. She doesn't suspect anything. She just needs a break."

"You're a fool," he said angrily, and walked out.

Lydia stared after him. "Tell me something I don't know."

Dear Reader,

The comment I received repeatedly from people who read this book when it was only in manuscript form was that it's "compelling." I hope that's true, because as I wrote it, the characters seemed to come to life, and the choices they made truly moved me. They prompted me to take a closer look at issues that have always intrigued me—what makes some of us do the things we do, believe what we do, accept or reject what others tell us is "right"? I don't pretend to have the answers to those questions. But I certainly enjoyed watching Hope draw her own conclusions.

The research for this story took me to Hillsdale and Colorado City, a small community straddling the Utah/Colorado border and inhabited by polygamists. Yes, as hard as it is to believe, they still exist. Many of them live there, in rambling houses that are purposely left unfinished. The only grocery store is a co-op, to discourage trade with outsiders. There is one gas station and a sprinkling of businesses. The people are unique, and I think visiting there added color to my story.

It was a pleasure to be able to work with such talented authors as the five who have written the rest of the books in THE BIRTH PLACE series—Darlene Graham, Roxanne Rustand, C.J. Carmichael, Kathleen O'Brien and Marisa Carroll. I hope you'll have the opportunity to enjoy their books, too.

I'd love to hear what you think of *Sanctuary* or any of my other work. Please feel free to contact me at P.O. Box 3781, Citrus Heights, CA 95611. Or simply log on to my Web site at www.brendanovak.com to leave me an e-mail, check out my news and appearances page, win some great prizes or learn about my upcoming releases.

Best wishes,

Brenda Novak

brenda novak

Sanctuary

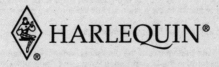

HARLEQUIN®

TORONTO • NEW YORK • LONDON
AMSTERDAM • PARIS • SYDNEY • HAMBURG
STOCKHOLM • ATHENS • TOKYO • MILAN • MADRID
PRAGUE • WARSAW • BUDAPEST • AUCKLAND

ISBN 0-373-71158-1

SANCTUARY

Copyright © 2003 by Brenda Novak.

This edition published by arrangement with Harlequin Books S.A.

® and TM are trademarks of the publisher. Trademarks indicated with
® are registered in the United States Patent and Trademark Office, the
Canadian Trade Marks Office and in other countries.

Visit us at www.eHarlequin.com

Printed in U.S.A.

To Thad, the youngest in the family
and a little boy who's larger than life. Thad, you might be
only six, but you already possess the heart of a lion.
The way you deal with the difficulties you face each day
leaves me shaking my head in wonder and admiration. You
go, sweetheart—nothing can ever stop a man with courage
like yours. If you forget everything I've ever taught you,
remember this: my love is everlasting.

Books by Brenda Novak

HARLEQUIN SUPERROMANCE
 899—EXPECTATIONS
 939—SNOW BABY
 955—BABY BUSINESS
 987—DEAR MAGGIE
1021—WE SAW MOMMY KISSING SANTA CLAUS
1058—SHOOTING THE MOON
1083—A BABY OF HER OWN
1130—A HUSBAND OF HER OWN

HARLEQUIN SINGLE TITLE
TAKING THE HEAT

PROLOGUE

The Birth Place
Enchantment, New Mexico
June, 1993

LYDIA KANE had keen, shrewd eyes. Hope Tanner stared into them, drawing strength from the older woman as another pain racked her. The contractions were coming close together now—and hard, much harder than before. Her legs shook in reaction, whether from pain or fear, she didn't know. She didn't feel as though she knew much about anything. She was barely seventeen.

"That's it," Lydia said from the foot of the bed. "You're getting there now. Just relax, honey, and breathe."

"I want to push," Hope panted. Though the baby wasn't overdue, Hope was more than anxious to be finished with the pregnancy. Lydia had put some sort of hormonal cream inside her—on what she called a cervix. The older woman said it would send her into labor. But the baby was proving stubborn. The pains had started, on and off, at sundown, and only now, when it was nearly four o'clock in the morning, were they getting serious.

More of God's punishment, Hope decided. She'd run away from the Brethren, refused to do what her father said was God's will, and this was the price she had to pay.

"Don't push yet," Lydia said firmly. "You're not fully

dilated, and we don't want you to tear. Try to rest while I see what that last contraction did.''

Hope stared at the ceiling as Lydia checked the baby's progress. She was tired of all the poking and prodding, but she would never say so. Lydia might think her ungrateful. After being alone for most of her pregnancy, wandering aimlessly from town to town, Hope wasn't about to do anything to anger the one person who'd taken her in. Lydia was so decisive, so strong. As much as Hope loved and admired her, she feared her a little, too. Lydia owned the birth center and had to be sixty years old. But she wasn't a soft, sweet grandmotherly type, certainly nothing like Hope's own patient mother. Tall and angular, with steel-gray eyes and hair, Lydia often spoke sharply, seemed to know everything in the world and had the ability to make other people—and apparently even events—bend to her will. She took command like Hope's father, which was an amazing concept. Hope hadn't known women could possess so much power.

''Is everything okay?'' Hope asked, weak, shaky, exhausted.

''Everything's fine.'' As Lydia helped her to a few more ice chips, the pendant she always wore—a mother cradling an infant—swayed with her movements and caught Hope's attention. Hope had long coveted that pendant. She craved the nurturing and love it symbolized. But she knew she'd never experience holding her own child so close. Not *this* child, anyway.

After mopping Hope's forehead, Lydia went back to massaging one of her feet. Lydia claimed that pressing on certain points in the foot could ease pain—she called it reflexology—but if reflexology was helping, Hope certainly couldn't tell. To her, its only value seemed to be in providing a slight distraction.

''It shouldn't be long now,'' Lydia assured her, but she kept glancing at the clock as though she was late for something and as eager for the baby to be born as Hope.

"I'd transfer you to the hospital if I was the least bit worried," she continued in the same authoritative voice. "This is dragging on, I know. But the baby's heartbeat is strong and steady and you're progressing. First babies often take a while."

Lydia had once mentioned that she'd been a midwife for more than thirty years. Certainly after all that time she knew what she was talking about. But Hope was inclined to trust her regardless of her professional experience. It was men who always failed her—

Another contraction gripped her body. Biting back a tormented moan, she clenched her fists and gritted her teeth. She didn't know how much more she could take. It felt as if someone had a knife and was stabbing her repeatedly in the abdomen.

Except for the music playing quietly in the background, the place was quiet. Parker Reynolds, the administrator, and the other midwives and clerical people who worked at the center were long gone. They'd left before Lydia had even induced her. She and Lydia were the only ones at The Birth Place. With its scented candles, soft lighting and soothing music, the room was meant to be comfortable and welcoming, like home. But this room, with its turquoise-and-peach wallpaper, Spanish-tile floor and wooden shutters at the window, was nothing like the home Hope had known. She'd grown up sharing a bedroom with at least three siblings, oftentimes four. If there were candles it was because the electricity had been turned off for nonpayment. And the only music she'd been allowed to listen to was classical or hymns.

"Good girl," Lydia said as Hope fought the impulse to bear down.

At this point Hope didn't care if she caused herself physical damage. She felt as though the baby was ripping its way out of her, anyway. She just didn't want to displease Lydia. The ultrasound she'd had several weeks earlier indicated she was having a girl, and Lydia had prom-

SANCTUARY

ised that her daughter would go to a good home. Hope didn't want to give her any reason to break that promise. Mostly because Lydia had painted such an idyllic picture of her baby's future. Her baby would have a crib, and a matching comforter and bumper pads, and a mobile hanging above her head. She'd have doting parents who would give her dance lessons, help her with her homework and send her to college. When the time was right, they'd pay for a lovely wedding. Her daughter would marry someone kind and strong, have a normal family and eventually become a grandmother. She'd wear store-bought clothes and listen to all kinds of music. She'd feel good about being a woman. Better than anything, she'd never know what she'd so narrowly escaped.

Hope wanted sanctuary for her child. She wanted it more than anything. After her daughter arrived and started her princesslike life, it wouldn't matter what happened to Hope.

She would already have given the only gift she could.

She would have saved her daughter from the Brethren.

"THE DEAL'S OFF," Lydia stated flatly, entering her office cradling Hope's new baby.

Fear nearly choked Parker Reynolds at this announcement. He glanced briefly at his father-in-law, U.S. Congressman John Barlow, who'd been waiting with him, before letting his gaze fall on the baby they'd come to collect. "Is something wrong?" he asked. "Is Hope okay?"

"Mother and baby are both fine, but—" she split her gaze between them "—it's a boy."

A boy... Parker's heart pounded in his chest like a bass drum. A boy could change everything. "Does Hope know?"

"I haven't told her yet, but—"

"Perfect!" his father-in-law interrupted. "You were worried how it would look to have Parker and Vanessa receive a newborn baby so soon after Hope gave birth. Now they won't have to relocate, and you won't have to hire a new administrator. There's no chance of anyone putting two and two together.''

Torn, Parker shoved his hands in his pockets and turned toward the window. After two miscarriages, his wife had never been able to get pregnant again. Now her health was too bad to continue trying. She was ill and miserable and so depressed she couldn't get out of bed even on good days. She claimed that having a baby would make all the difference, that it would give her the will to survive.

He believed it would. He believed it was his responsibility as her husband to save her somehow. But because of Vanessa's health, there wasn't an adoption agency anywhere that would work with them. This was his only chance....

''The baby's sex played a big part in her decision to give up the baby,'' Lydia explained.

''I don't give a damn if it did,'' John replied. ''She can't provide for a boy any easier than she can a girl. She's a seventeen-year-old runaway, for crying out loud. What can she offer this child?''

Parker felt his commitment to what they were doing waver even more. Two weeks ago, when he'd approached his father-in-law with this idea, it had all seemed so simple. Vanessa needed a baby. Hope's baby needed a family. Lydia needed money to keep the center afloat. But it didn't seem so simple anymore. It seemed almost surreal.

''Hope deserves the right to make an informed decision,'' he said.

''Like hell,'' John countered. ''She doesn't deserve a damn thing. From what you told me, Ms. Kane has housed her and cared for her during the last two months.''

''I had no ulterior motives when I took her in,'' Lydia said.

''I'm not here to argue about the purity of your motives," John replied. "Just keep the bargain. I've already paid you the money."

Lydia tightened her hold on the baby. "I'll pay you back."

"When?"

Parker knew that wasn't an easy question to answer. For the past six months the center had been inches away from closing its doors. The money had been spent on payroll and utilities and supplies.

"As soon as I can," she snapped.

"Considering that you pump every dime you have into this place, I don't think you're a very good credit risk," John said. "And I don't want the money back. I want the baby you promised us."

Lydia looked beaten as she gazed around the office. "This center has been my life," she said. "It's what I've fought for and loved for more than thirty years. But this time I've gone too far. What we're doing goes against everything I believe in."

"What we're *doing?*" John said. "You've already done it, Ms. Kane. You did it when you took my money." He motioned impatiently with one hand. "But you're making a bigger deal of this than it has to be. You're not doing anything that's going to hurt this baby's mother. So you've told her you're putting her baby up for adoption. In a way, you are. It might not be through a legitimate agency, but that doesn't matter? You—"

"Doesn't matter? How can you say that?" Lydia interrupted. "What we're doing is illegal, Congressman. You, of all people, should know that."

Parker's father-in-law assumed his "political" face. "The legality of the issue isn't the point here. The point is that this child isn't in any danger. He's going to a good home, and you and I both know it."

Lydia stared down at the baby for a long moment before lifting her gaze to meet John's. "Your daughter is ill. As much as I hate to say it, and as much as you two might not want to face it—'' here she gave Parker an apologetic glance ''—there's a chance she won't make it. That's why she couldn't get a baby through the regular channels.''

''You think I don't know that?'' Parker's father-in-law thundered, forgetting his ''let's smooth this over'' act. ''I know my daughter isn't well. That's why I'm not about to tell her she won't be getting this baby!''

Parker was watching their reflection in the glass, sometimes trying to see beyond the pane to the wooded landscape outside. He'd been tempted to jump in at several points and voice an opinion. But he wasn't completely sure if he agreed with John or with Lydia. He knew how badly his wife longed for a baby. He wanted to give her one. But now that the tiny infant he was supposed to take home had arrived, he was more bothered than he'd expected to be by the fact that he had no legal or blood right to claim him—more bothered than he'd expected about lying to young Hope. There was something so fragile, so innocent about the girl. Her pretty face lit up whenever she received the smallest kindness. Though part of him trusted that a baby would somehow help his wife improve, the rest of him felt lower than dirt for taking advantage of a vulnerable girl's desperation and trust—and letting his father-in-law buy something he had no right to buy. Especially because he'd grown up living just down the street from Lydia. He'd known her most of his life; she'd recruited him just after he'd graduated from college. He hated that he'd also taken advantage of her desperation to save the clinic.

''What difference does it make where the baby goes so long as he's well cared for?'' John asked Lydia. ''If you put the baby up for adoption, there's no guarantee he'll go anywhere better. At least you know Parker and Vanessa will love the child and care for him as their own.''

''It's still selling a baby,'' Lydia said, her shoulders drooping.

"Then pay me back someday if it'll make you feel better, but let Vanessa have her baby."

Pivoting away from the window, Parker finally broke his silence. He understood Lydia's pain, felt responsible for it. But they'd come too far to turn back. "Lydia, you know I'll give this child everything I have. And he might make all the difference to Vanessa."

She stared at him for several seconds before slowly crossing the room. "Then you'd better take him home," she said. "And I don't ever want to talk about this incident again. As far as I'm concerned, it never happened." With that she swept from the room, leaving Parker holding his son for the very first time.

CHAPTER ONE

Ten years later

GRIPPING THE STEERING wheel until the knuckles of both hands turned white, Hope Tanner drove into the very last place she wanted to be: Superior, Utah, population 1,517. Part of the town immediately brought back fond memories—the family-owned grocery where, when she was little, Brother Petersen had often given her a licorice rope; the elementary school she'd been permitted to attend for two years, the place she'd discovered art and that she enjoyed creating it; the town hall, with its tower and four-sided clock, which had always infused her childish heart with a sense of pride.

But there was also the meeting house with the hard pews where she and her twenty-nine siblings had sat for hours each Sunday to hear the Holy Brethren extol the virtues of polygamy and communal living, or the "principle" as they called it; Aunt Thelma's bakery, where they ordered the wedding cakes for each of her father's weddings; the old barn where—

Briefly, Hope squeezed her eyes shut. Not that memory, she told herself. Not for anything.

It had been eleven years since she'd run away from Superior, eleven *hard* years, but she'd survived, and she had an education now, a steady nursing job and a small rental house three hours away in St. George. As much as she missed her mother, she would never have come back to this place if not for her sisters.

Steering the old Chevy Impala she'd bought from one of her neighbors through the intersection that marked the middle of town, Hope turned left at the park, the easternmost part of which served as a cemetery, and swung into the gravel lot. Because it was barely noon and most members of the Everlasting Apostolic Church were still in church, the park was empty. But soon it would be crowded with women and children and possibly a few men, those who weren't sequestered at the meeting hall deciding who would give the sermon next week, whose daughter would become the plural wife of which elder, which family's claim for more grocery money was based on need and which on greed. It was Mother's Day, and on Mother's Day, after worship, practically everyone came out for a picnic. If Hope was lucky, she might see her sisters. If she was extremely lucky, she might even have the opportunity to talk to one or more of them while her father and the rest of the Brethren were still at the church.

Hope's hands grew clammy around her keys, and her heart seemed to rattle in her chest as she got out of the car and stepped into the shelter of some cottonwood trees, where she hoped to go unobserved until she was ready to venture forth. The smell of cut grass and warm earth permeated the air as butterflies, mostly black, fluttered from one daffodil to another. The gleaming white headstones in the neighboring cemetery seemed to watch her like a silent audience, waiting in hushed expectation for the drama of the day to unfold.

Turn around, go home, her mind screamed. *What are you doing? You've spent eleven years recovering from what happened in this place. Eleven years, for God's sake. Isn't that enough?*

It was more than enough, but Hope wouldn't let herself leave. Maybe Charity, Faith, Sarah or LaRee wanted out.

Maybe, sparse though her resources were, she could help them.

Fortunately, it wasn't long before she saw what she'd been waiting for—a group of women and children walking down the street, carrying bowls and baskets and sacks of food. They entered the park near the jungle gym in the far corner, and the children immediately scattered, laughing and calling to one another as the women made their way over to the picnic tables. Dressed in plain, home-sewn dresses that fell to the ankles and wrists—somewhat reminiscent of pioneer women—they wore their hair high off their foreheads and braided down their backs, and no makeup.

The Brethren frowned on any show of vanity or immodesty, just as they opposed modern influences that might entice their women and children away from the church, influences such as education or television. Consequently, few if any of these women had a college degree. Most hadn't graduated from high school. To outsiders, they pretended to be sisters or cousins to the men they'd married while living cloistered lives with very defined roles. Men worked and gave what they earned to the church, had the ultimate say in everything and took as many wives as they pleased. Women, on the other hand, were relegated to cooking, cleaning and bearing and raising children; they were threatened with eternal damnation if they were too ''selfish'' or ''unfaithful'' to share their husbands.

Hope was one of the rebellious. She hadn't been able to make herself comply with her father's dictates, hadn't been able to live the ''principle.'' Not for God. Not for her beloved mother. And certainly not for her father. In the minds of her family, her soul was lost. And maybe it was. Hope wasn't sure if she was going to hell. But she felt pretty sure she'd already been there.

She crept closer, staying among the trees as she began to recognize people. A thick-set woman in a blue floral dress looked vaguely like the first Sister Cannon, while the tall crone was probably one of Garth Huntington's wives. Raylynn Pugh Tanner, the youngest of her own father's wives—at least when Hope was around eleven years ago—stood in the middle of the chaos, as plain as ever with her wire-rimmed glasses and thin brown hair pulled into a tight braid. She wore a dress loose enough to make Hope believe she was either pregnant or had just delivered a baby, and was busy pointing to a willowy girl that Hope, at first, didn't recognize. "Don't put the desserts on that table, Melanie," she called. "Can't you see we don't have it covered yet?"

Melanie? Hope's fingers dug into the trunk of the tree she was using both for support and for cover. Melanie had been a baby when she'd left. Look at her now! How many more children had her father had? How many more women had he married?

The last Hope knew, Jedidiah Tanner had six wives. Sister Joceline—Hope had always been required to call her father's wives "Sister" because they were all daughters of God and sisters in His kingdom—was his first wife and had given him four boys and five girls. Sister Celia had followed Joceline, even though she was a few years older. Hope had once heard that Celia had difficulty conceiving. Or it was possible that after the initial newness of the marriage wore off, her father had simply refused to visit her bed. They'd never seemed particularly compatible, which made plural wives quite a convenience for a man. Jedidiah could simply go to the other side of the dilapidated duplex Celia lived in or to the trailer across the street and bed down with another of his wives. In any case, Celia only had two children, both girls. Sister Florence, her father's third wife, had six boys and two girls. Marianne, Hope's mother, had born five girls and, to her father's tacit disappointment, no sons.

Sister Helena had four boys and one girl, and Raylynn, the sixth and final wife—at the time Hope left, anyway—just had Melanie. Although they were separated by only two years, Hope had never liked Raylynn. From the beginning, she'd been bossy and outspoken, and had all but taken over the running of Marianne's household, at least when Jed wasn't around. A woman rarely had an entire house—or even mobile home—to herself, so Raylynn had come to live with Marianne, which had given Hope plenty of opportunity to get to know her.

The composed, ethereal Helena, however, who'd lived down the block in an old brick house built when the town was first founded in the early 1900s, was different. Hope had loved her. Unfortunately, Helena had always been Jed's favorite, too, which made her a pariah among his other wives and children. Hope and her mother had never been able to hold Jedidiah's partiality to Helena against her. Helena was too sweet, too withdrawn, as though she'd rather not be noticed at all. Even now, Hope saw her standing off to the side, staring into the distance, and wondered, as she often had as a young teen, what was going on behind the serenity of Sister Helena's face.

Hope forgot all about Sister Helena and the others the moment she spotted her own mother. Marianne was late joining the party and was trudging across the uneven ground in a dress so similar to one she'd owned eleven years ago Hope couldn't be certain it wasn't the exact same. Two girls, one about twelve and the other fourteen, tagged along behind her, bearing rolls and a ham, and Hope immediately realized they had to be her youngest sisters.

They'd grown so tall; she doubted she would have recognized them had they not been with her mother. Even Marianne had changed. Her clothes now hung on her like garments on an old wire hanger, and her hair was completely gray. She looked at least twenty years older, instead of only a decade.

Bitterness toward her father and guilt for abandoning her mother swelled inside Hope. She'd always been her mother's right arm and her only confidante.

Of all the places in the world, her family had to be

from here, Hope thought, watching her sisters deposit the ham and rolls on the table closest to them. By some counts, there were 60,000 practicing polygamists living in Utah, northern Arizona, Idaho, Montana and parts of Mexico and Canada. So Superior wasn't the only place where people practiced plural marriage. Most polygamists existed in relatively small communities made of up several families that espoused the same doctrines. But those doctrines weren't necessarily the same from group to group and had ventured far from the original Mormon beliefs that had spawned so many breakaway sects. The most conservative insisted sex was only for purposes of procreation. Others, like her family's church, believed a man could have sex with a woman at any time as long as she "belonged" to him.

Still, there were 1,517 souls in Superior, and only half of those were members of the Everlasting Apostolic Church. The chances of being born here, in this small community, had to be a billion to one.

Unfortunately, the chances of getting out were about the same.

The weight of her purpose finally propelled Hope back to the car, where she retrieved the flowers she'd cut from her yard for her mother. She had to make her presence known as soon as possible. She'd have a much better chance of an honest conversation with her mother and sisters while her father wasn't around. Considering the years that had passed since she'd last had contact and the way she'd left, it wasn't going to be easy to reach them, even without her father's interference. Her mother believed that God's acceptance required her to submit to her husband's will, which made it almost impossible to get her to listen to anything that didn't come directly from him or the pulpit.

Taking a deep breath, Hope walked resolutely toward the picnic area.

Sister Raylynn, with her eagle eye, noticed her first and

used her hand for shade so she could see better. Her jaw sagged, and, for an interminable moment, Hope felt the old fear and confusion return. The strictness of her upbringing, the emotional blackmail her parents and the leaders of the church had used to control her actions, the overwhelming competition she'd always felt for any crumb of her father's attention and the sermons railing about the fiery fate of the wicked—all those feelings and memories closed in, threatening to suffocate her. She could almost feel the flames licking at her ankles….

But then she saw her closest sisters. Charity, five years younger than Hope at twenty-two, had a child propped on one hip and a toddler at her feet. Faith, now almost nineteen, was pregnant.

Raylynn said something and pointed. Her mother stopped wiping the mouth of the child Charity held and they all turned to look, their faces registering alarm or surprise, Hope couldn't tell which.

Just as quickly, she felt her throat tighten and begin to burn. How she'd missed them. It had been forever since she'd last seen her family, but she'd carried them in her heart into a world that had little idea about who polygamists were or how they lived or—most especially—why they did the strange things they did.

Because of her background and her allegiance to these people, Hope had always stood apart. Alone. That aching loneliness had occasionally tempted her to return. But she could never rejoin them. If she couldn't live the principle at sixteen, she could never live it now.

"Hope, is it you?" her mother said, her voice faltering when Hope drew near.

Hope stopped a few feet away and tentatively offered Marianne the flowers, along with a tremulous smile. "It's me," she said. "Happy Mother's Day."

Her mother pressed one shaking hand to her bony chest and reached out with the other, as though to accept the bouquet or cup Hope's cheek. But Raylynn interrupted.

"Good, here he comes," she said. "It's okay, Marianne. You don't have to deal with this negativity. Jed's here."

Her mother's hand dropped, and dread settled in the pit of Hope's stomach as she looked up to see her father entering the park. A scowl generally served as his customary expression—anything less would have been frivolous—but his face darkened considerably when a little girl ran up to him and brightly announced, "Her name's Hope, Daddy. I heard her say it. Ain't she pretty? Ain't that a pretty name, Daddy?"

Her father passed the child without acknowledging her. Tall and imposing in an Abraham Lincoln sort of way, he still wore his beard untrimmed. Two gray streaks broke the black of it at each corner of his mouth, accentuating his frown. He'd lost a good deal of his hair; his face, on the other hand, hadn't aged a bit. Time couldn't soften his granitelike features any more than it could soften his granitelike heart.

"What is this? What's going on here?" he cried, his long legs churning up the distance between them. Next to him hurried her two uncles, Rulon, a taller version of her father, who had eight wives at last count, and Arvin, the runt of the family—and the man she'd refused to marry. Arvin was almost skeletal in appearance. The bones of his hips jutted out beneath a tightly cinched belt, and his chest appeared concave beneath his wrinkled white shirt. But at fifty-six, he still had his hair. Black and stringy, it fell almost to his shoulders. He was older than her father by a year, yet she would have been his tenth wife.

Hope's grip on the flowers instinctively tightened. She wanted to leave, but her feet wouldn't carry her. Not while Charity was standing in front of her looking so haggard and careworn at twenty-three. Who had her father arranged for Charity to marry?

"Hope's back," her mother volunteered in a placating tone as Jed reached them.

Her father's eyes climbed Hope's thin frame, the frame

she'd inherited from him. She knew he was taking stock of the changes in her, making special note of her khaki shorts and white cotton blouse. She was dressed like a Gentile, an outsider, and he wouldn't like that any more than he'd approve of the fact that her apparel showed some leg. She'd considered wearing a long dress, but that was too great a concession. She was part of these people, and yet she wasn't. She was an outcast. As much as she missed her sisters and her mother, the years she'd spent here seemed like another lifetime. She now knew the freedom of driving and making her own decisions, the power of education, the joy of being able to support herself. She lived in a world where women were equal to men. She could speak and be heard and have some prospect of making a difference.

That was what she wanted to give her sisters. A chance to know what she knew—that there were others in the world who believed differently from their father. A chance to get more out of life.

"Father," Hope murmured, but the old resentment came tumbling back, making the word taste bitter in her mouth. If not for his final betrayal, if not for his favoring Arvin's salacious interest over her happiness, maybe she wouldn't have done what she'd done in the barn. Maybe she wouldn't have had to pay the terrible price she'd paid.

"You have a lot of nerve showing up here on a day meant to honor mothers when you're guilty of just the opposite," her father snapped.

"I've never meant Mother any disrespect." Hope glanced meaningfully at Arvin. "I would have dishonored myself had I done anything different."

"You flouted God's law!" Arvin cried, her acknowledgment of his presence enough to provoke him.

"God's law? Or your own?" she replied.

"That's sinful," her father said. "I won't have you talking to Arvin that way. He's always loved you, was nothing but good to you. You were the one who wronged him.''

Briefly, Hope remembered her uncle's eager touches when she was a child. His long, cool fingers had lingered on her at every opportunity, and he'd always been quick to take her to the potty or clean a skinned knee. He'd scarcely been able to wait until she was old enough to bear children to ask her father for her hand.

''He had no right to press his claim once I refused him. I was only sixteen,'' she said.

Her father waved her words away. ''Your mother was only fifteen when she married me.''

''That doesn't matter. I would have been miserable.''

''Heaven forbid I should do something to displease such a princess!'' her father bellowed. ''Was I supposed to support you in feeling too good for a worthy man? Was I supposed to give in to your vanity? God will strike you down for your pride, Hope.''

''God doesn't need to do anything,'' she said. ''What you've done is enough.''

''Hope, don't say such things,'' her mother pleaded.

But the old anger was pounding through Hope so powerfully now she couldn't stop. ''What you've done in the name of religion is worse than anything I've ever even thought about doing,'' she told her father. ''You use God to manipulate and oppress, to make yourself bigger than you really are.''

Her father's hand flexed as though he'd strike her. He had beaten her a few times in the past—like the night she'd fled Superior—but Hope knew he wouldn't hit her now. Not in front of everyone. If he assaulted her, she'd have a legitimate complaint to file with the police, and the Everlasting Apostolic Church wanted no part of that. Though it was next to impossible to enforce the law, polygamy was, after all, illegal and there had been a few isolated cases in which polygamists had actually gone to prison, though mostly for related crimes and not for polygamy per se.

Still, the murmuring in the crowd that was quickly gathering told Hope she'd gone too far. She'd come with the intention of being diplomatic, of reassuring herself of her family's well-being and seeing if she could do anything to help her sisters. Instead, she'd disparaged the church and her father. But she couldn't help it. She was viewing their lifestyle with new eyes, and too little had changed.

"I'm going to have to ask you to leave," her father said.

It was a public park, but Hope didn't bother pointing that out. Her father had always believed that his power extended beyond the normal domain. Among his family and in the church, it did. For him, there was no world outside of that and, if she stayed, she'd only make matters worse for the others.

She glanced at Faith and Charity. "Anyone here want to leave with me?"

Her sisters stared at the ground. Her mother opened her mouth as though she longed to speak, but then clamped her lips firmly shut.

"All right, I'll go," Hope said when no one spoke, but Faith caught her by the arm.

"It's Mother's Day," she said, appealing to their father while clinging to her. "Can't Hope stay for an hour or two?"

"It's been so long since we've seen her," her mother added. "She doesn't mean what she says. I know she doesn't."

"Why does she have to leave at all? I think we should celebrate," Faith said. "You know the story in the Bible about the prodigal son returning. This should be a joyful time." She hesitated. "Even if she doesn't plan on staying long. At least we get to—"

"You keep out of it, missy. I'll not have her poisoning you, too," Arvin said, and something about the proprietary tone of his voice told Hope that Faith was more than just a niece to him now. Was that his baby her sister carried?

The thought made Hope ill. She'd come too late for Charity *and* Faith. A profound sadness swept through her as she gazed at her beautiful eighteen-year-old sister.

Again Faith wouldn't meet her eyes.

"I meant every word," Hope told her father.

"Then leave, and don't bother coming back," he said.

Hope took in the many women and children surrounding her—the adults, the teenagers, the babies and all those in between. "I won't. You have so many children, what's one twenty-seven-year-old daughter more or less?"

Dropping the flowers on the ground, she turned and stumbled blindly to her car. She couldn't save anyone here, she realized, swiping at the tears that rolled down her cheeks. They were too firmly entrenched in the lifestyle, too easily manipulated by the visions and visitations her father claimed to have.

Just as she used to be.

But when she reached the parking lot, the same little girl who'd called her pretty a few minutes earlier hurried out of the bushes and intercepted her before she could open the door of her car. The child had obviously been running and had to pause for sufficient breath.

"Faith said…" *pant, pant* "…to tell you to meet her at the cemetery…" *pant* "…tonight at eleven."

CHAPTER TWO

HOPE SAT ON ONE of the swings in the park, which was lit by a bright moon and the streetlight across the street, while she waited for Faith. Her sister had asked to meet at the cemetery, but Faith would have to pass the swings to get there, and Hope had no desire to go inside. Not because it was spooky in the Halloween sense. She didn't like Superior's cemetery because the stooped and weathered headstones represented the people who'd never escaped the yoke of the Everlasting Apostolic Church. Her mother would be buried there, and so would her sisters when they died, even though they'd never really lived....

"Hope? Is that you?"

Faith's voice came from the darkness behind her, and Hope turned. "It's me. Come have a seat."

Her sister moved into the moonlight, one hand braced protectively against her swollen abdomen, and Hope was struck by how far along Faith must be. Eight months? More?

Faith looked carefully around as though she feared being seen. "Thanks for coming."

"Do you want to talk somewhere else?" Hope asked. "We could go for a drive."

"No. If I get in that car with you..." Faith let her words fall off and took the swing next to Hope, using her feet to sway slowly back and forth.

If she got in the car, what? Hope nearly asked, but she didn't want to press Faith. She wanted to give her the chance to say what she'd come to say.

An old truck rumbled down Main Street. Hope could see it stop at the light glowing red near the corner of the park, then take off when the signal changed, but there wasn't much traffic in Superior, especially this late at night. The Everlasting Apostolic Church didn't believe in shopping or going out to eat on the Sabbath, so the few businesses that did open on Sunday closed down by five, even the gas station.

"So you can drive?" Faith asked when the rumble of the truck engine dimmed and the only sound was the creaking of their swings.

Hope nodded. "I learned how when I was nineteen."

"Where did you go today? After you left the park?"

"Up to Provo. I thought it might be more interesting to shop at a different mall."

"Provo's pretty far away."

"I had the time." With a deep breath, Hope studied her sister. "It's Arvin, isn't it?" she asked. "The father of your baby."

Faith's face contorted in distaste. "Yes. How'd you know?"

"It wasn't difficult to guess."

Silence.

"So how is it, being married to Arvin?"

"How do you think? He pretends to live the Gospel, but he's really arrogant and mean and stingy."

Somehow, even as a child, a sixth sense had warned Hope about the existence of a dark side beneath the eager smile Arvin had always offered her, together with the candy he carried in his pockets. Hope had done everything possible to keep her distance from him, which had eventually led to her outright rebellion. Faith, on the other hand, possessed a calmer, more long-suffering temperament. Hope had last seen her when she was only eight years old, but even then Faith had been a peace lover. A typical middle child, she was like a kitten that immediately curled up and purred at the first hint of praise or attention—the most patient and tractable of Marianne's five daughters.

And this was what Faith's good nature had brought her, Hope thought bitterly, staring at her sister's rounded stomach. Arvin's baby.

"Did Charity refuse to marry Arvin, too?" she asked. "Is that how it fell to you?"

Frowning, Faith cast Hope a sideways glance. "What you did eleven years ago embarrassed Daddy in front of the whole church. I don't think he wanted to push Charity into doing the same thing."

"She would have refused?"

Faith shrugged. "Charity's more like you than I am."

"Are you saying a woman should marry a man she detests for the sake of her father's pride?"

"No." Faith's swing continued to squeak as she moved. "Arvin always admired you. He'd been asking Daddy for you since you were small, and Daddy had already promised him, that's all. I'm just trying to explain why Daddy did what he did."

"I know why he did it, Faith. But that doesn't make it right. I was in love with someone else."

Her sister stopped swinging and scuffed the toe of one tennis shoe in the dirt, as though finally cognizant of the fact that the generous skirt of her cotton print dress had been dragging. "*That* was the other reason Charity didn't have to marry Arvin," she said.

"What do you mean?"

"I'm talking about Bonner."

The mention of Bonner's name sent chills cascading down Hope's spine. "What about him?"

"His parents came over a couple of years after you left and said they'd been praying about Bonner's future, and God told them Charity was to be Bonner's first wife. They said God wanted to reward him for not running away with you."

Reward him? For clinging to the safety of his parents

and their traditions, even though he didn't believe in them? For breaking her heart?

Hope told herself to breathe, to suck in air, hold it, then silently let it go. The pain would ease… "So Charity's married to Bonner?" she asked, her voice sounding small and tinny to her own ears. "Those are *his* children I saw with Charity today?"

"Actually they have three," Faith said. "You probably didn't see the oldest. Pearl, LaDonna and Adam."

Hope thought about putting her head between her knees to stop the dizziness washing over her, but she told herself that after eleven years she could take news like this. What she felt for Bonner had dulled into disappointment long ago, hadn't it? This was no more than she should have expected. "Does he have any other wives?"

"He had to take the Widow Fields."

"Because…"

"Because no one else wanted her, I guess. She petitioned the Brethren, and that's what they decided. It was sort of a consensus."

Hope didn't know what to say. Though Bonner wasn't yet a man when they'd pledged their love, only a boy of eighteen, she'd expected so much more from him. It was as though he'd never whispered those things to her in the dark, as though he hadn't helped hatch the plan that had culminated in so much heartache.

"He married JoAnna Stapley, too, about three years ago. And he's already asked for Sarah, when she's old enough," Faith added.

Mention of another sister caused Hope's scalp to crawl. "He wants Sarah?"

"Why not?"

"She's only fourteen!"

"She's so excited to get a husband under the age of forty she's willing to marry him now."

Hope sighed in disgust and resignation. "That's crazy, Faith. She's still a child. And he'll be thirty-two by the time she turns eighteen, which isn't so much younger than forty.''

"Maybe to the outside world it seems strange, but not here. You've been gone a long time.''

Too long. Or not long enough. Hope couldn't decide which.

"Why'd you come back?" Faith asked. "Was it because you were hoping that…maybe…Bonner had changed his mind?''

Hope touched her own stomach, once again feeling the phantom kicking of Bonner's baby in her belly. She'd thought a lot about Bonner over the years, had dreamed he'd change his mind and somehow find her, that the two of them would recover their child and become a family. But she knew that if he hadn't had the strength to leave before, with their love and their child at stake, he never would.

When Hope didn't respond, Faith grasped her swing. "I'm sure he'd take you back," she said. "I saw it in his face when Charity told him you'd been at the park.''

"You're mistaken.''

"No, I saw regret and…and pain.''

Whatever pain Bonner had suffered couldn't compare to what Hope had endured. That much she knew. "So you think I should become his…what? Fourth wife?" she asked, chuckling bitterly. "That'd make Jed happy.''

"It would," Faith said earnestly.

Hope shook her head. "No, it would smack too much of me finally getting my way, and he couldn't set that kind of precedent. He still has two daughters to coerce into marriages they may not want. Maybe he's even planning to give them to Arvin.''

Faith visibly cringed. "I don't think so. He's not very pleased with…with the way Arvin treats me. Deep down, he knows you were right about Arvin. Daddy's just not ready to admit it.''

How many daughters was it going to take?

"How'd you get away tonight?" Hope asked. "I can't imagine that after seeing me in town, Arvin would stay anywhere but with you."

"He and Rachel, the seventeen-year-old Thatcher girl, were married a week ago, and he hasn't tired of her yet. He likes his women young—real young, Hope. He would hardly leave me alone the first year we were married. But then I got pregnant. He finds my swollen belly... unappealing, so now he almost always sleeps elsewhere."

"Does that bother you to know he's with others?"

"No, I'm grateful. I can hardly stand it when he touches me," she said with a shudder.

Bile rose in Hope's throat at the thought of her eighteen-year-old sister not being young enough for Arvin. Or maybe it was the mental image of him touching Faith in the first place that bothered Hope so much. "We should call the police," she said. "If Rachel's not eighteen, that's statutory rape."

Faith's shoulders slumped. "I can't do that to Daddy. It would bring too much negative publicity on the church and hurt families who are trying to live the principle the way it's meant to be lived."

Hope had some questions as to how the principle was meant to be lived in this day and age. But she understood that Faith would be much more sympathetic to the church's beliefs than she herself would, especially after being away so long. "Sexual predators shouldn't be tolerated in any community. Even one as tightly knit as this," she said, sticking with a line of reasoning Faith could not refute.

"I don't think you can call him a predator," she said. "Rachel married him willingly enough. And he's careful not to touch anyone who isn't his wife."

"Are you sure about that? What about his children?"

"I don't think he's hurt any of them," Faith said, but

the lack of conviction in her voice made Hope more than a little nervous.

"Have you talked to Jed about your suspicions?"

"What suspicions? I said I don't think he's hurt any of his children."

"You're worried that he might."

Her sister didn't answer right away.

"Faith?"

"Okay, I tried to talk to Daddy about some of the things Arvin's said to me, but he didn't want to hear. Arvin's his brother and a pious church member."

"Pious?" Hope scoffed.

"He pretends to be, especially to the other Brethren. And you know the police won't do anything. You've heard Daddy say it a million times: 'This is America. It goes against the principles on which this country was founded to persecute people for their religious beliefs. We're just living God's law. Are we supposed to forget what our God has told us just because man decides we should?'

Hope was willing to concede that respect for religious freedom might be a small part of the reason the police typically left polygamists alone. But she knew politics were at work, too. In 1957, the last time authorities had made any kind of concerted effort to stamp out polygamy, television stations had aired newsreels of fathers being torn from their crying wives and children, and public sentiment had quickly turned against the police and their efforts.

"The police will help if we can prove that children are being abused," she said.

"That's the problem. I have no proof. Just this nagging sense that something isn't right with Arvin."

Hope had experienced the same nagging sense eleven years ago. But it was tough to convict someone on suspicion alone.

"They love you, you know," Faith said out of nowhere, spinning the conversation in a new direction.

"Who?" Hope said.

"Daddy. Bonner. Maybe even Arvin."

"I doubt that."

"Well, Daddy does at least."

"There's no room in a heart filled with such beliefs."

"I know he's passionate about the church, Hope. But he'd let you come back. You just have to show him you're willing to repent."

Hope had already repented. She repented every day—for trusting an eighteen-year-old boy who said he loved her more than life. And for being financially unable to care for the child he'd given her. But she knew that wasn't the kind of repenting sweet, innocent Faith was talking about. "And that embarrassment you mentioned earlier?" she said. "How could Jed forgive me for something so monumental?"

If Faith picked up on the sarcasm in Hope's voice, she gave no indication. Her face remained as solicitous as ever. "He'd have to forgive you, Hope. The Bible says, 'For if you forgive men their trespasses, your Heavenly Father will also forgive you. But if you do not forgive men their trespasses, neither will your Father forgive your trespasses.'"

Hope knew what the Bible said. Verse after verse had been drilled into her from birth. She'd scarcely been allowed to read anything else. But she hadn't so much as glanced at a single page in the entire eleven years she'd been gone. Because of the way the scriptures had been used—as a tool to force her into a life she didn't want—just the sight of the black simulated-leather binding made feelings of claustrophobia well up in her. "Seventy times seventy," she muttered.

"That's right," Faith said. "If you come home, the Brethren will insist that Daddy forgive you, even if he won't do it on his own. And then you and Bonner can be together at last.''

She and Bonner… ''Along with a couple of my sisters and the Widow Fields?''

''Is that so bad?''

''Maybe not to you.''

''Then marry someone else, someone who refuses to live the principle, too. Maybe someone who's not even a member of the church. There're people here in Superior who don't believe in plural marriage. And there're other towns close by. You don't have to separate yourself from us completely.''

''I thought marrying outside the church precludes me from heaven,'' Hope said just to hear her sister's response.

''I don't know, Hope,'' Faith said. ''I don't pretend to know much about heaven anymore. If there is one, I'm having a tough time believing in it. Since I married Arvin…well, Mother would say that my faith is being tested.'' She offered Hope a weak smile. ''But I'm not so certain everything the church teaches is really true. If it is, why are we the only ones who believe it? Surely we're not the only people on earth who are going to heaven. Anyway, I know this much—family is all we have in this life. And we've missed you. Daddy might have thirty-five children, but Mother has only five, and you're one of them. She hasn't been the same since you left.''

Hope couldn't help reaching for her younger sister's hand. They'd lost eleven years they'd never be able to recover and she regretted the pain she'd caused her mother. ''Faith, I appreciate what you're saying, I really do,'' she said. ''I didn't leave here because I wanted to. But I can't come back. If I don't live the principle, Jed would never let me associate with you. He's too afraid I'll pull you and the rest of his children away from his beliefs. Besides…'' Hope hesitated, unwilling to barrel on for fear she'd upset her sister.

''Besides what?'' Faith prodded.

"I don't want to come back here," Hope admitted. "I can't live in a place where guilt is used to motivate my every action. I can't submit my will to a man's, because I no longer believe women are inferior. I can't believe our sole purpose here is to procreate, not when we have so many other talents and abilities. And I can't believe God has so little compassion for His daughters that He would expect us to give more to our husbands than we get in return."

Silence met this announcement. Hope felt slightly embarrassed about the passion that had rung through her voice, and knew that what she was saying would probably sound radical to her sister. But she'd spent many years agonizing over what she believed and what she didn't, and she could hardly feel indifferent about her conclusions.

"I'm not going to say I think you're wrong," Faith said, "because I don't know."

"Then how do you do it?" Hope asked. "How do you stay here and let Arvin come to your bed?"

"I've been telling myself the dissatisfaction I feel is Satan tempting me away from the truth but—" she tucked her dress around her legs "—you've probably already guessed it's not working. If it was, I wouldn't be here right now. I'd be protecting myself from your 'dangerous influence,' as Daddy told us all to do after we saw you today."

"That was generous of him," Hope muttered. "I guess he feels a little differently about prodigals than the father in the Bible did, huh?"

"He said the prodigal in the Bible was humble and repentant." She turned her face toward the cemetery. "If it makes you feel any better, I don't think it was easy for him to spurn you today."

Hope didn't want to debate the issue. She had almost no feelings left for her father. She'd never had many positive ones to begin with. "What does Mother say about your situation with Arvin?"

"She claims having a baby will help. But she admitted the loneliness will probably never disappear."

"Don't you think that's a tragedy?"

"What?"

"To expect to be lonely your whole life, when you're beautiful and healthy and only eighteen?"

Faith bit her lip as she seemed to consider Hope's words. "I think she sees it as a burden we, as women, must band together and carry," she said at last.

"Why?" Hope asked.

"For a greater reward later on, after this life."

"You just told me you're not sure the church's teachings are correct. That means your sacrifice might be for nothing."

No response.

"You don't have to stay here," Hope said. "There's a whole world out there, Faith."

"What about Mother? And my sisters? I have nieces and nephews and friends here."

Hope noticed she didn't mention her husband or their father.

"You can't live your whole life for other people," Hope said. "You have to let them make their decisions, and you have to make yours."

"But I'm not as strong as you are, Hope. I'm not sure I can make it on my own. And sometimes what I hear in church really speaks to me, you know? Sometimes I think Daddy has to be right."

"So did I," Hope said. "Maybe he's not wrong about some things. I believe it's important to live a good life, to be honest, to serve others, to develop your talents. But is this the best place to do that? What about your baby? If it's a girl, do you want her to have a plural marriage? To endure the emotional starvation of sharing her husband with who-knew-how-many other women. To have no hope of living without so much guilt she can hardly function?''

The moon bathed Faith's troubled face in silver when she tilted her head to look at Hope. ''Were you able to give your baby anything better?''

''I hope so.'' Hope leaned her forehead against the cool metal chain above her right hand. ''I have no guarantees, but at least I improved the odds.''

''So you're okay with knowing you'll never see your own child?''

Faith's question was certainly blunt, even ruthless in a way, but there was no condemnation in her voice, only a sincere desire to plumb Hope's regrets, to see how she'd lived and to know if the outside world was truly better.

''There are times I'm not okay with that at all. But I was promised she'd go to a good family, and I still trust the people who told me that.'' Hope pictured the arresting face of the young administrator of The Birth Place. Parker Reynolds had been there to encourage her at a pivotal point in her life. And Lydia Kane, so alive with over sixty years of intense, passionate living, had set the supreme example of what a woman could be. Together, they'd inspired Hope to pull her life together, regardless of the obstacles in her path, and become an obstetrics nurse. But she'd had to leave Enchantment behind to do so. She couldn't live somewhere that would forever remind her of the child she'd given away, forever tease her with the possibility that she might someday bump into her daughter.

''What are you thinking about?'' Faith asked.

Hope steered her mind away from that long-ago place of adobe buildings, red sunsets, brisk clean air and pine-scented mountains. ''Just that I'm glad my baby won't have to go through what I went through,'' she said. ''Adoption provided her with a complete family, one that had the means to take care of her. But things are different for you, Faith. You wouldn't have to give up your baby.

You'd have a place to live, food to eat, a chance to go to school. That's why I'm here. To help you, if you want my help."

Uncertainty clouded her sister's face.

"Don't you ever dream of leaving?" Hope pressed.

"All the time," Faith whispered.

Hope's pulse leaped at the longing in her voice. "Then tell me what you want most out of life."

"I want…" Her sister scuffed her toe in the dirt again. "Never mind," she said. "It doesn't matter."

Wrapping her arms around the chains of her swing, Hope leaned back to stare at the sky. "It matters, Faith. Dreams always matter. See those stars? You need to pick one and shoot right for it."

Faith gazed up at the night sky. "The star I want is too far away."

"Not if you really believe in it."

"I want to feel good about myself," her sister said softly. "And…and sometimes I dream of having a man of my own. A *young* man, who'll devote his whole heart to me and our children." She laughed in a self-deprecating manner. "I know it sounds vain and selfish, and Father would say I deserve to lose my salvation if I can't be happy with a good, God-fearing man, regardless of his age. But I don't love Arvin, Hope. I want to love the man whose children I'm bearing."

Her last words were spoken so reverently they sounded almost like a prayer. "Every woman should have that right," Hope said.

"No, those are evil thoughts, and I'm evil for thinking them."

"They're not evil," Hope argued. "And neither are you." Standing, she reached out to Faith. "Come with me. I'll take you home and tomorrow I'll show you a whole new world."

Faith's eyes went wide. "I can't, Hope. As much as I want to—"

"Faith, you're miserable. How long can you really expect to last? Don't wait until you have more children. Then it'll only be worse. You'll feel even more trapped."

Faith twisted the gold band on the finger of her left hand. "But I've made promises."

"What about the unspoken promise of a mother to her child? *Your* promise to *your* child?"

She closed her eyes. "I hear what you're saying, Hope. Part of me believes you're right. I just—"

"What?"

She looked up again. "I don't know if I can do it. It goes against everything—"

"Do it for your baby."

"And if I regret leaving?"

"You won't," Hope said.

The confidence of this declaration seemed to be just what Faith needed, because she straightened as though feeling a sense of resolution. "Okay." She stood up and took Hope's hand. "Let's go. Let's get out of here fast, before—"

"Before what, Faith?" a man's voice interrupted. "Before your husband finds out?"

CHAPTER THREE

IT TOOK HOPE a moment to make out Arvin from among the long shadows of the trees. When she did, her palms grew moist.

"It'll be okay, Faith," she murmured, her heart pounding.

Faith looked like a deer caught in headlights. "Arvin, I—"

"You're what?" he interrupted. "You're planning to run out on me in the middle of the night? Is that what you're doing here?"

"I'm sorry," Faith said. "I know it isn't right to leave this way. But I'm not happy, Arvin. I haven't been happy since we married. I think you know that."

"What, you're not satisfied with having me in your bed? You want some Gentile rutting between your legs?"

Faith jerked as though he'd shot her, and Hope stepped between them. "That's vulgar, Arvin. Below even you."

"Vulgar." He chuckled. "She's so prim and proper, no one will want her. Look at her. You think some other man is going to desire a woman who's bearing the child of her own uncle?"

"How dare you try to belittle her for what you—"

"You might be my uncle, but you're also my husband," Faith said at the same time. "I haven't done anything wrong."

Hope tried to bar him from coming too close to Faith, but he stepped around her. "They're not going to care about your version of right and wrong, Faith. They don't understand the principle. The outside world will think you're a freak, a freak without an education or any way to support yourself. They'll have no use for you or our baby. Is that what you want? To be a laughingstock? To have no one?''

"She'll have me," Hope said.

"You stay out of this. It's none of your affair," he growled. "You belong here, Faith. Don't let Hope paint pictures of dreamlands that don't exist."

"Don't listen to him," Hope said. "I've painted no dreamland. Arvin is the only freak I know. Let's get out of here." She tugged on her sister's arm, eager to get them both away before Arvin tried to stop them physically, but Faith resisted her efforts.

"What if he's right, Hope? What if I don't fit in?" she asked. "I can't expect you to take care of me and my baby indefinitely."

"You'll fit in just fine," Hope said. "When the baby's old enough, you'll go to school and learn to support yourself and your child. There's nothing to worry about. I'll take care of you as long as you need me. You'll see. Come on."

Still, Faith hesitated. "That's asking a lot of you, Hope, and I feel so lost already...."

"What about your poor mother?" Arvin asked, his eyes shining like obsidian in the darkness. "Are you trying to break her heart? You've seen what Hope's already done to her. Now you're going to do the same thing?"

"I don't want to hurt anyone," Faith said.

Hope gave Arvin a look of disgust. "Stop pretending. You're not worried about our mother. You're only worried about yourself."

"Oh, yeah?" he countered, and those shiny eyes seemed to stab right through her, eliciting more of the revulsion she'd felt toward him even as a girl. "I have eleven other wives. I don't need an eighteen-year-old girl who knows nothing about pleasing a man. Why, she's so frigid I practically have to pry her legs apart.''

Faith gasped, and Hope raised a defensive hand as if she could ward him off. ''Then let her go, Arvin,'' she said. ''She doesn't love you. She never has.''

''And give you what *you* want? After the way you've treated me? Like hell!''

Hope couldn't believe her ears. Unless she'd missed her guess, this wasn't about Faith; he didn't desire her, he didn't need her, and he certainly didn't want her. This was about the past. ''See, Faith? He's just trying to get back at me. We need to go.''

''Faith, come home with me,'' Arvin said, his voice imperious. ''Right now, before I feel the need to go to the rest of the Brethren and complain about your behavior.''

Hope wished she could wipe the smug expression from Arvin's face. Obviously he thought he'd win the tug-of-war between them. She was afraid he would. But what could she do? Faith was of age and pregnant. She needed to make her own decisions.

''I said we're going home,'' he said even more forcefully.

Her sister glanced at the parking lot where Hope's Impala waited. ''I live in a house with two of your other wives,'' she finally said, ''who don't seem to like you a whole lot more than I do. I don't have a home.'' With her back ramrod-straight, she turned and started toward the Impala.

Hope felt a rush of pure adrenaline and hurried after her. Faith was actually going through with it. She was leaving Arvin, Superior, the Everlasting Apostolic Church!

''You'll be a pariah,'' Arvin called after her.

''Don't listen to him,'' Hope murmured.

''I won't let you come back here!'' he shouted. ''You've just kissed your friends and family goodbye, not to mention your eternal salvation. You're going to rot in hell, Faith, right along with Hope!''

Hope opened her mouth to tell him he'd be there, sweating right along with them, but Faith turned and spoke before she could. ''I'd rather go to hell with Hope than spend one more night with you,'' she said, and got in the car.

Stunned, Hope scrambled into the other side, started the engine and peeled out of the lot.

THEY TRAVELED south without speaking, the thrumming of tires on pavement the only sound for more than an hour. Hope finally turned on the radio, hoping music might soothe the raw emotions jangling inside her and take her mind back to where it was before she'd returned to Superior. But when Faith's gaze cut toward the radio, she quickly flipped it off. She didn't want Faith to feel the shock of having stepped outside her sheltered existence quite so soon. Superior had regular radio stations of course, but the Everlasting Apostolic Church encouraged parishioners not to listen to the ''devil's music,'' and Hope guessed Faith was one of those who obeyed.

''You can listen if you want,'' Faith said politely as the quick spurt of music died.

The tone of her sister's voice gave no indication of what Faith was feeling, which made Hope uneasy. Tears would be good at this point, she thought. But after Hope had left Superior, she hadn't been able to cry for a year, and she saw no sign of tears on Faith's face, either. Maybe it was a Tanner thing.

''I'm fine with having it off,'' Hope said. ''I wasn't thinking.''

Headlights bore down on them from the opposite direction. A truck passed, and then they were once again alone on the road. Hope peered nervously in her rearview mirror, as she'd been doing since they left, just to be sure. She certainly didn't want Arvin, or anyone else, following her. She'd spent too long making a safe home for herself to compromise it now.

"You going to be okay?" she asked, sending her sister a worried glance.

Faith sat in the same position she'd taken when they left—legs clamped tightly together, back straight, hands folded primly on her belly. "I think so."

Hope adjusted the heater because it was getting too warm in the car, and at last forced herself to ask the question she knew she should pose before they went any farther. "Are you having second thoughts, Faith? Do you want me to take you back?"

Her sister stared through the windshield without blinking, and Hope imagined she was watching the broken yellow line in the center of the road rush past. Each break took her farther from her home, farther from everything she'd ever known, farther from everything she'd ever believed she would do....

Finally Faith shifted her weight and eased further into the seat. "No."

Hope sighed in relief. *Don't worry. It'll get easier as the days and weeks pass,* she wanted to say. *I've been there.* But now wasn't the time to go into what the future would or wouldn't hold. It was nearly one in the morning. Her sister had to be exhausted. And if Faith's feelings were anything like Hope's when she'd run away, she was too confused to make sense out of anything.

A few more miles and Faith's eyelids drooped until her lashes rested on her cheeks. As her breathing evened out, Hope began to relax, too. Faith's situation might be similar to the one she'd been in eleven years ago, but Hope silently promised that it would end differently. Faith would get to keep her baby. She'd never experience the ache Hope felt every time she thought of the infant she'd borne but was never allowed to hold. She wouldn't have to wonder if she'd made the right decision about giving up a child she would have loved with her whole heart.

She would, however, have to lie about her baby's father.

The words Arvin had flung at them in the park came immediately to Hope's mind, making her cringe. *You think some other man is going to desire a woman who's bearing the child of her own uncle?…You're a freak…They'll have no use for you or our baby….* The bastard. He'd made her a freak. And while Faith was swallowing her distaste and submitting to him because she believed it was God's law, Hope felt sure he was delighting in the perversion of having church-sanctioned sex with his own niece.

Highway 14 came up on her right. Hope automatically made the turn that would take her to I-15 and then on to St. George. Her glowing instrument panel indicated she was speeding again, but she was too engrossed in her thoughts to care. The genetic connection between Arvin and Faith was unfortunate, for Faith and the child's sake. But everyone had secrets. Hope had managed to keep her own past a secret from almost everyone, except the people at The Birth Place—Lydia Kane, Parker Reynolds and the others employed there.

What was one more skeleton in an already crowded closet?

AFTER ANOTHER HOUR and a half, the adrenaline that had kept Hope alert through the entire drive ebbed, and her eyes began to burn with fatigue. When she finally turned down her quiet residential street of small brick homes, she was longing for bed and a few hours of unconsciousness before trying to help Faith face the future. Hope had insulated herself from others by focusing on becoming functional and productive—and to a certain extent, being a chameleon. She blended in. She didn't make waves. She withheld the part of herself that knew pain. But helping Faith meant she'd have to engage emotionally, and that frightened her more than anything. What if Faith couldn't reject the teachings of the Brethren? What if she gave up and went back? What if Faith clung so tightly to the past that even Hope could no longer escape it?

Hope didn't want to be thrust into that environment again, didn't want to think about Superior and her days there, because doing so only revived old heartaches. Images and memories of Bonner sometimes hovered close enough as it was. He was so tied to thoughts of her baby…

Hope hit the garage-door opener and let the car idle in the driveway while she waited for the door to lift. So what if the man she'd loved had married her sister? It didn't really change anything. It just created a jumble of emotions Hope hadn't felt in a while—and something more. Something akin to…envy?

It wasn't envy, she told herself. How could she envy Charity, who'd looked so pale? Sure, she had Bonner's children, but Hope had control of her own life. Nothing was worth relinquishing that. What she felt now was the sting of her father's betrayal. That he'd let Charity marry the man she'd begged him to let *her* marry spoke volumes about Jed and his lack of love for his ninth child. Had he given her and Bonner his blessing, they would've become husband and wife. She would've stayed in Superior and raised her child as part of the family.

But then she would have remained a member of the Everlasting Apostolic Church. Which wasn't so good, she decided. Bonner had claimed he had no desire to take any other woman to his bed, ever. Yet he hadn't been strong enough to make good on his words by leaving with her. And he'd gone on take three wives!

Maybe her father and Bonner had done her a favor. Hope knew she couldn't have stood by and watched Bonner marry again and again, couldn't have welcomed those other women into her home and into her husband's bed. This way, she was out of Superior and the strictures of the church. She was living a normal life that promised far more than she would've had if she'd stayed. And now she had Faith.

She glanced at her sleeping sister as she parked in her small detached garage and cut the engine, recalling the times she'd read the Bible to her, or braided her hair, or curled up in the same bed on Christmas Eve because Faith was too excited to sleep. They never received much for Christmas—gifts detracted from the true meaning, according to her father. But they were filled with expectation all the same, if only for the little presents they gave each other.

Her last Christmas at home, Hope had earned extra money taking in ironing so she could give Faith the beautiful Barbie doll her little sister had seen in the store window and long admired. Her father had immediately condemned the gift as being too frivolous and expensive, but the joy on Faith's face when she tore off that wrapping paper made Hope believe her money had been well spent. Later that night, she'd found Faith's most prized possession on her pillow—a plastic journal with a small lock and key. The pages that had already been used had been torn out and replaced by some roughly cut scrap paper. A short note written in Faith's childish scrawl told her she wanted her to keep the journal.

And here they were eleven years later. A lump swelled in Hope's throat. Faith might have been overlooked by others, but she'd always been Hope's favorite. More sensitive than the rest, she'd always soothed Hope.

"Faith, we're home," she said, gently shaking her shoulder.

Faith blinked and sat up. "I should have kept you company on the drive, Hope. I'm sorry."

"No. It was better that you slept, better for the baby."

Her sister's gaze circled the garage. For a moment she looked completely bewildered. "This is your house?"

"Just the garage. And I don't own it. I rent."

Faith climbed out, following wordlessly as Hope led

her around to the front of the house, where she nearly tripped over Oscar, a large gray cat, who screeched and ran for cover.

"What was that?" Faith asked as he slipped into the hedge separating her house from his owner's and crouched to glare at them.

"That's Oscar," Hope said.

"Your cat?"

"He belongs to my neighbor, but I think he's trying to move in with me. He comes over all the time."

"Do you feed him?"

"Occasionally. Mr. Paris doesn't mind. I guess we sort of share him. Oscar generally won't let anyone but Mr. Paris touch him, anyway, so it doesn't matter much. He just hangs out on his own." A cat after her own heart, Hope added silently.

Bending, Faith held out her hand to coax him closer, but he was still put out by his close call. Whisking his tail in a show of irritation, he didn't budge.

Hope unlocked the front door and swung it open. "He's not very friendly, but I admire his independence."

"I like cats." Faith peeked into the house. "Do you live alone?"

"I've had roommates in the past, but ever since I started making enough to afford the rent, I've been living alone," Hope said, holding the door.

Faith still hesitated at the threshold, glancing toward Oscar as though she'd rather hide out with him in the hedge. Probably the idea of moving in with Hope made a decision that had been somewhat impulsive now seem permanent. "So you've never been married or...or anything?"

"No. No husbands, no live-in lovers, no steady boyfriends."

Faith finally stepped into the living room. "And you're not seeing anyone?"

Hope thought of Jeff, her neighbor's son from down

the street, and the doctors, male nurses and other hospital staff who asked her out on occasion. She knew they talked about her, perceived her coolness as a challenge. But no one had managed to pique her interest. She wanted a husband and family eventually, but the moment whoever she was seeing began to push for commitment, she felt such a terrible panic she broke off the relationship. "Not really," she said.

"But you're so pretty."

Hope chuckled. "I guess I'm a little jaded," she said, nudging her sister farther inside.

The house smelled of the fresh flowers Hope routinely cut from her garden in back and kept in a small tin bucket on the kitchen table. She liked the contrast of fragile versus resilient, old versus new, delicate versus careworn.

Hope flipped on the light. "What a beautiful home," Faith breathed, almost reverently.

Hope took a moment to see her surroundings through Faith's eyes. The house was old. It still had its original hardwood floors and plaster walls, but had been remodeled so that the front room, which had once been a porch, was enclosed by a series of paned windows. The rooms were spacious, despite the fact that the house was only about a thousand square feet. The kitchen opened into the family room, both of which could be seen from the front entrance. An office, set off by double doors, opened to the left. The hall that led to both bedrooms branched off to the right.

"Did you decorate this place all by yourself?" Faith asked.

Hope nodded. "On weekends I search the classifieds looking for treasures, and I often pick up a piece of furniture for a fraction of its value. I fix and refinish wooden items in the garage, if I want the grain of the wood to shine through. Or I paint or stencil on various pieces I find, like that old church pew in the kitchen."

"It's lovely," Faith said.

Hope dropped her keys on the counter. "An old widower down the street owns the house, but I take good care of it, so he pretty much lets me have free rein."

Faith continued to walk through the main rooms before pausing in front of an arrangement of cross-stitch samplers on the kitchen wall. Large and elaborate, there was one for each season. "These are great," she said.

"Thanks." Hope liked to cross-stitch and collect odds and ends. Her dishes, silverware and linens were all mismatched antiques or one-of-a-kind items, like the Flow-blue plates and creamers from seventeenth-century England that adorned the white, built-in shelves on either side of the fireplace in the kitchen/living room.

"You must make a lot of money to live like this," Faith said. "I've never seen anything more charming."

"I don't make a lot of money," Hope said with a laugh, "but I grew up in the same household as you, remember? I know how to stretch a dollar."

Faith cocked an eyebrow at her. "You're better at it than I am."

"Don't be too hard on yourself. This is just my version of *The Boxcar Children*. Remember that book? I used to read it to you when you were little."

"I do," Faith said. "It was my favorite."

"This might sound silly, but when things got really tough for me after I left Superior, I used to pretend I was one of those children, finding or making what I needed out of the things other people discarded." She moved into the kitchen to check the answering machine on the breakfast bar. No calls. Not unusual.

"I can't believe you've done all this."

"It's nothing." Hope changed the subject because her sister's praise made her feel guilty for having so much when her family had so little. "You said you were living with two of Arvin's other wives. Which ones?"

Faith paused next to the black-iron baker's rack where

Hope stored her pasta and cereals in uniquely shaped jars. "Do you remember Ila Jane?"

"That old battle-ax?"

A smile flickered at the corners of Faith's lips. "She's the only one of us who ever dares put Arvin in his place. He likes her cooking but doesn't bother her for anything else, and she's happy that way. Being around her was actually the best part of being married to Arvin. She took me under her wing, like another daughter. Her oldest is close to my age, anyway. But I'm not fond of Charlene, Arvin's second wife. She lives with us, too. Her children are especially difficult, like her, all except little Sarah. Sarah's only seven, but Charlene ignores her, so she spends most of her day with me."

"Is Charlene still pretty?"

"Pretty enough, I guess. She's given Arvin ten kids, so she's done well by him."

Hope no longer agreed with using that kind of measuring stick for a woman's success, but she knew it would take a while for Faith to understand and adjust, so she said nothing. "Does he spend much time with Ila Jane or Charlene?"

"No, or his children, either. When he moved me into that old house on Front Street—"

"Not the big yellow one," Hope interrupted. "We always thought that house was haunted, remember? We'd dare each other to ring the bell, and then we'd run."

"That was when the Andersons lived there, and old lady Bird, Sister Anderson's mother, used to sit rocking in the window of the attic for hours."

"I take it she's passed away."

"Oh, yes, and her son was excommunicated for stealing from the storehouse. That's how Arvin got the house."

"So that's where you've been living?"

"For the past few months. When he moved me in with Ila Jane, I knew he was putting me on a shelf."

Hope rummaged through a glass-fronted cupboard for

two mugs. "And you think it's because of the baby? You said something earlier about your condition being 'unappealing' to him."

"He claims he's trying to leave me in peace, since pregnancy can be so uncomfortable. But I know he's not really interested in doing me any favors. Arvin doesn't work that way."

"No kidding," Hope added.

"He's probably just sidetracked for the time being, what with marrying Rachel and everything." She sank onto a stool at the counter.

A million biting comments about Arvin rose to Hope's lips, but she voiced none of them. Setting the cups on the counter, she said, "I thought maybe I'd make us some hot cocoa before bed."

Faith shook her head. "None for me, thanks. I'm too tired. All I want to do is turn in."

Hope put the cups away, secretly grateful Faith had refused her offer. She was almost ready to drop. "Your room's just down the hall," she said, her sandals clicking on the floor as she moved through the house turning on lights. Stopping at the first room on her right, which was decorated in Battenburg lace and pink with yellow accents, she waved Faith inside.

"Nice," Faith said as she stood at the foot of the bed and gazed around.

"Make yourself comfortable while I get you a nightgown and a toothbrush," Hope said at the door. "Tomorrow we'll go shopping for clothes and toiletries."

"You don't have to go to work?"

"Not until evening. I'm a nurse, so my hours vary. Tomorrow I have the night shift."

Her sister plucked at her skirt, reminding Hope of a nervous habit their mother used to have.

"I know this must feel strange, Faith," Hope said, "but you'll be comfortable here, I promise. We'll buy everything you need tomorrow."

"But isn't it going to be expensive to replace everything I left behind?"

"It won't be too bad. I've got the money."

Faith still seemed ill at ease, so Hope tried to combat her insecurity with a confident smile. "Don't worry about anything."

"Okay." She started to turn down the bed, and Hope moved toward her own room to get the promised articles, but her sister called her back.

"Hope?"

"Yeah?"

"What happens if you get sick of me? Or we run out of money, or…whatever?"

Hope's heart twisted. How vividly she remembered what it was like to feel as though the ground beneath her feet might crumble at any moment. She was still protecting herself from that possibility, wasn't she? That was why she worked so hard to make her house a home. So she'd feel safe and protected.

"I might get sick of you, and you might get sick of me. But that won't change the fact that we're sisters, Faith. You'll always be welcome here. We'll work together to build lives we're both happy with, and we'll help each other get through the tough times."

"Why?" Faith asked suddenly. "It's been eleven years, Hope. Why bother with me when you have all of this?"

All of this. By most people's standards, Hope's home wasn't anything special. But Faith had known only overcrowded trailers and duplexes and old houses with bad plumbing, all of which had been filled to bursting with children, secondhand clothing and shabby furniture.

"I know this will probably sound crazy to you, because you feel you're forsaking God by leaving Superior, Faith. But I believe He's put me in the position of being able to help you for a reason. I *want* you here, and Charity and the others, too, if they ever want to come."

Faith smiled, and on impulse Hope walked back and

hugged her. "It's good to be with you again," she said. "Whatever the future holds, we'll get through it together."

"I don't think it's going to be easy," Faith said, clinging to her.

"No," Hope agreed. "It won't be easy. But nothing worth having ever is."

CHAPTER FOUR

HOPE AWOKE to the sounds of someone moving around in her house. At first, the noise made her go tense with fear. But then she remembered she now had her sister living with her.

Excitement poured through her veins and mingled with something more difficult to define—not dread exactly, but foreboding. Hope didn't want to go back to the way she'd felt eleven years ago, didn't want to relive the loneliness, the fear or the struggle, even vicariously. But her sister's happiness was worth the sacrifice. What frightened Hope wasn't the difficulty of what lay ahead so much as the possibility that, at any point, Faith could give up and return to Superior.

"Faith?" she called.

The hall floor creaked as her sister came to stand in her open doorway. She was fully dressed, had already scrubbed her face and fixed her hair and it was only—Hope glanced at the clock by her bed—seven-thirty.

"You anxious to go shopping or something?" she teased. "The stores don't even open until ten."

"I just...I'm used to getting up early. I usually have work to do, especially now that it's planting season. You should see the big plot Ila Jane and I have been preparing for our garden. We're going to grow tomatoes and zucchini and corn and—oh, you name it—everything, even our own pumpkins for Thanksgiving." She seemed to realize what she was saying and finished weakly, "At least, we were."

Hope shoved herself into a sitting position and motioned for Faith to join her on the bed. "I have a big garden in back," she said. "I grow a lot of flowers, some that I import all the way from Denmark."

"Really? Why in the world would anyone need to buy flowers from so far away?"

"They're dahlias and they're beautiful. Wait till you see them. I usually grow a vegetable garden, too. Maybe you'd be willing help me with it this year."

Her sister's face brightened at the mention of such familiar work. She'd probably been wondering what, exactly, she was going to do now that there wasn't an army of children to care for. In a polygamist household, it wasn't uncommon for the wives of one man to share responsibility for all his children, regardless of who belonged to whom. The camaraderie the women enjoyed sometimes offset the lack of attention they received from their husband—not that every household was able to achieve this type of peaceful cooperation. Catfights broke out all the time. Some of the wives banded together against others or treated certain children with marked prejudice. But in Hope's little house, the silence alone was probably enough to make Faith feel as though she'd lost contact with the real world.

"I—I thought I'd read the scriptures," Faith said, her voice a little tentative. "But of course I wasn't able to bring mine, and…and I notice you don't have any lying around."

Scriptures. Hope barely refrained from wrinkling her nose. Before bringing Faith home, she'd purposely avoided any reminder of her past. There were times she wished she could be like the rest of the Christian world, or most of it, anyway, and think kindly on religion, but it had been eleven years since she'd sat through a sermon. The prospect of entering a church, *any* church, made her feel as though she couldn't breathe. If she ever got married, it would be in Vegas.

"I'm sure I have some here somewhere. I'll dig them up and you can keep them in your room and read them whenever you'd like," she said, knowing it would be useless to explain her aversion to all things religious. Faith would only fear that she was the devil, as her father claimed. Even Hope didn't understand the overwhelming anxiety she felt when faced with the Bible, a church, a clergyman or even an overzealous missionary type. Not all her memories of gospel-related things were bad. Once, when she was a child, her mother had taken her and her sisters to Salt Lake, where she encountered a vagrant for the first time. He was mostly blind, slightly deformed, definitely filthy and almost skeletal in appearance. A woman in a conservative black suit and high heels hurrying past them on the sidewalk clucked her tongue and muttered something under her breath about how pathetic he was. But her mother stopped and gave him the last of their money. When Hope asked why, she said, "Jesus loves him, and so must we."

"But he's so pathetic," she'd replied, feeling old beyond her years as she mimicked the other, more sophisticated woman. Her mother had smiled gently and lifted her chin. "That's only on the outside, little Hope. Jesus doesn't care about that."

Hope had felt humbled and loved then. If Jesus could love a beggar, surely He could love a little girl with flyaway brown hair and scabby knees, who often had her mouth washed out with soap for losing her temper and saying things she wasn't supposed to say to her father's second wife. But even the warmth of that memory wasn't enough to send her back into a church. The Brethren and her father had poisoned that part of her during her teen years, when they'd grown more and more controlling. Or maybe she'd lost her faith when she'd given up her baby. After all, that was when she'd felt as though whatever light she'd been trying to shelter inside her had finally winked out.

"What would you like for breakfast?" she asked, getting out of bed and heading to her closet for a robe. She'd hoped to sleep in after the emotionally exhausting day and night they'd spent. Especially because she had to work later on. But she couldn't leave Faith on her own.

"I need a favor," Faith said.

"Anything. What?"

"Don't treat me like a guest, okay?"

Hope blinked at her in surprise. "I wasn't. I was just…"

"I know, and I appreciate it," Faith replied. "But I won't be able to make it if I don't feel as though I'm carrying my own weight, or at least contributing in some way that's valuable to you."

"Are you kidding? You're going to work your…" Hope had been about to say, "butt off." She'd been living around Gentiles long enough to have incorporated their more popular expressions and speech patterns. But her sister had not and would be shocked, even by such mild vulgarity. So she finished, "…fingers to the bone in that garden I mentioned."

"That's fine," Faith said, still perfectly serious. "That's what I need. That's what I want."

"Great." Hope's smile was brighter than her mood warranted. This was going to be even more difficult than she'd thought. Until she and Faith became acquainted again and learned how to be comfortable around each other, things were going to be awkward. "Why don't you make breakfast while I shower, then?"

"Okay."

"I'll have two fried eggs and toast. Everything's in the kitchen. Just rummage around to find what you need, and if you get really stumped, holler."

"I'll be fine."

Hope kept the smile on her face until her sister disappeared down the hall, then let her shoulders sag as she sank back onto the bed. What were they in for? Her life and Faith's had taken completely opposite paths. Now they were so different that Hope wasn't sure they'd ever be able to find common ground. What if taking Faith away from Superior had been a mistake they'd both live to regret?

She'd never know whether she could help Faith if she didn't try, she decided. She just needed to take things one day at a time. And this day, they were going to buy clothes.

With a deep, bolstering breath, Hope got up and headed for the shower.

"FIND ANYTHING you like?" Hope asked, getting to her feet to take the stack of clothes Faith had carried into the dressing room several minutes earlier.

Faith bit her lip as she regarded the maternity jeans, T-shirts and jumpers Hope had selected for her to try on. "No, not really."

"Why not?" Hope asked. "Nothing fit?"

The voices of people passing the store in the mall outside droned in the background. By the time Hope had shown Faith around the garden and the house, then taught her how to use the microwave, dishwasher, washing machine and dryer, it was nearly noon. Activity at the mall was just beginning to peak.

"Everything fit," Faith said. "It's just that…well, I thought maybe I'd rather sew a few items for myself."

Hope nearly groaned. Not more of the dowdy dresses that would instantly mark her as belonging to a polygamist community. "Faith, what's wrong with these clothes? They're comfortable and practical and—"

"They're too…stylish," Faith replied. "I don't want to be vain, Hope. It's not right." She spoke in a whisper because the saleswoman hovered close by—but not because she wanted to help them. The moment they'd entered the store, the woman had watched them with contempt and the kind of curiosity one typically felt when viewing something fascinating yet distasteful, like maggots on meat. No doubt Faith's appearance had given them away. Colorado City and Hillsdale, a large polygamist community straddling the Arizona-Utah border, was less than an hour's drive away. The people of St. George saw more than their share of polygamists, some of whom lived right in town. The women were especially easy to spot because they typically wore pants beneath the voluminous skirts of their dated dresses, along with a pair of old tennis shoes.

But familiarity didn't necessarily breed acceptance.

"A little style never hurt anyone," Hope insisted, and turned to challenge the saleswoman's stare.

The saleswoman crossed her arms, as though she had a right to gawk at them.

"Maybe we should go somewhere else," Faith said.

Protectiveness, and pride, wouldn't allow Hope to leave just yet. She'd been away from Superior long enough to understand, to a degree, the woman's fascination, but such rudeness was inexcusable. "No, we have as much right to be here as anyone. Pick out a few things."

"I don't want anything. I just need some fabric and—"

"We'll get you some fabric and you can sew as many dresses as you like. Just pick out something you'd want if you weren't worried about everything the church taught you."

With a frown, Faith delved into the stack and came up with a plain pair of maternity jeans. Then she grabbed a top off the rack that resembled something an eighty-year-old woman would wear—an eighty-year-old woman with no taste.

"I said pick what you'd want if you *weren't* worried about the church," Hope said in exasperation, and selected a denim jumper and a cap-sleeve periwinkle blouse. "This okay?"

Faith shrugged.

"Good enough." Hope piled the rest of the clothes on

the chair in which she'd sat and carried the ones she planned to purchase to the cash register.

The saleswoman took her time sauntering over. "This everything?" she asked, her voice flat.

"For now," Hope replied.

The woman started scanning the merchandise, but paused to glance over at Faith. "Disgusting," she muttered.

"Excuse me?" Enough was enough. "Did you say something? Or were you simply proving that you're as small-minded as I suspected from the start?"

"It's okay, Hope," Faith murmured at her elbow, obviously embarrassed.

"It's not okay with me," Hope replied.

The woman's jaw dropped. Usually polygamists visited the mall in groups, stuck close together and ignored the whispers and derision they encountered. Hope had seen them scurrying about, sometimes pausing to gaze longingly in a store window that sold merchandise they'd never permit themselves to buy. In the past she'd always tried to ignore them because she didn't want to acknowledge her roots. But being with Faith revealed her as surely as a sign hanging overhead.

Something mean and ugly flashed in the other woman's eyes. But a second salesperson, who must have been away at lunch or on break, walked into the store, and the woman ringing up Faith's clothing immediately changed her attitude. "I didn't say anything," she said, her attention now strictly on what she was doing.

Hope paid for the clothes, grabbed the sack and, with Faith scurrying to keep up, stalked out of the store. She had half a mind to complain to the manager. Except she knew that causing a fuss wouldn't do anything to help her sister. Faith had been taught to turn the other cheek, even when confronted with ridicule. Hope, on the other hand, believed that valuing herself as an individual and setting boundaries for others who didn't set boundaries for themselves went farther toward fostering respect.

She'd become a master at setting boundaries, especially with men.

"Is everything okay, Hope?" Faith asked. "You're not mad at me, are you?"

Hope realized she was striding through the mall as if her life depended on it. Slowing, she forced a smile. "Everything's fine. I just figured that woman should be told her behavior wasn't appreciated, that's all."

Faith nodded uncertainly, so Hope took her arm, anxious to get out of the mall quickly because the stares they drew grated on her nerves.

"Is this going to be too hard for you, Hope?" Faith asked. "I don't want to be a thorn in your side. Is having me around worse than you expected?"

Hope wasn't sure what she'd expected. She'd returned to Superior out of love and a sense of duty. She'd gone back as soon as she'd felt emotionally capable of making the trip. Now she feared she wasn't as prepared as she'd hoped.

"You're not a thorn. I want you around, no matter what," she said, which was true for the most part.

"I hope so. Because I can't let go of everything I've been taught. I'd lose...I'd lose too much of *me*. You understand that, don't you?"

"I understand that the world is a very different place from Superior," she said.

"The world is Satan, trying to bring you down," Faith said.

Hope thought of Lydia Kane and Parker Reynolds and what they'd done for her ten years ago, and the people she worked with at the hospital now, who often went above and beyond the call of duty. She thought of 9/11 and the firefighters, and those people on the plane that crashed in Pennsylvania, and the smaller acts of generosity and courage she witnessed on an almost daily basis. "I'm afraid that's too simple an answer, Faith."

"Then I don't understand."

Because she hadn't lived in the real world. Yet. "In many ways, it's easier to live the Brethrens' teachings than not live them," Hope said. "Then you always know what's right and wrong—or at least you think you do. Because they've made all your decisions for you. And now…you have to start thinking for yourself."

THAT NIGHT Hope's shift at the hospital seemed to drag on forever. They had two mothers in labor, several newborns in the nursery and an ob/gyn who wasn't responding to his page. But despite concerns that she or Sandra Cleary, her supervisor, would have to deliver the baby if the doctor didn't arrive soon, Hope couldn't keep herself from reflecting on Faith. Soon her sister would be doing exactly what the two women in rooms 14 and 15 were doing—giving birth. Then she'd have a newborn in the house, as well as a sister with whom she'd had no contact for almost eleven years—

"Hope, can you visit Mrs. Walker's room?" Sandra asked. She had her head down and was busy finishing up some paperwork at the nurses' station. "She's signaling for us."

"Of course." Hope visited Room 14, where she'd already spent much of her time since coming on duty at ten. Mrs. Walker asked if they'd heard from her doctor yet. Hope had to tell her no.

"What happens if he doesn't get here?" Mr. Walker asked, worry creasing his forehead.

"Everything will be fine," Hope assured him. "I've been a nurse for five years and Sandra's been here longer than I have. Between us, we've seen hundreds of births and even delivered a few babies. And there's always the emergency physician on duty downstairs." She didn't add that he'd only be able to help if there wasn't someone with a more pressing condition—like a heart attack—in the emergency room. She figured that was a little too much information at this point.

They seemed to accept her words, probably because they had no choice, and Hope fetched Mrs. Walker another blanket to keep her legs warm.

"I'll be right back," she said, and went to the nurses' station to see if Sandra had heard anything from their missing doctor.

"Not yet," she responded, tucking several strands of shoulder-length brown hair behind one ear. "I swear, if we have to deliver this baby…"

If they delivered the baby, the stress would probably take a year off their lives, yet they'd make their normal salaries, nothing more. The doctor, who'd most likely turned off his pager, would still receive his full fee. Considering all the things that could go wrong…

Hope didn't even want to think about all the things that could go wrong. "He'll get here," she said as confidently as possible, and glanced at the clock. Was it too late to call Faith? Hope hated leaving her alone so soon. She'd dug a Bible out of her attic for Faith to read before bed, hoping that might help her sister acclimate. But Hope's world was so foreign to Faith, she could be feeling pretty lost. She could even be weakening and thinking about going back….

Unfortunately, it was past midnight. Too late to call. And Mrs. Walker was signaling for a nurse again.

Heading back to room 14, Hope told herself to quit worrying. Somehow, everything would work out for the best.

HOPE'S EYES were gritty with fatigue as she drove home from the hospital the following morning. She'd had to stay a couple of hours beyond her usual shift because Regina Parks, one of the morning nurses, had called in sick right in the middle of a surprise, preterm delivery.

At least Mrs. Walker's doctor had shown up in time to actually earn his fee. After that, everything had gone smoothly—until the emergency that had kept her late. A teenage girl had arrived at 6 a.m., already in advanced labor. Fortunately, the emergency doctor had been available to help, and the baby, a boy, took his first breath just minutes before Hope left. The baby was tiny, barely four pounds, and had respiratory problems, but the doctor thought he was going to live.

Hope remembered the young mother's excitement over her infant and wondered how Lydia had ever inspired her to become an obstetrics nurse. When faced with the normal scenario of appropriately aged mothers, attending fathers and supportive families, she could usually do her job without letting things get to her. But every once in a while someone like this young teenager came in—someone who invariably pulled her back to the day she herself had given birth. Then such a powerful longing gripped her, she could barely function. She'd told Faith she felt confident that her daughter was living a princesslike life. But there was no way to know for sure. Hope could only assume the best, and pray. As far as she'd drifted from organized religion, she still prayed about that. And she still dreamed of meeting her child, of touching the little girl she'd secretly named Autumn, if only just once.

Forcing her attention away from the empty ache she felt whenever she thought of Autumn, Hope stretched her neck to ease the tension knotting her muscles and pulled into the garage. With any luck, she'd find Faith in good spirits and be able to get some rest. She felt as though she could sleep for a week if—

The sound of voices reached her ears as she got out of the car and approached the house. Was it the television? She wanted to believe it was, but a flash of movement inside the front windows told her she and Faith had company.

CHAPTER FIVE

AFTER RUSHING to get inside before whoever had come could drag Faith away, Hope stood in her doorway as though transfixed. It was Bonner. After so many years, she'd begun to think she'd never see him again. She'd certainly never expected him to show up on her doorstep.

He'd changed. Of course, he was only eighteen when she'd seen him last; she should have anticipated some differences. But Bonner had done more than grow a couple of inches and put on a few pounds. Unlike most of the other men in the church, his thick dark hair was neatly trimmed and his face cleanly shaven. His clothes were modern and his teeth straight, despite the fact that few polygamists ever bothered with braces. And his eyes...

Actually, his eyes were the same. Maybe that was why his presence hit her so hard.

Slowly, he rose to his feet. Next to him, Arvin did the same.

Arvin's presence came as much less of a surprise. Hope had worried that he might crop up again, somehow give them trouble. She had not considered Bonner's involvement.

"What's going on?" she asked, finally looking at Faith.

Faith folded her arms in a cradling, protective manner. "I'm sorry, Hope," she said. "I...I felt I should call Mother, let her know where I was and tell her we're okay. She said she was really grateful I did—"

"And then she sent Arvin after you."

"I just wanted to give her some peace of mind."

"Your mother did the right thing," Arvin declared, his attention on Faith. "Now *you* need to do the right thing. I'm your husband, after all."

"You're her uncle," Hope clarified. "Nothing more."

"You'd bastardize your sister's child?" he cried. "Listen to her, Bonner! See what she's become? She's trying to make a mockery of my marri—"

"Arvin," Bonner interrupted, his tone sharp, "calm down and let me handle this."

To Hope's amazement, Arvin quickly backed off. "Fine. You take care of it, Bonner. I'm just...I'm angry, that's all. She had no right to take my wife and child away. I've never done anything to Hope."

Bonner spared him an irritated glance, and Hope braced herself for whatever he might say. He was the only man she'd ever loved. She'd had a few sexual encounters since they'd created Autumn, but those experiences had been, without exception, unsatisfying and mechanical.

"You look good, Hope," Bonner said. "But then, you were always beautiful, more beautiful than any other woman."

"You can say that to me when you're married to my sister?" she asked, her stomach churning with leftover emotions she'd rather not name.

"You want me to lie?"

"I want you to go."

"Only if Faith goes with us," Arvin interjected.

Another pointed glance from Bonner shut him up. "I know you have no reason to hear me out, Hope, but I'm only asking for a few minutes of your time. That's all. Surely what we shared warrants that much. Is there someplace we could talk?"

Hope felt tears sting her eyes, but she absolutely refused to shed them. She'd quit crying over Bonner long ago. "I have nothing to say to you."

"Just a few minutes," he said. "I want to make things right between us."

There wasn't any way to make things right. Autumn was gone. Bonner could never restore what he'd taken from her.

But he'd been only eighteen....

Finally Hope gave a brusque nod and led him out to her back porch, where she sat in one of the two wrought-iron chairs. She would've offered him the other chair, but she could barely bring herself to look at him.

"It's nice out here," he said. From the corner of her eye, she could see his gaze sweeping the flower garden, the birdbath and hummingbird feeder.

Hope's throat felt thick, as though she couldn't speak. She turned her attention to the huge, colorful heads of orange, purple and pink dahlias and tried to draw strength and peace from their beauty. She inhaled the smell of moist grass and freshly turned earth. This was her haven, the safe place she'd created.

But her past had caught up with her.

"Say what you came to say," she said, hoping for a quick release from the intensity of the moment. Her fatigue wasn't helping.

"Look at me."

Did she have to? She forced her eyes to meet his.

"I'm sorry," he said simply, his expression somber. "I know I hurt you. I was young and stupid, and I'm sorry."

Hope didn't know what to say. She'd lost Autumn, and *now* he was sorry? "Not half as sorry as I am."

"Then come home with me."

Her heart skipped several beats. "What?"

"I've never stopped loving you, Hope. I've prayed and prayed that you'd come home eventually, that you'd come home to *me*."

When she spoke, her voice was barely audible. "You've got to be kidding."

"Things have changed. I have more power in the church. No one will mistreat you if you're my wife. Everyone will forgive and forget, and things will finally be as they should've been in the beginning." He propped his hands on his hips as though he'd thought it all out and arrived at a decision she could only agree with. "I've already received your father's blessing. He gave it to me before Arvin and I came here. I want to take you home and marry you. Come back where you belong."

Where she belonged? Hope wasn't sure there was such a place. She'd thought she belonged here, in her little house and pretty garden, but now she wasn't even sure of that.

"Hope?" he pressed when she didn't respond.

"I can't."

"Of course you can."

"It's been eleven years, Bonner. What we had is gone."

"I don't think so."

Hope clenched her hands in her lap. "I'm afraid it is."

"Is there someone else, then?" he asked.

How ironic that he'd pose that particular question. "You're the one who's married," she said.

"I have more than enough room in my heart for you."

"I'm afraid I'm not willing to join the parade going through your bedroom."

He grimaced. "It's not like that. I treat my wives well. And I'd treat you especially well. I'd give you every minute I can—"

"Meaning you'd deprive my sister of the attention she's currently getting? Or her children? Or maybe you were talking about one of your other wives, like the Widow Fields. You never asked for her, anyway, right?"

He fell silent for a few moments. "You've changed."

"In more ways than you realize."

"You're as wicked as they say."

Hope blanched but didn't respond.

"I offer you true love and salvation, and you jeer in my face."

"I don't need you to save me."

"You're making a mistake, Hope. You're going against everything you've ever been taught. There must be an echo left that tells you what you're doing is wrong."

"The only echo I hear is when you told my father you'd abide by his decision to give me to Arvin," she said.

His jaw tightened and his eyes narrowed. "Are you trying to rub my nose in it? I told you, I was young—"

"And I was younger."

"So you can't forgive me. That's what this is all about."

"No, this is about wanting more out of life than what you have to offer."

He rocked back as though she'd slapped him. "But I told you. I have power in the church now. I can do—"

"Pretty much whatever you want," she finished for him. "That's what frightens me."

Color flooded his face, and she thought Bonner would reveal just how full of himself he'd become. But he only looked down his nose at her as though she was the biggest disappointment of his life. Then he went inside.

Hope followed, wondering what he was going to tell Arvin.

"Let's go," he said as soon as he reached the living room.

It was obvious that Faith had been crying. Hope felt a flash of guilt for leaving her alone with their uncle.

"What do you mean?" Arvin said, his jaw going slack. "Isn't Hope coming back?"

Hope saw anger and accusation in Bonner's glance, as if *she* had somehow wronged *him.* "No, she'd rather go to hell, just like her father said."

Her father had always had such confidence in her.

"Well, Faith's coming," Arvin nearly shouted. "Faith, get your things."

Faith didn't look as though she trusted her own voice. She shook her head, instead of speaking, and Arvin's face contorted. "You do as I say. I'm your husband, you hear? When I tell you to do something, you mind. Now, get out to that car."

The clap of his hands sounded like a gunshot. Faith jumped and started toward the door, but Hope caught her by the elbow. "She's only leaving if she wants to. Not because you think you can treat her like some kind of slave." Turning to Faith, she purposely softened her voice. "You don't have to go with him, Faith. I'm here. And I'm not afraid of him. I won't let him do anything you don't want him to do. You don't have to worry about that. But if you *want* to go back, now's your chance."

Dashing a hand across her cheeks, Faith wiped fresh tears on the skirt of her dress and moved closer to Hope. "I don't want to go back," she said. "I don't *ever* want to go back."

The vehemence in her sister's voice told Hope she meant what she said. Surprise and relief flooded her in equal measure. But there was still the issue of Arvin and Bonner in her living room. And the fact that she'd been lying when she said she wasn't afraid of them. It might have been a long time since she'd lived under the Brethren's authority, but her parents had struck a double blow—they'd sent Bonner, whose presence completely unnerved her, and Arvin, who made her skin crawl.

Squaring her shoulders, she projected as much confidence as she could muster. "Then that's it. I'm afraid it's time for the two of you to go."

"Like hell!" Arvin cried. "Faith's not staying here."

"I'll call the police if you don't leave this minute," Hope replied.

Arvin took a step toward her, looking as though he'd gladly wring her neck, but Bonner intercepted him. "Let's go. She's a child of the devil. I guess the Lord was looking out for me all those years ago."

Arvin shook off his hand. "I'll make you pay for this, bitch," he snarled. "I'll make you so sorry, you'll—"

"Arvin, that's enough," Bonner cut in. "Let's go."

"This isn't over," Arvin replied. "This isn't over by a long shot."

"Hope didn't do anything. I did," Faith said, but no one seemed to hear her above Bonner's more strident voice.

"She'll pay a heavier price than you could ever exact," he announced. "The Lord will take vengeance upon her soul."

"I know He will, because I'm going to help Him," Arvin said, and swaggered out.

Bonner glanced at Hope, and the emotion in his face frightened her almost as much as Arvin did. Not because he looked crazy. But because he looked so sane and could still curse her as though he could command even God. The power he held in the church had obviously gone to his head. And to think that for an instant she'd been half-way tempted to give up the fight and go back to her roots! How could she have wavered?

Because she still remembered the way he made her feel, she realized. She'd been dead inside since she'd left him. She wanted to feel *something* again, to forget…

But not with Bonner. Lifting her chin, she glared at him in return until finally, thankfully, he left.

IN THE WAKE of Bonner and Arvin's departure, the silence felt palpable. The temperature was already rising—would hit the mid-eighties later in the day. The early warmth of spring promised another blistering summer like the last one, when St. George had known week-long stretches of 110 degrees or more. But it was the quality of the silence that felt strange to Hope, not the heat; the stilted silence and the realization that after eleven years, she'd just confronted the one man she still dreamed about.

"I'm sorry he came," Faith said finally.

Her words seemed to ripple through the air, forever

moving outward, just like the consequences of what had happened when she was only sixteen....

"It's not your fault. Bonner should have known better," Hope said, trying to throw off a nagging sense of loss. Regardless of how hard she wished things had ended differently a decade earlier, she couldn't do anything to change the situation now. She'd lost the innocence that had allowed her to experience such all-consuming love.

"Are you really over him?" Faith asked.

The answer was complex, Hope knew. Because of what Bonner had meant to her, she wasn't sure she'd ever be completely over him. What had happened had cut her too deeply. But she wasn't about to admit that to Faith.

"I am," she said, thinking she might as well make it simple, even in her own mind. The nuances of lost love and regret didn't change anything.

Moving to the couch, Faith squatted close to the floor and held out one hand. "Here, kitty, kitty," she crooned. "Come here. It's okay. They're gone. You don't have to be afraid."

For the first time, Hope realized that Oscar was inside the house. He hovered, partially concealed, between the couch and chair, obviously on edge and ready to bolt at the slightest provocation. "What's Oscar doing in here?" she asked. "I've never been able to entice him across the threshold."

"I encouraged him with a piece of meat this morning. I wanted the company. He actually sat in my lap and let me pet him. But Bonner and Arvin rang the doorbell while I was trying to get a burr out of his coat, and he panicked." Faith indicated a couple of deep scratches on her wrist.

"Huh," Hope snorted. "Poor thing."

Faith arched a brow at her sarcasm. "He only scratches when he's frightened, Hope."

"Then he must be downright terrified most of the time."

"He'll learn to trust me. I like him."

"If you want a cat, we can get you a decent cat," she said. "One that won't shred you to ribbons. There are definitely easier animals to love than old Oscar."

"No." Faith gazed thoughtfully at her scratches. "I want this cat. I think he needs me."

Faith had been in the house less than two full days, and she'd already adopted poor Oscar. What was wrong with Hope that she refused to get attached, even to a cat?

"I'm proud of you," Hope said.

"Because I want Oscar?"

"Because you can still risk loving. And because you're made of sterner stuff than I thought."

Her sister flipped one braid over her shoulder. "You expected me to go back, didn't you."

"I did."

"I *was* tempted, but only because it's not fair to bring all this negative stuff back into your life. I saw the way you were looking at Bonner. I feel terrible that—"

"Don't," Hope said. "I don't want to talk about it."

Faith turned to Oscar, who crept warily closer. "Were you telling the truth when you said you weren't afraid of Arvin?"

"Not really," Hope said. "Were you telling the truth when you said you called Mother just to let her know you were okay?"

A faint smile lit her sister's face. "I guess, deep down, I knew she'd send someone for me. Leaving Superior behind suddenly seemed too frightening." Her smile disappeared. "But when I saw Arvin, I felt like there was a giant steel ball sitting on my chest. I knew he'd want to establish his claim on me as soon as we got home. He'd probably spend the next several nights with me to show me how powerless I am. And the thought of being that powerless scared me more than the fear of a future without the rest of my family. When I realized that, and then thought about my baby having no better father than Arvin, I knew I was wrong, that I *had* to go through with this.''

"What'd Arvin say while Bonner and I were out back?"

"He was sort of nice at first. He told me the place wasn't the same without me.''

"And when you didn't rush to the door to leave with him?''

Finding a more comfortable position on the floor, Faith made soft clicking noises, still trying to coax Oscar closer. "He said Ila Jane needed my help with the garden.''

Oscar, seemingly less threatened now, sniffed in the direction of her outstretched hand.

"He used Ila Jane because he knows you love and respect her,'' Hope said. "He knows you care about the garden, too.''

Faith didn't respond. She crooned to Oscar, who hesitated, inches away from her hand, then swished his tail and brushed up against her.

Hope shook her head as she watched the two of them. Maybe Faith would make a more successful adjustment to regular life than she had. At least Faith still had her ideals.

CHAPTER SIX

HOPE CALLED IN sick that night. She'd slept almost the entire day, but she still had a headache, and she couldn't leave Faith by herself. Not again. Not after Arvin's visit. His vile threats still echoed in her mind. Now that he knew where they were, she was afraid he might act on those threats. He might have earlier if Bonner hadn't been around.

Bonner. His face and voice immediately appeared in her mind. *I'm sorry, Hope…*

"Hey, I'm talking to you." Faith put a hand on her shoulder.

"Hmm?" Hope blinked as the familiar surroundings of her kitchen materialized. She'd just drifted off, she realized.

"I'm going to have a cup of herbal tea. I asked if you wanted me to make you one."

"No, thanks." Hope gazed down at the list she'd been making at the table—a list of all the things they'd need to purchase before Faith's baby was born. They'd already talked about getting her a good doctor. The polygamist community was a tight-knit one that survived mostly on welfare. When a member fell ill or was seriously injured, he or she typically came to St. George for treatment and relied on the state to pay the bill. But prenatal care was something else entirely. The Brethren believed it immodest and immoral to allow an outsider, especially a man, such intimate access to their wives. So a few of the older women acted as midwives and gained knowledge as they gained experience. Faith had been examined by Sister Belinda and Sister Rosie, she said, both of whom claimed that her baby was coming along just fine. But she'd never been to a licensed doctor.

Hope was anxious to make sure she saw one soon. It was probably too late to worry about such things as iron deficiency or testing for gestational diabetes. But there were still a million things that could go wrong if Faith didn't receive the proper care. Besides, Hope wanted an accurate due date; they didn't need any surprises.

"I think we should get a monitor," she said, trying to return to the spirit of their planning. "It would come in handy if the baby was napping and we were out in the garden or the garage."

"Monitors are expensive," Faith replied from the counter, where she was making her tea.

Hope shrugged. "Only thirty or forty bucks."

"That's expensive."

"It's affordable, Faith." Hope put down her pen to rub her eyes. It was nearly eleven and she was ready to head back to bed. "We're not trying to support an army. Just the three of us," she went on, taking up her pen again. "We'll get by. So stop talking about the expense of everything. It'll only make you feel indebted, and I don't want that. You'd help me if I needed it, wouldn't you?"

The insecure expression clouding her sister's face disappeared. "Of course."

The kettle began to whistle. Faith lifted it off the stove. Hope had tried to show her how to use the microwave, but evidently, she wasn't quite ready to make the transition to the electronic age. They'd grown up in a house built in 1910, without a dishwasher or a microwave.

The telephone rang as soon as Faith poured her tea. Hope wondered who might be calling so late, but nodded for Faith, who was closer, to pick it up.

"Hello?"

Hope continued to study her list. If they were careful,

they could possibly purchase a crib at a secondhand store or a garage sale. They might even be able to find a—

"Who is this?" A shaky quality filtered through Faith's voice, causing Hope to glance up—and notice that the color was quickly draining from her sister's face.

"Is this Sarah?" Faith said. "Sarah, what's wrong?"

Hope shoved away from the table to round the counter. "What is it?"

Faith ignored her. "Are you hurt, honey? Sarah, is it you?" Suddenly she dropped the receiver onto the counter.

"What happened?" Hope asked.

Faith rubbed her arms as if she was cold. "Someone was crying."

"Was it Sarah? What did she say?"

"Nothing. It sounded like a little girl, but…but I think Arvin was there, too." She stared at the phone as though it had turned into a snake. "I think he was hurting Sarah," she said, her words coming out in a terrified rush.

"Is Sarah Charlene's daughter? The one you mentioned before?"

Faith nodded. "She…she has a harelip. She doesn't really fit in and Arvin's never been very good to her. But she has the sweetest disposition and…" Faith pressed a fist to her lips.

"Whoever that child was could've been crying for any reason," Hope said. "She could have been crying for a drink of water, Faith. You don't know she was being hurt."

"But Arvin's capable of hurting children. I know he'd hurt Sarah if he thought it would bring me home."

Hope slipped her arm around Faith. She wouldn't put it past Arvin to hurt a child, either. But she and Faith weren't exactly in a position to do anything about it. They couldn't give in and go back, because then he really *would* have all the power. "The whole thing was probably a hoax, Arvin's attempt to manipulate you into coming back," she said, trying to comfort her.

Faith remained stiff and unyielding. "What was I thinking?" she asked. "He'll never let me leave. He'll hurt the people I love."

"No," Hope insisted. "Sarah's probably fine. Most likely she's in bed asleep and that was some other child. It could even have been a crank call."

"I d-don't think so."

"If it was Sarah, then Jed…er, our father, will take care of her. He wouldn't let Arvin hurt anyone. In Superior, there are some lines even men can't cross, right?"

"Not many," Faith whispered. "And how would Daddy know?" Her fearful eyes were riveted on Hope's. "It's all about secrets, isn't it? The kind we're taught to keep everyday."

The phone began to beep from being left off the hook, but Hope refused to place it back on its cradle. She wouldn't allow Arvin the chance to harass them any more tonight. He'd done enough damage.

"What should I do?" Faith asked.

"Nothing," Hope said. "There's nothing you can do. At least we can still get hold of Mama. I wasn't sure of that until you called home." Not all households in Superior had phones. Many members of the Everlasting Apostolic Church didn't have sufficient credit to convince the telephone company they'd pay the bill. But some of the more powerful Brethren managed to get one, usually by putting the account in the name of one of their children. When Hope was still living at home, having a phone had been something of a status symbol.

"Daddy had the phone company install one at Sister Helena's house and tried to take Mama's out. But Mama wouldn't hear of it. It's the only time I've ever seen her fight him on anything."

"And he gave in? Why was having a phone so important to her? She doesn't care about impressing people."

"Are you kidding?"

"About what?"

"I think she's been waiting for you to call. Getting rid of the phone meant you never would."

Faith's words hit Hope like a hard-packed snowball to the chest. She'd wanted to call so many times, most of all when she delivered her baby....

But she couldn't think about the hurts that refused to heal. She couldn't let them stop her, especially now. She had Faith to consider. For the baby's sake, if for no other reason, she couldn't let Arvin coerce her sister into coming back to him.

"We'll call Mama in the morning and tell her what we heard," she said. "She'll do what she can. Maybe we'll contact Jed, too." Hope cringed at the thought of that, but she'd do anything to protect an innocent child.

Faith took a deep breath and visibly pulled herself together. "See what I've brought you? Nothing but trouble."

"Arvin's the one who's causing all the trouble."

Her sister didn't respond.

"Faith? It's not you. It's Arvin. And he's just trying to scare you. You can't let him, or he wins."

"Is that what you really think?"

"It is."

"Okay."

Hope squeezed her sister's shoulder. "That's the spirit. Sarah's fine."

"I hope so."

"We'll call and check on her in the morning."

"That would help."

Hope retrieved Faith's tea and handed it to her. "You going to be all right?"

Faith took one sip, then put the cup down. "Yeah, but I'm pretty tired. I think I'll turn in."

"That's probably a good idea." Hope watched her sister go, worried about the stiffness in her posture. She was pretending to be fine, but Hope knew that telephone call had disturbed her deeply.

"Damn Arvin. Damn him to hell and back," she muttered fiercely once her sister had disappeared down the hall.

Dumping Faith's tea in the sink, she set the cup in the dishwasher and went to check the doors and windows. Occasionally, if it was hot and there was a cool breeze, she propped open the front door and let the evening air sift through the house. It brought with it all the spring smells she loved so much—fresh-cut grass, anise, rosemary. She lived on the kind of street where everyone knew everyone else, most went to the same church, which was located only a block away, and no one worried about crime or violence.

But tonight she didn't care how safe her neighborhood *normally* was, or how welcome a breeze might be. She was going to lock up.

Oscar darted between her legs, nearly tripping her as she passed through the living room. He'd been in for most of the day, had even allowed Faith to feed him. But the expectant meow he gave her at the door told Hope he was definitely ready to go out.

"Here you go," she said, opening the door and holding the screen.

The cat fled past her, loped across the yard and disappeared into the shrubs separating her place from Mr. Paris's.

Hope took the opportunity to look around. No strange cars were parked on the street. No movement or noise broke the stillness. Mrs. Crandall's porch light, two doors down, cast strange shadows on the lawn. But that wasn't unusual. Mrs. Crandall left her light on every night.

Overall, it looked like another quiet night in her peaceful neighborhood.

A HEAVY THUMP woke Hope long before dawn. She lay in bed, straining to hear above the sound of her own breathing, her nerves tingling from the sudden awareness flooding through her. What was that? Faith? Was she up?

Hope angled her head to see down the hall, hoping a glimmer of light would indicate it was her sister moving around. But the darkness beyond her bedroom was so complete she had to blink several times to be sure her eyes were actually open.

"Faith?" she called softly.

No response.

Kicking off the covers, Hope got out of bed and started moving carefully toward the hall. It was probably nothing, she told herself. But the memory of Arvin's threats and the call they'd received earlier made the back of her neck prickle.

Surely Arvin wouldn't reappear so soon. Surely he wouldn't do anything that could actually injure someone.

Surely? Hope realized she wouldn't put anything past her uncle. He'd considered himself above the law for so long, who could say what he'd do? He believed Hope had wronged him for the second time, and he'd promised revenge. Just what his idea of "making her pay" was, Hope didn't know. But she wasn't going to let him surprise her. Or hurt Faith.

Creeping through the house, Hope stood at Faith's door, grateful to find it open, and peeked in. Faith already had more privacy than she'd ever experienced. She probably saw no need to close her door at night.

The window to the left of the bed faced the side yard, where a line of cottonwood trees blocked most of the moonlight. After a few seconds, however, Hope managed to make out her sister's form. Faith was still in bed, sleeping.

So what was the noise she'd heard?

She tiptoed down the hall toward the kitchen and living room, where the windows would allow in more moonlight. The phone was still off the hook from earlier, so Arvin couldn't call them again. She hoped she'd be able to establish service right away in case they had an emergency on their hands.

There isn't going to be an emergency. I'm overreacting, she told herself. But that didn't ease the sick feeling in her stomach. Nor did it replace the bigger question: if Arvin *was* back, what might he do?

Hope recalled the fierceness of his anger the night he found out she was pregnant with Bonner's baby. Her father had called Arvin from the church, wanted to meet him at the house to discuss the problem. But Arvin arrived first and screamed every vile name he could think of at her—whore, slut, child of hell. He would have struck her, if not for her mother.

Faith had once said she believed Arvin was in love with Hope, but Hope knew better. Ever since she'd grown old enough to avoid and deny him, he'd become obsessed with the idea of forcing her to submit to him. But he'd never loved her.

The numbers of the digital clock on the microwave lent the kitchen an alien greenish glow. While Hope watched, 2:34 became 2:35. They hadn't even been sleeping three hours. But three hours was long enough to drive from Superior to St. George. Arvin could easily have returned to Superior with Bonner this morning, placed the call Faith had received before bed, then slipped away undetected. One wife would simply assume he was with another, and the other Brethren wouldn't have a clue.

Keeping to the walls and darker corners, Hope looked through the glass doors that opened into the backyard. With the porch and all the old trees back there, it was difficult to see much beyond a few murky shapes—the garden gate, the grill, the lawn furniture. Fortunately, nothing moved.

She held still for several seconds, waiting, listening.

She was about to go to the front, when another thump shot a jolt of adrenaline through her system.

It had come from the side yard, where she kept her garbage containers on a small concrete slab poured specifically for that purpose.

Hope made a feeble attempt to convince herself that it was only Oscar, searching for food scraps among the refuse. Or engaging in another of his many fights. St. George wasn't particularly concerned with animal control. There were plenty of strays. But the only sound was that ominous thump. No hissing or growling.

Hope's eyes cut to the phone. She darted across the kitchen to hang it up—and nearly jumped out of her skin when she heard a voice behind her.

"Hope? Is everything okay?"

She whirled to face Faith, standing at the entrance to the hall, only her silhouette visible in the darkness.

"Faith! What are you doing up?" she whispered harshly, flattening one hand against her chest as if she could slow the pounding of her heart.

"I heard something," she said softly. "Did you?"

Hope nodded.

"What is it?"

"I don't know."

"It could be Arvin," Faith said. "Maybe we should call the police."

"You don't really think he'd do anything…serious, do you?"

"He's strange," Faith admitted. "Sometimes he was kinder than I expected him to be. But I don't think he was feeling very kind when he left here today. And he's more often cruel."

Cruel wasn't good. Not when they were hearing things that went bump in the night. Hope's fingernails curled into her palms. "What kind of cruel?"

Before her sister could respond, the doorknob on the

back door began to jiggle and Hope felt her knees go weak.

"It's him. It's got to be him," Faith said. "Call the police."

Hope hung up the phone, but even after she'd waited several seconds, she couldn't get a dial tone. Wasn't she waiting long enough? Or had Arvin cut the line?

The doorknob stopped rattling. A dark shadow moved past the closest window. "Get down," Hope whispered, trying to give the telephone another chance to work.

Faith crouched down and crawled over just as Hope put the receiver back to her ear. No dial tone. *Shit!*

"What's wrong?" Faith demanded. "Call the police. I don't want him to get inside. I don't want him—"

"He can't get in," Hope said breathlessly. "We'll be fine." She hurried across the floor to reach the cupboards and took out the biggest knife she owned.

"What are you going to do with *that?*" Faith asked.

"Protect us. Go to the bathroom and lock yourself in."

"I'm not leaving you here. It's my fault he's doing this. If I go back with him, he'll stop. Maybe I should just—"

"You're not going anywhere you don't want to go," Hope said. "And at this point, he'd probably punish you, anyway. He could hurt the baby."

Standing on legs that felt far too rubbery to support her, Hope made it to the window without falling and raised a hand to the glass so she could stare out. The back porch was empty now. At least it *appeared* to be empty.

"Is he gone?" Faith asked.

Hope doubted Arvin had driven three hours just to make a little noise. "I can't tell."

"Maybe I should turn on a light."

"No! If we turn on the lights, he'll be able to see in, but we won't be able to see out."

"At least he'll know we're up and around, that we know he's here."

"I get the impression he doesn't care if we know. He

might even *want* us to know. It might be part of whatever game he's playing. We're alone. He's already cut the phone line.''

''What are we going to do?'' Faith asked.

''Anything we have to,'' Hope responded. Anger and determination were finally coming to her rescue, lending her strength. She would not allow Arvin to terrorize them. She'd come too far to fall back into the pit of fear and intimidation from which she'd escaped.

''Stay here.'' Hurrying into the living room, Hope pressed her nose to the front window. She'd been hoping to spot Arvin, to see what he might be up to, but she hadn't expected to come face-to-face with him on the other side of the glass.

With a startled cry, she jumped back and dropped the knife.

''Hope? Are you okay?'' Faith asked as the knife clattered to the floor.

''He's right outside. I saw him.'' She scrambled to reclaim her weapon, then held it tightly in one ice-cold hand as she hovered near the window to peer out again. This time she saw nothing.

''Is he still there?'' Faith breathed, coming up behind her.

''I can't tell where he is. But he can't be far.'' She banged on the window to draw his attention. She didn't really want to come face-to-face with him again, but keeping him in front of her was definitely preferable to wondering whether he was sneaking around some other part of the house, trying to break in. ''Flip on the porch light.''

She heard the floor creak as Faith made her way to the switch by the front door. A moment later, the light came on, and Hope saw Arvin standing on the porch, looking about as sinister as a man could look, with his straggly hair, gangly body and cadaverous cheeks.

''I've called the police,'' she shouted loud enough for

him to hear. "If you know what's good for you, you'll head back to Superior now."

He grinned, revealing less than the normal allotment of teeth. "Pretty tough to do that without a phone, ain't it, Hope?"

Hope tightened her grip on the knife. "I have a cell phone. Welcome to the twenty-first century," she said, and wished with all her heart that it was true. Unfortunately, she socialized so little she'd never seen any point in purchasing a cell phone—but he didn't know that.

His smile disappeared. Darting forward, he slapped his hand against the window.

The glass shook. Faith screamed and sank to the floor. Hope automatically raised the knife—and pretended she hadn't nearly lost control of her bladder.

"Harassing us isn't going to do you any good," she said. "Faith's not leaving with you. She's *never* going back. You might as well accept it and go home, where you can continue to pretend you're God."

"As far as she's concerned, I am God," he said. Then he laughed, and it was creepy enough that Hope shivered.

"You're crazy. I hope you know that."

"You'd better hope I don't get in there," he said. "Because you know what I'm going to do to you? I'm going to do what I've wanted to do since you were nine years old. I'm going to show you what you've missed over the years, pretty baby. And maybe when I'm done, you'll be carrying my child, too. Just think, you and Faith could both be—"

Suddenly Arvin turned. Hope searched the darkness behind him and found Mr. Paris hurrying across the lawn, wearing a pair of old pants with his pajama shirt tucked halfway inside and holding Oscar in the crook of one arm. Her neighbor stopped at the edge of the flower bed in front, which brought him just inside the circle of light shed by the porch fixture.

"What's going on here?" he said. At least, that was

what Hope thought he said. He wasn't as close to her as Arvin was, and she had to strain to hear him.

"Mind your business, old man," Arvin said. "This has nothing to do with you."

For fear of what might happen to her unsuspecting neighbor, Hope flew to the door, unlocked it and stepped outside. Mr. Paris had no way of knowing he was dealing with a man whose mind was warped by too much inbreeding.

"Who're you calling old?" Mr. Paris said. "Looks like the pot calling the kettle black. And what are you doing here, anyway?" He eyed the knife Hope still held in one hand, and Hope felt a little sheepish. She wasn't sure she could've used it. It had just seemed like her only defense option at the time.

"Doesn't appear to me like you've been invited," Mr. Paris finished.

"He wasn't invited," Hope said. Trying to convince Arvin to move on before there was any kind of altercation, she added, "The police are already on their way."

"She's got my wife," Arvin said, his voice suddenly plaintive. "I'm just trying to get my wife back."

Mr. Paris squinted at him, then at Faith, who'd come out and was standing just behind Hope. "Looks to me like she'd be better off with a fella closer to her own age." He hiked up his pants. "I think you oughtta leave."

A light came on across the street, and Mrs. Hortichek stuck her head out her screen door. "My Lord, what's going on over there, Hope? You'd think the world was coming to an end, what with all the racket."

"I'm sorry. It's nothing, Mrs. Horticheck," Hope said. "You can go back to bed."

"I would if I could sleep," she snapped, and slammed her door.

"I'm going to call my father in the morning," Hope told Arvin. "I think he'll agree with me that you've finally lost your mind and give Faith his blessing to leave you."

"That's what *you* think," Arvin said. "You'll never turn my own brother against me. If you so much as try—" he glanced malevolently at Mr. Paris "—no senile neighbor will be able to save you." He gave Faith a hateful glance, then disappeared into the darkness, leaving Mr. Paris blinking after him.

"Who's he calling senile?" her neighbour said. "I do believe that man has a screw lose."

An engine roared to life near the end of the block, followed by the squeal of tires. "Or two or three," Hope said with a sigh. "Thanks for coming over."

"Are the police really on their way?" Mr. Paris asked eagerly. A visit from the police was big news in their neighborhood. The last time anybody called for emergency help was when Mrs. Fernley's electric wok shorted out and set her kitchen on fire only days after Hope had moved in. That night, the entire neighborhood had stood on the lawns and watched the firefighters do their work. Some folks still talked about it fondly, as though they'd never enjoyed themselves more.

"No, not really," she said. "Sorry to disappoint you."

Hope made a mental note to purchase a cell phone at the mall the following morning, said good night to Mr. Paris and ushered Faith inside. But the next day, she knew a mere cell phone would never be enough. Arvin wasn't going to back off—he'd left her a little reminder that he'd probably be visiting again soon. And that things might not end so well next time.

When she opened the front door to retrieve the paper, there on her front step was Oscar the cat.

But he was no longer breathing.

CHAPTER SEVEN

HOPE KNEW she couldn't let Faith see Oscar, which made the distasteful job of removing the cat's corpse, cleaning up the blood, and notifying poor Mr. Paris that much more difficult, because it all had to be done in secret. After eleven years of cautious, calculated movements, her entire life seemed to be veering out of control. But she couldn't think of anything she should've done differently. She'd had to go back to Superior; she probably should have gone years ago. She'd had to bring Faith home with her; Faith had no one else to help her. And she'd had to send Bonner and Arvin away in no uncertain terms.

Still, she felt responsible for Oscar's death and even a little guilty for not loving him more when she'd had the chance. Except, now more than ever, she didn't want to love anything. Love was a dangerous, risky venture.

Take Oscar and Faith, for example.

"HE *WHAT?*" Bonner said.

Hope drew a shaky breath and glanced at poor Mr. Paris, who was sitting at his kitchen table, so shocked by what had happened that he hadn't even removed his muddy boots after helping her bury Oscar. "He...he killed my neighbor's cat."

"He mutilated him," Mr. Paris added, his voice ringing with outrage. "What kind of sick bastard does that to a defenseless cat?"

"It wasn't Arvin," Bonner said. "He drove back to Superior with me, and I was with him most of the day."

"Were you with him last night?" she replied.

"No, but…I can't imagine he'd kill your neighbor's cat. What does your neighbor have to do with anything?"

"They exchanged a few words after Arvin cut the phone line and started harassing us last night. I'm sure Arvin wasn't too pleased about the interference."

"Still," Bonner said, "what's the point of murdering a cat?"

"He was sending me a message." Hope closed her eyes and shook her head. She'd had no better luck convincing her parents. Her mother had said she'd look out for Sarah—grudgingly, because agreeing to do so acknowledged that Arvin might be dangerous—but Jed wouldn't even hear her out. She and her father had started to argue almost immediately, and he'd hung up. Which was why she'd called Bonner. Bonner had heard Arvin's threats yesterday. She'd hoped, because of that, he might listen to her and realize how dangerous Arvin was. "He left the cat on my doorstep."

"I'm sorry about that, Hope, but I don't know what you think I can do."

"I want you to convince the Brethren that Arvin is unstable. He's going to hurt someone, Bonner. Someone has to do something."

"What? He hasn't hurt anyone yet. You think the Brethren are going to excommunicate him for killing a cat? I don't think they care about some cat in St. George. Anyway, it's your word against his, and I don't have to tell you how they view you right now."

They? She knew Bonner viewed her the same way now. "You could tell them what he said yesterday."

"And he'd tell them he was just angry, that he didn't mean it."

She dropped her head in her hand and rubbed her throbbing temple. "Faith has every right to leave him, Bonner."

"I can't agree with you there," he said. "I don't believe in divorce. You know that. And Faith is carrying his child.''

''Which means what?''

''It means there's nothing I can do. I can't tell him to stay away from his own baby. How would I enforce it even if I did?''

That was the problem. The police had told her basically the same thing. She could file a restraining order against Arvin, but there was no guarantee he'd respect it. As much as she'd hoped the police or someone in Superior might be able to help, there wasn't anything anyone could do. No one could watch Arvin around the clock. No one could ensure that he wouldn't return and...

She stared at Mr. Paris's slumped shoulders, regretting that his kindness last night had cost him his pet. She knew he'd eventually adjust, maybe even get a new cat. He was a tough old guy. But she and Faith couldn't go on living next door, wondering when the other shoe was going to drop.

She had to do something. And she had to do it right away.

''WHERE HAVE YOU been?'' Faith asked, poking her head out the door as Hope removed her gardening boots.

Hope positioned her boots carefully on the back porch so she wouldn't have to look at Faith. Her mind still held the image of Mr. Paris's face when she'd had to tell him about Oscar, and it was making her eyes burn and her throat ache.

She couldn't let herself care. If she cared, she'd be hurt. And she'd already promised herself that she wouldn't let anything or anyone hurt her again. But it didn't seem to help.

She struggled to speak around the lump clogging her throat. ''I was just out pulling weeds.''

''I checked the garden a few minutes ago.''

''I was helping Mr. Paris with his garden.''

"Are we still going shopping today?"

Shopping. For what? Hope no longer felt safe in her own house. She certainly couldn't bring a newborn baby here. What if Arvin returned while she was at work? Or got inside the house while they were sleeping? If he came after the baby was born, he'd steal it, at the very least. At the most...

The memory of Oscar's mangled body made her cringe. Blinking against the tears that blurred her vision, she said, "Not today. We need to pack. We're going away for a while."

Faith's head snapped up. "What are you talking about? The baby's due soon."

"I know. But we can't stay here. Arvin..." She cleared her throat. "He could come back."

"I thought we were going to call our parents, see if they'll do something to stop him."

Hope had already tried that and knew it was futile. Even if their parents and Bonner were supportive of her and Faith, which they weren't, Arvin would have plenty of opportunity to harass or harm them. Staying put was simply too big a risk to take. Especially with the prospect of a new baby...

"I called Mama and Jed this morning."

"And? What did they say? Did they agree to look after Sarah?" she asked anxiously.

"Mom said she'd make sure Sarah was fine, but..."

"What?"

"I think Arvin is more dangerous than I realized."

"What do you mean?"

Hope brushed the dirt from her jeans because focusing on something so trivial helped. "That we should just disappear. And we should do it today."

Faith put a hand to her chest and stepped back. "How can you say that? What about your job?"

"I'll just have to tell them that I'm in the middle of a

family emergency and can't come back to work for an indefinite period of time."

"And they'll accept that?"

"They might."

"What if they don't?"

"A good obstetrics nurse can find work just about anywhere."

"But if you leave like this, the hospital won't give you a recommendation," Faith said.

"That's not necessarily true. I've never been late. I've rarely missed a shift. And I've often worked through holidays and weekends so others could have time off. My supervisor has always been very complimentary of the way I handle my job. She might overlook the lack of notice."

"But you'd be leaving more than your job. What about your home?" Faith glanced around the room, and Hope couldn't help but follow her eye, taking in all the things she'd sewn or painted over the years. Everything was so carefully arranged. She'd been comfortable here. Safe.

But she wasn't safe anymore. And neither was Faith.

"I'm sorry, Hope. This is all because of me," she said. "I shouldn't have come."

"Yes, you should. You just shouldn't have called home. I hope you know better than to ever do that again." Seeing the distress on her sister's face, Hope backed off. Faith was only eighteen. Considering her lack of experience and the emotional turmoil of the past few days, what she'd done was perfectly understandable. "But if I were you, I might've done the same thing," she said. "In any case, it's not going to help us if we waste time feeling bad about past mistakes. We need to start planning for the immediate future."

"How?" Faith fiddled with the end of her braid, and Hope wished she could get her to leave her hair loose or cut it. "Where could we go? Salt Lake?"

Hope closed and locked the door behind her. "I know a place," she said. "It's in New Mexico."

"But I've never been outside Utah. How do you know this place?"

"It's where I had my baby," Hope said. She didn't add that it was where Autumn might be living now, as a ten-year-old girl.

THE DRIVE WAS long and hot. It was spring in other parts of the world, but the Arizona desert felt like summer, especially because the air conditioner in Hope's car had broken down shortly after they reached Cedar Ridge. By the time they hit the Petrified Forest National Park near the Arizona–New Mexico state line, Hope's shirt was stuck to her back and her temper had grown short. They'd taken most of the day yesterday to move her things into storage. Then they'd spent the night at a motel, because she didn't want any more unpleasant surprises from Arvin, and at five o'clock this morning they'd set out. It had been a stressful couple of days.

"I still don't understand why you wouldn't let me ask Mr. Paris if I could bring Oscar with me," Faith grumbled, bringing up the subject they'd argued about several times already.

"I told you, Mr. Paris would never have let him go," Hope said.

"I thought Mr. Paris didn't really care about him."

Hope had thought *she* didn't really care about him, either. As much as she didn't want to face it, she'd found out differently when she discovered his lifeless body on her porch. "You can't go up to someone and simply ask for his pet," she said.

"You said Oscar just hangs out on his own. That hardly sounds as though Mr. Paris would care a whole lot if he came with us."

Hope propped her elbow on the door and sighed. "It

would be harder to find a place to rent with a pet,'' she said, searching for reasons.

Faith turned toward the window, still brooding about not being able to bring the cat, and they lapsed into silence again. Overall, they hadn't spoken much. There hadn't been a lot to say now that they were both leaving their former lives behind. Hope wasn't sure how long they'd stay in Enchantment. She was afraid it might prove too painful to be back, that she'd find herself searching the face of every girl anywhere close to Autumn's age for a possible family resemblance. But she'd given up the house in St. George because she knew she could never return and feel secure.

Fortunately she'd had practice in leaving things behind. Which was why she'd been able to drive away with only a simple phone call to the hospital.

Poof. The past eleven years of her life had disappeared as quickly as the first sixteen. Only this time she'd briefly considered calling a few people to say goodbye. Jeff, the man she'd been dating on and off, a couple of nurses with whom she'd worked, a few neighbors. At least she'd seen Mr. Klinger and Mr. Livingston from down the street when they'd come to help her move everything into storage. She'd said a private goodbye to Mr. Paris. She hadn't asked him to help her move, because she didn't want Faith to find out about Oscar. And the rest of her friends and neighbors…

The rest she wouldn't think about, she decided. Just like she wouldn't think about Oscar. Or Arvin. Or Bonner…

To her chagrin, the list was getting rather long.

''You look tired,'' Faith said.

She'd had too little sleep over the past few nights to recover after only one fairly solid block of eight hours in a motel. But she couldn't ask Faith to drive. Faith didn't have a license. The men in the Everlasting Apostolic Church did all the driving. It was one more way to keep their women powerless and dependent.

"I'm fine," she said. "How about you?"

"I'd be better if Oscar was here."

"Would you shut up about Oscar?" Hope snapped.

Faith's lips thinned. She folded her arms and stared straight ahead.

Hope rested her head on one hand, wishing she'd held her tongue. "Sorry."

"It's okay. I know what we're doing isn't easy for you, and it's all my fault."

"It's not your fault. It's our parents' fault, and it's not easy for either of us." After all, Faith was moving for the second time in a week, after having lived her entire life in the same small town.

"Do you think we're making the right decision?" Faith asked.

"We're staying safe. I think that's a pretty good idea."

Hope could feel Faith studying her. "Can you tell me about the place we're going? It seems so—" she gazed out the window at the desert, which stretched on either side of them as far as the eye could see "—flat."

"Enchantment is nothing like this," Hope said, remembering the deep cool forests of the Sangre de Cristo Mountains, the snow-covered peaks, the rapid streams that cut through the sparsely populated area. The Rio Grande Gorge wasn't far from the Enchanted Circle north of Taos, where the small, resortlike town of Enchantment was located, and the whole area smelled of pine and piñon. "It's high wilderness, but it's sort of touristy, with cute little shops and lots of ski-rental places."

"Where will we stay?"

"We'll find someplace to rent." Hope hadn't had time to make any arrangements, but Enchantment had protected her once. She had confidence it would do so a second time—and take Faith in, as well. When she'd said good-bye to Lydia Kane and Parker Reynolds ten years ago, she'd assumed it would be forever. Lydia had told Hope to be happy, to emotionally release the child she'd given up, start over someplace new and never look back. And Hope had taken that advice to heart.

But forever never seemed to last that long. Hope had thought Superior was behind her forever, too.

"How will we live, now that you don't have a job?" Faith asked.

"I told you, I'll find work."

"Where?"

"There're plenty of hospitals and doctor's offices in New Mexico. If there's license reciprocity between New Mexico and Utah, I'll be better off. But if there isn't, I can always work in another capacity until I'm able to get licensed again."

"But how are we going to get by until you find something?" Faith asked. "I heard you on the phone with your landlord. You lost your last month's rent because you couldn't give thirty days' notice."

"But I left the place in such great shape, I'll get my security deposit back. That's better than nothing."

Hope shifted to relieve a cramp in one leg. She'd been driving for nearly ten hours, and sitting in the same position for so long was making her stiff and uncomfortable. "We can live off my savings—for a while."

It sounded like a precarious existence even to her, but Faith didn't comment on that. "What about all your furniture and stuff? The things you put in storage?"

"It'll be waiting for us when we need it."

"When will that be?"

Hope wished she could say. "I'm not sure. Let's just wait and see what happens in Enchantment."

Faith tilted her head back onto the headrest. "How do you know so much about Enchantment, Hope? Did you stay in New Mexico a long time?"

Long enough for Enchantment to change her. "Not for very long, but I really liked it."

"So…is this a bit like going home?"

"Not exactly."

Faith's lashes lowered to her cheeks. Hope thought she'd fallen asleep until she spoke again. "What's it like to make love?" she asked out of the blue.

Hope glanced at her sister's swollen tummy. "You know what it's like."

"I'm not talking about sex."

Hope lifted her eyes to her sister's delicate-featured face. She wanted to say it was all the same, but that would be a lie. She and Bonner had been young, fumbling virgins, but what they'd shared had been far more satisfying than anything she'd experienced since. She knew the distinction between love and sex about as well as anyone.

"Making love is...sort of a spiritual experience," she admitted. "It's giving everything you've got, physically and emotionally, and it's better than—" she struggled for something to compare it to but came up empty "—anything," she finished lamely.

"Do you think we'll ever find husbands and have regular families?"

The sun was beginning to set on the desert, creating a spectacular display of gold and orange streaks in the rearview mirror. "Probably," Hope said, infusing some optimism into her voice for her sister's benefit. The fact that she could drive away and leave a nice guy like Jeff behind without a single remorseful thought told her *she'd* probably never marry, but she hoped Faith would. "It shouldn't be hard for you. You're young and beautiful."

Faith pulled on her seat belt. "You're prettier than I am. And you're not *that* old."

Maybe Hope wasn't old, but she certainly felt like it. She felt as ancient and dried up as the arid landscape through which they were driving.

THEY STOPPED for the night in Albuquerque, then drove on the following morning. The road narrowed as they began climbing through the mountains, the scenery far different than that of the desert through which they'd traveled yesterday. Towering bluffs and sheer drop-offs overlooked green, pine-filled valleys that often included stands of aspens. The earth had darkened to the color of coffee grounds, and everything smelled so…fresh.

Hope rolled down her window to let the wind blow through her hair as they started to descend into the valley where she knew they'd find Enchantment, sitting among the mountains like a jewel in the palm of God's hand. The tight curves of the road eventually straightened, name of the highway changed to become Paseo de Sierra, and soon she could see the town just ahead.

"Are we there?" Faith asked sleepily, rousing herself from a nap as Hope slowed to heed the lower speed limit.

"This is it."

"It's beautiful."

Hope took a deep breath, mentally embracing the town like an old friend. Other than an A-frame building with a sign that read Outdoor Tours posted near the door, a few new T-shirt shops and a drive-in restaurant called the Sunflower Café, the place hadn't changed much. There was the newspaper office, with its glass front and gold writing in the window, the small, square post office with its flag flying, the timber-and-adobe police station a few doors down connected to the library and the Chamber of Commerce, and the drugstore, which doubled as a video-rental store—all just as they'd been when she left. The American Legion Hall looked as though it had recently received a fresh coat of white paint, and the bougainvillea blooming in front of the Morning Light Bed-and-Breakfast had taken over considerably more ground, but that was it. Even the dusty trailer park at the far end of town hadn't changed. Ten or fifteen single-wide mobile homes, most at least twenty years old, still sat on hard-packed earth, which turned into a muddy mess with the first snow.

Hope wondered if Zach Vaughn still lived in the trailer park. She'd once bumped into him at a pivotal point in her life—at Slim Jim's, a small, dark steakhouse where the thick wooden tables were lit mostly by candles and the steaks were as big as the plates. Zach was a burly guy who had her beat by eight years or more. She'd had no romantic interest in him, but she remembered being impressed by the fact that he was driving truck and had a place of his own. Probably because she'd believed that if she could just find a home, she might be able to keep her baby.

It was a closer look at the Lazy H Trailer Park, however, that had convinced her to go through with the adoption. She'd wanted to give her baby a better start than that.

"Is something wrong?" Faith asked.

Amazed that she could still remember Zach's name from that brief encounter, Hope pulled her attention away from the trailer park and blinked at her sister. Already, they were nearing the end of town. A campground and a few rental cabins were nestled in the trees a little farther off, but she and Faith didn't have any camping gear, and if they were going to rent a cabin, they needed to go to the real-estate office in town.

"No, nothing. I was just thinking about getting something to eat. You hungry?"

Faith shrugged. She was still shy about saying when she wanted or needed anything. Hope suspected it was because her sister didn't have any money and hated being such a liability, so she pushed the food issue, although she wasn't particularly hungry herself. Being back in Enchantment was evoking too many bittersweet memories.

"Should we try the Sunflower Café?" she asked.

"Sounds good."

Hope flipped a U-turn and pulled the car into the small corner lot of the Sunflower Drive-in. "Looks like they have a little dining room off to the side where we can eat. Since we don't really have anywhere pressing to go, I think I'd prefer that. How 'bout you?"

Faith was wearing a frown and clicking her nails together. "Do you think Arvin's been back to St. George?" she asked, instead of answering.

"It's possible."

She put a hand on the door latch but didn't get out. "What do you think he'll do when he sees we're gone?"

"What can he do?"

"He can come after us."

Hope cringed at the memory of lifting Oscar's bloody body from her doorstep. "Don't worry. He won't be able to find us."

"Are you sure?"

Hope had rarely spoken of anything connected to New Mexico. She doubted there were even two people in St. George who'd remember her ever mentioning the state, let alone the town.

"I'm sure," she said, but she knew there were ways of tracking a person that had nothing to do with word of mouth. She had to be able to get her mail somehow, which meant she'd eventually need to have it forwarded to a post-office box—preferably one she could reach without having to drive too far. She was going to need her last couple of paychecks and tax documents and final household bills. And as soon as she started working again, opened a new checking account or applied for a Visa card, there was always the chance that her new address would be picked up by one or more of the various credit-reporting agencies.

Whether or not Arvin ever found them would depend a whole lot on how badly they wanted to lead a normal life—and how smart and determined he was. But Hope thought he'd get frustrated and give up before coming anywhere close. At least, she was praying he would. Because something about the craziness in his eyes the last time she saw him made her suspect that if he ever found them again, he wouldn't content himself with killing another poor cat.

CHAPTER EIGHT

HIS GARDEN-NUT burger long gone, his plate pushed to the side, Parker Reynolds sat in the same booth at the Sunflower Drive-in that he claimed most Fridays, reading the *Arroyo County Bulletin*. He had a busy day waiting for him at the birth center—he'd already had a hectic morning—but he'd taken such a late lunch he decided to pick up Dalton from school before returning. His son usually went home with his best friend, Holt, and played at Holt's house until Parker came to get him just before dinner. But the two seemed to be having some trouble getting along lately, and Parker thought it might be a good time to give them, and Holt's mother, a break.

Not that Dalton was going to be especially pleased about returning to work with him and being surrounded by a bunch of women at the clinic. A fifth-grader at the local elementary school, he was still fully immersed in the "Ew, gross" stage of male maturation. Anything delicate, pink or too sentimental was adroitly sidestepped and treated with the same crinkled nose of disdain as a dog pile. If he was taking a little longer to emerge from this stage than most boys, Parker couldn't really blame him. As Holt's mother often pointed out, he was being raised on pure testosterone.

The masculine nature of everything they did had started out as more of an oversight than anything else. Parker's job required him to work nearly fifty hours a week at The Birth Place, where he was surrounded by mothers and babies and midwives. He was ready for a good burger and a game of football by the time he quit work.

But his son's intolerance of anything the least bit feminine was quickly becoming a concern. Because Parker's wife had died when Dalton was only two, Dalton didn't remember his mother, and his only living grandmother, his mother's mother, didn't provide much of a feminine influence. Wife of Congressman John Barlow, she behaved more like a power-hungry man than a woman. Oh, she loved Dalton, all right—fiercely. But Amanda was too ambitious to spend much time with him.

Which left Parker to lament that his own mother had succumbed to a stroke shortly after he and Vanessa were married. She'd been the nurturer in his life and had remained close to him even during his teenage years, when his father couldn't say a nice thing about him. His father's disdain for the stupid things Parker did as a teenager— which were the same things most teenagers did—turned out to be rather ironic, however. After Parker's mother died, his father married a woman half his age who behaved more like a high-school girl than an adult.

Parker grimaced at the thought of Phoebe. With her shallow outlook on life, bleached-blond hair, breast implants, expensive tan and collagen-swollen lips, she was hardly the kind of influence Parker wanted for Dalton, any more than Amanda was. Fortunately his father and Phoebe lived in Washington and weren't too concerned with visiting—

The bell over the door jingled as two women entered the enclosed portion of the drive-in, and Parker glanced up. With a population nearing five thousand, Enchantment was large enough that he didn't know everybody, yet small enough he could expect to run into a familiar face or two almost every time he came to town. Today had been no different. He'd passed Rhoda Strand, the dental hygienist over at Herb Calloway's office, on his way in.

He didn't recall ever seeing this obviously pregnant

young woman before. She blocked his view of the other woman who was with her, but he quickly returned his attention to his paper. He didn't want her to think he was staring. Past experience had taught him that pregnant women were sensitive about that kind of thing. From what he'd seen at the clinic in his twelve years there, pregnant women were sensitive about everything.

"Oh, good, it's health food," one of the women said. "What do you want to order?"

"I'm not sure. I might get a nut-burger if it isn't too big. We had a late breakfast."

"That was in Albuquerque. It's been a while."

"You're the one who only picked at your food."

"I ate plenty."

Bored, he looked up again—and nearly shot out of his chair. He hadn't recognized the pregnant woman and still didn't, but he definitely knew the woman with her. Though he hadn't seen Hope Tanner in ten years, he hadn't forgotten her name or her face and knew he never would. How could he, when he had a daily reminder?

What was she doing back in Enchantment?

Standing, he gathered up the paper, tossed it in the metal rack the Sunflower provided for the purpose of sharing the news and tried to hurry out the door. He'd wait for Dalton in the parking lot of the school and pray that Hope was just passing through.

"Parker, don't you dare leave that plate on the table," Myrna chastised from behind the order window.

Parker came to the drive-in often enough that the hired help knew him by name, but he pretended not to hear. He was planning to make a clean getaway—until the two women at the counter turned and he saw the recognition in Hope's eyes.

"Parker Reynolds," she said.

Parker cleared his throat and pretended to have difficulty recalling her name. When they'd first met, he'd been married about three years and was already dealing with a sick wife. Hope had been a pregnant teenage runaway. From her perspective, he wouldn't have much reason to remember her. "You're…"

"Hope Tanner," she supplied, smiling the same smile he could easily have pictured without ever seeing her again—because his son's was exactly the same. "Don't you remember me?"

"Of course. It's just…it's been a while."

"Ten years, actually."

If only ten years were enough…

"Where have you been?" he asked.

"I've been living in St. George, Utah."

And now for the *big* question…

"What brings you back here?" he asked, working to keep his tone conversational.

She nodded toward her pregnant companion. "This is Faith, my sister. As you can tell, she's close to her delivery date. I'm taking her to see Lydia, where I know she'll be in good hands."

"I'm sure Lydia will be happy to meet her," he said, even though he knew that Lydia would, if anything, be less pleased to see Hope than he was.

"Are you still working at the clinic?" she asked.

He nodded, suddenly wishing he'd moved on long ago. He'd planned to, just to be safe. But then Hope's baby had turned out to be a boy, she'd left town and, almost at the same time, his wife had taken a turn for the worse. After the steady decline that ended in Vanessa's death, it suddenly seemed absurd to leave a well-paying job—a job where he felt he was making a difference in the world—a comfortable home and a neighborhood where he knew everyone on a first-name basis. Especially when his in-laws insisted he had nothing to fear, and Lydia was so certain Hope would never be back.

"That's wonderful," she said. "Then we'll probably see you again this week."

"I guess so," he said, which was the best response he

could muster. His mind kept telling him that everything was okay, that she didn't know anything. But his conscience wasn't willing to write it off quite so easily.

HOPE STARED after Parker Reynolds as he left, feeling a little hurt. He'd meant a great deal to her ten years ago, as a mentor and a friend, but their association must not have had any value to him.

"Who was that?" Faith asked, following her gaze.

Hope forced herself to turn away and collect the red plastic baskets containing the nut-burgers they'd ordered. When she was pregnant, she'd sometimes hang out after her appointment with Lydia in hopes of seeing Parker at the clinic—and was always rewarded with a smile or a kind word. Once, when everyone was closing up and getting ready to leave for the day, he'd even called her into his office and given her a brand-new coat, simply because he thought hers was looking threadbare.

"He's the administrator at the birthing center," she said, carrying her food to an empty table.

"So he worked at the center when you had your baby?"

"Yeah."

"How could he?"

"What do you mean?" Hope stepped over one of the benches permanently affixed to a table and sat down, trying to come to terms with her disappointment. Faith perched on the other side, sitting sideways in deference to her big belly.

"He doesn't seem old enough to have been working ten years ago," she said, sliding her burger closer. "Shouldn't he have still been in school or something?"

"He's not *that* young, Faith." Hope added some ketchup from the center of the table to her bun. "He's got to be at least thirty-five."

Her sister spoke around her first bite. "How do you know?"

"Because he'd already graduated from college and was married when I met him."

"Oh." Faith wrinkled her nose as she swallowed. "He's married? I didn't see a ring."

Hope managed a laugh, despite the hollowness that had engulfed her since Parker's lackluster reception. "You haven't even had the baby yet. Don't tell me you're shopping for a man already."

"It doesn't hurt to keep an eye out. Don't you think he's handsome?"

Of course Parker was handsome. A woman would have to be blind not to notice. He was a rugged, outdoorsy type who dressed casually in jeans and flannel shirts. Tall and athletic, he seemed comfortable in his own skin. And his eyes were particularly attractive. They were almost as dark as his hair, which was a rich coffee color, surrounded by long, thick lashes any woman would envy. But Hope had never considered him *handsome* handsome. Not in the way Faith meant it. Not as in *personally* appealing. And he was married, to the daughter of a congressman, no less!

Still, she thought he'd cared about her as a friend. Now she wondered if she'd meant anything to him at all. He didn't even remember her name.

"I guess," she admitted grudgingly, and started on her meal.

PARKER SLAMMED the door as he entered Lydia's office, only belatedly realizing that he'd used considerably more force than necessary. The crash that reverberated through the clinic sounded especially loud against the quiet music playing over the intercom.

Lydia Kane dropped her pen and lifted her piercing gray eyes. "What's gotten into you?"

Parker jammed his hands in his pockets and began to pace. He wasn't sure exactly what to say. He and Lydia shared a secret, but to a certain extent, they pretended it was a secret they kept from each other, too.

"Hope's back," he said simply, and knew the moment he said it that despite the years, last names were unnecessary.

Lydia's eyes narrowed as the color drained from her angular face. But she didn't lose her poise. Lydia never lost her poise. At seventy-three, she still had the energy of a much younger woman and more drive than most men. Her razor-sharp intellect and shrewd business decisions generally reflected that. But she'd made one mistake. And Parker feared what might happen to both of them if word of that mistake ever got out.

"How do you know?" she asked.

"I just saw her. In town."

Before Lydia could respond, there was a tap on the door and Trish Linden, the receptionist, poked her head into the room. "Is everything okay?" she asked, as though the slamming door had immediately brought her trotting down the hall.

Lydia gave a curt nod. "Everything's fine, Trish." Her voice remained calm, controlled, but Parker noticed the whitening of her knuckles as she clasped her hands on the desk.

It wasn't like Trish to pry. She hesitated for only a second before retreating and closing the door.

"What's she doing in town?" Lydia asked.

"Her sister's pregnant. She's bringing her to the center."

Lydia had her shoulder-length steel-gray hair pulled back in a ponytail that suddenly seemed too tight. "*That's* what brought her back? How far along is the sister?"

Parker crossed to stand in front of her, resting his knuckles on the edge of her desk and leaning into them. "She looks about ready to deliver. I think Hope even said something to that effect."

Lydia stood and clutched the rose-colored pendant she

wore like a talisman. "Fine. We'll deliver her sister's baby, and then all three of them will go back to wherever they came from. It's been so long. Surely Hope has built a life somewhere else by now. She's probably married or…or has a good job or *something*. She was such a beautiful girl, with so much potential. If her sister's as close to term as you say, they could be gone within a couple of weeks, a month at most. A month's not that long."

Another knock sounded on the door. "Come in," she said, her voice bearing a trace of irritation.

Dalton stepped into the room, looking a little unsure of himself. "Sorry to bother you, Aunt Lydia," he said with a shy yet placating smile. "But I need to talk to my dad, and it can't wait."

"What is it?" Parker asked.

"Miguel brought his sister in for her monthly checkup. They're just about to leave, and he said I can ride along with him in his police car for a couple of hours until you get off work, if that's okay with you."

Parker didn't want Dalton to go anywhere right now, not even with a sergeant on Enchantment's police force. But he knew his emotions were pretty scrambled. Hope's reappearance had left him reeling.

"Let him go," Lydia said in a low voice. "You're worrying about nothing."

Parker had heard those words before. From his father-in-law ten years ago. He didn't believe them now any more than he had then. But he couldn't regret the arrangements he'd let Congressman Barlow make. He loved Dalton, and it was too late for regret. The only thing he could do now was guard the secret. As bad as he felt about certain aspects of the situation, some things were better left in the past.

He nodded grudgingly and Dalton dashed off, leaving the door open.

THE PUNGENT SCENT of fresh-cut wood, combined with furniture polish and a hint of smoke and ashes, hit Hope the moment the leasing agent opened the door of the rental cabin—and won her over even before she had a chance to walk through the kitchen and bedrooms. Nestled in the crook of two mountains only fifteen minutes outside Enchantment, the narrow A-frame was small, but ideal for her and Faith. Here they would enjoy the warm days and cool nights of a high wilderness summer amid the shade of surrounding pines and the gentle sway of the long grasses on the slope down to the lake.

"Fortunately it's the off-season, so this cabin is renting at a fraction of its usual price," Peggy Jane, the leasing agent, said.

Hope turned to see Faith's reaction and caught a hint of a smile. Her sister liked it, too. What wasn't to like? For a rental, the place was clean and nicely decorated. Overstuffed leather couches with Western-style rivets faced a distressed-pine entertainment center and a potbellied woodstove. Thick Navajo rugs covered much of the gleaming, wood-plank floor, and pictures of cowboys in black metal frames graced the walls. The lamps, made of the same black metal twisted into interesting designs, perched on primitive, roughhewn tables, which added a great deal to the Southwestern flavor. And an assortment of baskets hung from the wall below the loft that would be Hope's bedroom—since Faith would have too difficult a time climbing the ladder to get there.

"It's lovely," Hope said. "Are you sure the family who owns it won't be needing it this summer?"

"The Loreys have three teenage boys who usually come only during ski season," Peggy Jane replied. "The last time I talked to Mrs. Lorey, she said they were going to be spending the summer abroad."

"Look at the bathroom," Faith said from down the hall. "It's bigger than I thought it would be. And my bedroom has a spectacular view of the lake."

Hope joined her at the junction of bedroom and bath

and saw a simple bathroom decorated in blue with a sand-colored tile floor, and a bedroom with the same rugs and wide-plank floor as the living room. A king-size bed sat beneath a large watercolor print of a Native American woman making pottery. An old-fashioned wardrobe was tucked into one corner, and a small dresser sat to the right of the door. The window Faith had mentioned took up almost the whole of one wall and showed the sun glistening on the water. Hope could hear the quack of ducks and the call of some other bird she couldn't name.

She'd almost forgotten how beautiful Enchantment was.

"The kitchen's sort of small," she said, trying to contain her excitement.

"We can make do with that, don't you think? To the Boxcar Children, this would be a real find," Faith said, grinning.

Hope slipped her hands into the pockets of her denim Capris. "This isn't exactly roughing it." She felt certain she could find something cheaper. If she wanted *really* cheap she could rent a trailer at the Lazy H. But she and Faith needed something positive to cling to right now. They also needed a nice place for the baby. Given her desperate circumstances, it was a matter of pride that she could afford such nice accomodations for her second stay in Enchantment.

She turned to Peggy Jane, who'd followed them into the bedroom. "We'll take it."

"Wonderful. I just need you to fill out a rental application and give me a couple of references from past landlords. Then we'll run a quick credit check."

A feeling of unease swept down Hope's spine. As soon as Peggy Jane contacted her references and identified who she was and where she was calling from, her old landlord, Orlis Deets, would know where she'd gone. He was only one person, a widower who lived alone and suffered too badly from arthritis to go out much, so her whereabouts wouldn't become common knowledge among the folks who knew her in St. George. But she'd be linking her past to her future with at least that one thread....

She thought of Arvin and the other Brethren and how unsophisticated they seemed. Though the men had much more contact with Gentiles than the women did and sometimes, like Bonner, attended university, they shied away from the outside world whenever possible. Arvin, especially, clung to the church and the social framework it provided because it gave him a feeling of acceptance and power she doubted he'd find anywhere else. Even if he managed to figure out where they'd gone, he wouldn't have an exact address and certainly wouldn't take the time or trouble to search further. Would he?

When she hesitated, Faith's eyebrows knitted together. "A credit check isn't a problem, is it, Hope?"

Hope took a deep breath and managed to smile. "No, of course not."

They were eight hundred miles from Superior. Surely they were safe.

CHAPTER NINE

"HOW WAS SCHOOL today?" Parker asked his son, tossing the football to him in a perfect spiral.

Across the half-acre yard, Dalton caught the ball against his chest and launched it back. "Good."

"You and Holt getting along okay?"

Dalton shrugged, darted to the right for another catch and then returned the football.

Parker held onto the ball hoping to get more than just a shrug from his son. Body language was typically good enough; Parker didn't think life had to be complicated with too much detail or explanation. But Holt's mother, Melody Rider, had pulled him aside last week to tell him that Dalton was having a problem expressing his feelings, and Parker planned to correct that. He didn't want Dalton to have any problems. He loved his son more than anyone in the world. "I asked you a question."

"Holt's a dork," Dalton said.

Parker felt the scowl he wore so often lately settle back onto his face. "That's not a very nice way to talk about your best friend."

"But it's true," he said in a sulky voice.

Dalton didn't sound very repentant, but Parker was tempted to let it go. His son *had* expressed himself quite effectively, and that was the whole point of this conversation, wasn't it? Anyway, it was tough to get too angry over a sentiment that echoed what Parker had thought for years. Holt could be fun, even charismatic at times, but he was basically a mama's boy who tended to pout at the drop of a hat, bragged about athletic ability he didn't possess and always had to be the center of attention. Calling him a dork certainly wasn't very nice, but said it all about someone like Holt.

"You used to really like Holt," he said. "What's changed?"

"He's turning into a big—" Dalton seemed to consider his word choice more carefully "—baby."

Parker threw the ball again, a little long this time, and it bounced into the bushes. "Can you give me an example?"

Dalton waited until he'd recovered the ball before responding. "He started crying the other day at school just because Anthony stole his homework and ran off with it."

"What would you have done?" The ball landed in Parker's hands with a satisfying *thwump*.

"I would've chased Anthony down."

"What if he wouldn't give it up?"

The ball was in flight again. Dalton's eye homed in on it as he said with absolute certainty, "He'd give it up."

"How do you know?" Parker asked.

Dalton made a spectacular diving catch. "What'd you say?" he asked, coming to his feet.

"How do you know he'd give it up?"

"Because he knows what I'd do to him if he didn't."

Parker winced. This was exactly the kind of tough talk that had him worried. Although his son didn't fight often, he'd been involved in a couple of skirmishes at school, enough to lend credence to Melody's assertion that Dalton might be dealing with his emotions in the wrong way. "You don't solve problems with your fists, Dalton. We've talked about that before."

His son gave him a "get real" look. "In *that* type of situation you do. I'm not going to tattle to the teacher. And I'm sure as heck not going to start crying, like Holt did."

Parker knew he should probably take a stronger stance

against violence. But he knew that if he was ten years old and facing the same dilemma, he wouldn't tattle or cry. Whoever took his paper would give it back upon demand or else. And Parker wasn't dishonest enough to pretend differently. Which was at least part of the reason he was so inclined to believe what others were telling him—that he needed to find a mellowing influence for his son. He and Dalton were too similar for him to provide any kind of counterbalance.

Briefly he thought of Hope Tanner, her medium-brown hair windblown around an oval face that harbored the most striking eyes he'd ever seen. Although hers were more hazel than green, Dalton's eyes had a similar shape.

Would Hope have been a good mother? Would Dalton have been better off with her?

She couldn't give Dalton any more than he'd already been given, Parker told himself, and shoved her out of his mind, promising himself that she'd soon be gone.

"It's okay for a boy to cry over *some* things, don't you think?" he asked, tossing the ball.

"Like what?"

"Like…missing his mother," Parker said.

Dalton dove for the next ball and came up with grass stains on the knees of his jeans, which were nearly worn through. "I don't miss my mom. I don't even remember her." He thought for a moment. "I guess it would be okay for a guy to cry over having his arm chopped off, though. Or if his best friend got shot or something."

Parker's surprise nearly made him miss Dalton's next throw. "It doesn't have to be that dramatic," he said, managing to cradle the ball to his chest.

"I'm not sure what you're trying to say, Dad," Dalton said with a frown. "I'm not going to cry over a homework paper, even if you want me to."

"Not over a homework paper," Parker said. "Just…just if you ever feel like you need to get something off your chest. You probably think that's the sort of stuff guys take to their moms, but I hope you know you can always come to me.''

Dalton's hesitation in answering told Parker he still wasn't sure about this conversation. ''Whatever,'' he said at last. He was probably hoping Parker would drop the subject, but Parker hadn't made any real headway, and he wasn't willing to give up yet. For some reason, it was important he compare favorably with the parent Hope might have been.

''I know you think crying is just for girls,'' he persisted, ''but that's simply not true. We all feel the same things, and there's no shame in it.''

Dalton eyed the ball Parker had tucked under his left arm as if to say, *Can't we just play ball?* ''Are you okay, Dad?'' he asked, instead.

''I'm fine, why?''

''You're acting funny. You don't have any bad news for me, do you?''

''Of course not.''

''You're not going to start crying, are you? Because I definitely wouldn't like that. It would be too—'' he made a face ''—weird.''

Parker hooked a thumb in his pocket, feeling a sense of relief he hadn't expected. Evidently his son didn't want him to be the soft, sensitive type. ''You can relax. I'm not going to start crying.''

''That's good.'' Dalton sounded relieved, but still a little unsure. ''Is it Grandpa and Phoebe? Are they coming to visit again?''

Now, that really would be a tragedy, Parker thought. ''No.''

''Then what's the problem?''

Parker sighed and wiped the dirt from his hands onto his jeans. So much for helping Dalton get in touch with his feminine side. ''No problem. I think there might be a golf classic on TV.''

''Good,'' Dalton said. ''Let's go watch it.''

OTHER THAN A SMALL television-and-VCR combo in one corner that was playing Disney movies for the children and a large Navajo rug covering the Mexican-tile floor in front of the fireplace at the other end of the waiting area, The Birth Place looked exactly the way Hope remembered it. Even the distinctive scent of some expensive, woodsy potpourri mingled with herbal tea took her back ten years.

"This isn't anything like the hospital-type of atmosphere I expected," Faith said, staring wide-eyed as she and Hope stood just inside the entrance. "It's sort of…homey."

"It's supposed to be homey. That's the appeal," Hope said, but her stomach was knotting as the sights and sounds evoked another part of her life, one she'd cast aside. The Birth Place had once symbolized safe harbor for her and her baby. Now it was connected to a loss so great Hope couldn't determine whether she was happy to be here or not. For her, the center was probably a better place to remember than to visit. But she knew Faith would be in good hands with Lydia, and there was some small comfort in familiarity.

The woman at the reception counter looked to be about forty-five. Of average height and weight, she had short, dark hair, which she wore in a no-frills style, and an unremarkable face. She smiled as they approached, and Hope noted her name tag. Trish.

Hope couldn't recall anyone by that name. Presumably she hadn't been working at the center when Hope had given birth to Autumn. Devon, Lydia's granddaughter, had been the receptionist then.

"Can I help you?" Trish said.

Hope returned the smile. "Is Lydia here?"

"I'm pretty sure she is. She was in her office a few moments ago."

"Would you please tell her Hope Tanner would like to see her?"

"Sure. I'll be right back."

They waited as Trish hurried down the hall to the right of the waiting room, her comfortable-looking orthopedic shoes squelching as she walked.

"Do you think she'll remember you?" Faith asked in the ensuing silence.

"I think so." Hope glanced at the various women sitting in the soft leather couches and accent chairs of the waiting room. Two obviously pregnant women chatted next to three toddlers playing with toys from a box by the television. On the opposite couch perched a woman with a newborn.

Hope watched the woman gently rub her baby's head—and hated the envy that snaked through her.

"Hope?"

Turning, she saw Lydia at the mouth of the hall, wearing a white blouse, a long skirt with a beaded belt and several pieces of turquoise jewelry. A few more wrinkles lined her lean, angular face, but her high cheekbones were just as flattering as they'd always been, her eyes just as keen. Somehow Hope doubted the clarity of those eyes would ever change. Lydia was willpower incarnate.

"Hello, Lydia," she said.

Lydia closed the distance between them and hugged her, the silver bangle bracelets at her wrist clanging with the motion. But she'd hesitated just long enough to let Hope know she wasn't entirely pleased to see her.

Feeling a stab of disappointment similar to the one she'd experienced with Parker Reynolds, she told herself it was because Lydia thought she was making a mistake in returning to the past, even now. But the situation had changed. Hope had a reason to come back, a compelling reason. Surely Lydia would see that, once she understood.

"What brings you to Enchantment, dear?" she asked before her blue-gray eyes slipped curiously to Faith.

"This is my sister, Faith. She's due in a couple of weeks. Well, actually we don't know *exactly* when she's due. We think it's in a couple of weeks. I was hoping you'd be able to take her on as a client. I can pay the regular fee this time," she hastened to add.

"I was never worried about your inability to pay the last time," Lydia replied, tucking back a long strand of silver hair that had fallen from her ponytail. "Money is valuable to me only in that it keeps the center open and running so I can do what I love most."

The sincerity that rang through those words evoked a sense of nostalgia in Hope. She, too, loved helping new babies come into the world. Lydia's passion for life was what had inspired her to become an obstetrics nurse in the first place. If nothing else, it felt good to return to the source of that ambition.

"Hello, Faith. I take it you're from Superior," Lydia said, the gravity in her voice when she mentioned their town indicating she hadn't forgotten what it signified.

Faith nodded.

"Well, you're certainly welcome here. I don't deliver many babies anymore. I'm too busy sitting on the board of directors and overseeing everything else. But I can set you up with one of our other midwives, if that's okay."

Faith looked to Hope, and Hope said, "That's fine."

"Good. Why don't the two of you come on back so I can put you in a room? I think it would be wise to establish what we're dealing with before we go any further."

They followed Lydia to a room off a corridor that was now, to Hope's surprise, L-shaped. The center had changed more than she'd originally thought. This section of the building, containing a series of larger rooms and what looked like another office, was obviously a recent add-on.

"You've expanded," she said. "Things must be going well."

"They are. We've had our ups and downs over the past ten years, but we're still afloat and delivering more than sixty babies a year. We now have three full-time midwives and one who works, like I do, as sort of an overflow person when we need her."

"That's good to hear." Hope felt a certain awkwardness between Lydia and her and wished it would disappear. "I can't wait to see Devon again. She must be one of your full-time midwives."

At the mention of her granddaughter, Lydia's lips thinned and her face paled. "No, Devon lives in Albuquerque now, where she has her own practice as a certified midwife."

Hope came to a stop. "She does? But she always talked about working here with you until you retired and then taking over the—"

"She changed her mind," Lydia broke in. Her stiff posture told Hope not to probe further, but Hope had difficulty believing there could be any estrangement between grandmother and granddaughter. Lydia and Devon had always been so close. Devon had spent almost every summer working at the center, usually as receptionist.

Realizing she'd made some sort of blunder, Hope started walking again and said the first thing that came to mind. "I ran into Parker Reynolds in town yesterday. He told me he's still working here."

"He's been with us ever since he graduated from college. I knew better than to let him get away back then, and I know better than to let him get away now." Lydia waved them both toward an upholstered couch that matched the pink and mauve of the wallpaper. "He and Kim Sherman, our accountant, are the most practical people on staff. They keep us on track when it comes to meeting our goals." She leaned against the golden oak cabinets surrounding a small sink close to the door but still seemed…tense.

"How's Parker's wife?" Hope asked. "I remember she was quite ill."

"I'm afraid she died a couple of years after you left."

"I'm sorry to hear that," Hope said, wondering how Parker had dealt with the loss.

Lydia poked her head into the hall to ask a woman wearing a denim jumper to get her a new-client chart. "Tell me what's happened in your life," she said as the woman hurried off. "When you left, you were only seventeen. Now look at you."

Hope felt a twinge of pride at what she'd managed to accomplish. "Thanks to you, I'm an obstetrics nurse."

Surprise registered on Lydia's face. "You became a nurse? That's wonderful. But I certainly can't take any credit for it."

"Of course you can. Without you—"

"I had nothing to do with it," Lydia said briskly, raising a hand as if hers was the last word on the subject. "But I always knew you'd land on your feet, Hope. You were so bright, so capable, despite everything you had working against you."

"You took me in when I had nowhere else to go, Lydia. I'll never be able to thank you enough for that."

Lydia briefly closed her eyes. "Don't thank me," she said, then promptly changed the subject. "So, are you married? Engaged? In love?"

Hope felt far less proud of her personal life than her professional accomplishments. She might have moved on since Enchantment, in some ways, but in others... "None of the above, I'm afraid."

"And you, dear?" Lydia asked Faith.

Faith opened her mouth, closed it again and shot a helpless look at Hope.

"She's not married," Hope supplied.

"I see."

"I *am* married. Sort of," Faith corrected. "I mean, my baby's not illegitimate or...or anything."

Before Lydia could respond, the woman she'd spoken to in the hall a minute earlier returned with a manila file folder. "Here you go, Lydia."

"Thank you. Gina, come in for a second. I want to introduce you." Taking Gina's arm, Lydia guided her farther into the room. "This is Hope Tanner, an old friend of mine, and her sister Faith. This is Gina Vaughn, our newest midwife." She indicated Hope with a wave of her hand. "Hope, Gina used to be a nurse, as well."

"Vaughn," Hope repeated, the name jogging a memory. "I met a truck driver by that name when I lived here ten years ago. You're not related to Zach Vaughn, are you?"

"I'm married to him," she said, but there wasn't much enthusiasm in her voice and Hope could hardly picture the two of them together. Not much bigger than a twelve-year-old, Gina had long, straight auburn hair, a few freckles across her nose and a healthy glow to her skin. She looked like the energetic, outdoorsy type, not typical of the women who generally hung around the Lazy H Trailer Park.

"It's nice to meet you," Hope said.

Gina murmured the same sentiment and started to leave, but Lydia detained her. "Actually, Gina, I was hoping you'd take Faith on as one of your clients."

Gina's gaze immediately lowered to Faith's bulging midsection. "Of course. I'd love to. But...isn't she already working with someone?"

"No. She's new in town and has yet to be seen—by anyone."

If Gina was surprised that Faith had had no previous prenatal care, she didn't let it show. They saw all kinds at the clinic—those without medical insurance, those too stubborn, lazy or indigent to take proper care of themselves, even those who'd initially planned on having the baby completely on their own.

"When's the baby due?" Gina asked.

"That's what we're about to find out," Lydia replied. "We need to see what her cervix feels like. She might have started dilating already. It looks like the baby's dropped. Hope, would you mind waiting outside?"

"Of course not." Hope squeezed her sister's arm on her way out. "It won't be any big deal," she said. "I'll be in the lobby, okay?"

She didn't wait for a response. She trusted Lydia implicitly and wanted to communicate that to Faith. Closing the door behind her, she headed down the hall. She was thinking about Lydia's rather subdued reception when she rounded the corner and was nearly bowled over by Parker Reynolds.

"Whoa," he said, catching her before she could fall. His hands felt strong and sure on her upper arms, but the hard line of his jaw suggested he wasn't any more pleased to see her now than he'd been the day before. Maybe Enchantment wasn't going to be the haven she'd anticipated. Maybe it was expecting too much of these people to welcome her a second time.

Quickly regaining her balance, Hope stepped out of his reach. "Excuse me," she muttered. "I didn't hear you coming."

"No problem," he said, but she could sense that there *was* a problem of some sort as he checked the hall behind her. "Where's your sister?"

"She's in the exam room with Lydia."

"So Lydia knows you're here?"

She nodded.

"How long until the baby's born?" He sounded as though he couldn't wait.

"That's what they're trying to determine."

"You mentioned it would be soon, though, right? A couple of weeks, maybe?"

What did it matter to him. "That's a good guess." Hope cleared her throat. The hero worship she'd once felt for this man was difficult to forget. Maybe he was acting like a stranger, but he still *looked* like the Parker Reynolds she remembered so fondly. The Parker Reynolds who'd given her a coat that cold spring. The Parker Reynolds who'd playfully teased her when she'd been lonely and slipped a twenty into her purse on at least two different occasions—at a time when finding twenty bucks was like unearthing a pot of gold.

Hope wondered if she should say something about his wife. She wanted to, but he seemed so remote.

"How long are you planning to be in town?" he asked.

She and Faith had nowhere else to go. There was a chance they'd settle here, if she could get a good job, but she was reluctant to say so. Parker hadn't minded her as a poor, pregnant runaway, but dealing with her as a full-grown woman seemed to be a different story. "That depends on Faith."

"Of course." He slid his hands into the pockets of his jeans.

Hope thought of Faith saying how handsome he was. She tried not to agree, but he looked particularly good today in his red sport shirt with the cuffs rolled back and his dark hair falling across his forehead.

"Well, I'll see you some—" she started to say, but he asked at the same time, "Where are you staying?"

"At the Lorey cabin."

"Nice place."

"We like it there."

"You've changed. A lot," he said, surprising Hope with the sudden switch in topic.

"I've grown up."

His eyes ranged over her. "Yeah, that's pretty tough to miss."

Hope raised her eyebrows, wondering what exactly he meant by that. "Excuse me?"

"You married?" he asked.

"No."

"Engaged?"

"No. I've never been married or engaged."

"So you've been on your own all this time?"

Hope knew lives didn't get much more "alone" than hers had been. "I guess you could say that."

"You just seem so…"

"What?" she prompted when he hesitated.

"Different."

"From what?"

"From before," he said, and walked away.

"Yeah, well, you've changed, too," she muttered to herself as she watched him disappear into an office. "And it doesn't look as though it's for the better."

CHAPTER TEN

A FEW MINUTES later, Parker sat at his desk, staring at the spreadsheet Kim Sherman had provided, even though he wasn't really seeing it. He needed to focus on the fund-raiser The Birth Place sponsored for SIDS research every summer and okay the proposed budget. With only six weeks to go until the event, time was getting short, and they were running into some significant snags.

But he couldn't stop thinking about Hope Tanner. She wasn't a down-and-out runaway anymore. She was an adult, who seemed surprisingly capable and confident. Only her eyes revealed her difficult past. They reminded him of deep dark pools, glasslike on the surface but churning with a powerful undercurrent. He knew she'd acquired that guarded look by suffering through more than her share of hard luck and difficulty. What bothered him now was wondering whether he'd added to her pain....

She'd been planning to give up the baby, he told himself. Lydia had started to make the arrangements even before he'd gotten his father-in-law involved.

But the question of whether Hope would have given up her baby if she'd known it was a boy had always haunted him. Maybe she would've felt she could raise a boy without risking the things she most feared for a daughter. Maybe she could actually have done a decent job. Which meant he'd robbed her of Dalton.

He pictured Dalton as a chubby baby, jamming his finger into his mouth. Then as a toddler running around the house and making one mess after another. Then as a kindergartner learning to read and showing wonder over something as simple as a bee or a butterfly. Those memories were precious to him. Irreplaceable. They were memories Hope didn't have.

But despite the clandestine way it had all come to pass, Parker had fallen in love with Dalton the very instant he'd gazed down at him in Lydia's office. It was Dalton who had softened the loss he'd felt when Vanessa died. It was Dalton who'd filled his life and his heart for the past ten years. He generally tried not to think about Hope. But now she was back, and the guilt he'd suppressed and justified for so long spread through him like a cancer.

"You going to be through with that anytime soon?" Lydia said from the doorway.

Parker blinked and looked up. "When's Faith due?"

"I've scheduled her for an ultrasound with Dr. Ochoa at his office, but from what I can tell she's about thirty-seven weeks."

"Thirty-seven weeks," he repeated. "That means we only have three or so weeks to go."

"Exactly."

"We can make it for three weeks," he said, to bolster his spirits as much as Lydia's.

"Except I'm not sure Hope and Faith will be leaving after the baby's born," she said slowly.

The sick feeling Parker had experienced since bumping into Hope at the Sunflower Drive-in intensified. "What do you mean?"

"According to Faith, she and Hope are sort of on the run."

"From what?"

"From Faith's husband—" she arched a brow "—who's also her fifty-six-year-old uncle."

"God, not the polygamy thing again."

"Hope and Faith have three other sisters who live in their hometown and twenty or thirty step-siblings."

"Do you think Hope and Faith are in any real danger?"

She folded her arms and leaned against the lintel. "That's tough to say. They didn't go into a lot of detail. Faith's trying to leave her husband, and he's not very happy about letting her go. That's it."

"Hope told me she's been living in St. George, not Superior."

"She visited Superior for the first time only a couple of weeks ago."

"Then that's good," he said, feeling a measure of relief. "That means she's established a life separate from Superior. She might not have a husband or a family to bring her back to St. George, but what about a job? She has to make money somehow."

"She was an obstetrics nurse, but she quit her job at Valley View Hospital just before they fled St. George."

Lydia's words effectively doused his relief, but he wasn't willing to give up easily. "That shouldn't change anything," he insisted. "If they're on the run, they probably won't stay much longer than we originally thought, whether they return to St. George or move somewhere else."

"I have no idea what they'll do." She crossed the room to straighten an impressionistic painting of a woman cradling a child. "But if word of what we did gets out, it'll ruin the clinic," she said, keeping her eyes on the painting. "It's exactly what we deserve, of course, you and I. But I hate the fact that other people will suffer with us." She finally turned back to him. "People like Dalton."

"Word won't get out," he said. "After ten years of loving my son, I'm not about to lose him."

THE WIND ROSE up that night, tossing branches *clack, clackety-clack-clack* against the cabin. Hope had awoke a couple of times, but she heard the blustering and buffeting mostly in her subconscious and later blamed it for her dreams.

"What's wrong?" Faith asked, shuffling into the

kitchen in a pair of slippers they'd bought after leaving the birthing center yesterday.

Hope stirred another spoonful of sugar into her coffee. "Nothing."

"You look tired. Didn't you sleep last night?"

"A little. I dreamed a lot."

"About what?"

She'd dreamed about Arvin pressing his face to the glass of the cabin's front window and then using his shoulder as a battering ram, trying to get inside. But that dream wasn't the one that bothered Hope most. The dream that bothered her most had been about Autumn.

"A lot of things," she said. "You know how piecemeal dreams can be."

"It's probably because of all the recent changes in your life. Since I came back to St. George with you, you've lost everything."

She'd lost her home and her job, but Hope wasn't nearly as sad about those losses as she'd expected to be. Now that she had Faith with her, she realized that, emotionally at least, she'd been treading water all those years in St. George. She'd been anesthetized by routine and determination. Now she knew hurt and worry and loss again, but she was also glad to find she could still care.

"I like it here," Hope admitted, pushing her bad dreams to the back of her mind. A few dreams, no matter how unnerving, were a small price to pay to keep Faith and her baby safe. "What about you, Faith? Are you okay in Enchantment?"

Her sister took a seat at the table, rested her arms on her round belly and stretched her slipper-shod feet out in front of her. "You know I feel guilty for leaving Mama and Charity and LaRee and Sarah behind. But the more days I spend away from Arvin, the more I'm experiencing this—" she shook her head, wearing an expression of wonder "—almost intoxicating sense of freedom. More and more, the thought of going back makes me feel…ill."

"You can't worry so much about what the people we meet are going to think of you, though," Hope said.

"What do you mean?"

"Yesterday you didn't have to tell Lydia that your baby isn't illegitimate."

"My baby *isn't* illegitimate. I was married before I went to Arvin's bed."

"It wasn't a legal marriage, Faith."

"It was to me."

"I realize that. But you can't go around explaining that you're from a polygamist colony in Superior."

"Why not? You just said I shouldn't care what other people think."

Hope's spoon clinked against her cup as she stirred a little more cream into her coffee. How could she make Faith understand that it was better to leave the past behind *completely?* "For the most part that's true," she said. "But you also have to protect yourself. You don't want to be treated like a freak, and you don't want the taint of your upbringing to spill over onto your baby."

"Because my baby might be tainted in some way is exactly why I don't want anyone to think he or she is illegitimate."

"Most people these days don't shun illegitimate children, or even unwed mothers." She put her spoon down. "Let's make this simple, okay? There aren't a lot of divorced eighteen-year-olds, but I suppose there are a few. Why don't you tell everyone you're divorced?"

Faith leaned forward. "You're saying I should *lie?*"

Hope wondered how she could make this more palatable to her sister. "Not really," she said. "I just don't think you should mention Arvin or your background to anyone. If someone asks, you should have a story already prepared."

Faith toyed with the empty place mat in front of her. "A story. That's lying."

Evidently, there was no way to sugarcoat it. "I guess it is."

"Lying is a sin."

"I know that."

"You don't think it matters?"

"It matters more that you erase what's happened to you in the past and clear the way for a better future. Superior is really nobody's business."

Silence. "Faith?"

"It isn't anybody's business," Faith admitted after a few seconds.

"Why don't you say you're from the Salt Lake area? That isn't such a stretch, since you've been there. If anyone probes deeper, you could tell them you just graduated from Murray High."

"But I already told Lydia the truth."

"That's okay. I'll talk to her. Just don't tell anyone else, okay?"

Another long pause.

"Do you understand?" Hope prodded. "Are you with me on this?"

Finally, her sister nodded and Hope felt the beginnings of a smile. Faith was stronger and more mature than she'd ever dreamed, even if she was a bit of a Goody Two-shoes. "Thatta girl." She knew she was pressing her luck, but she couldn't help adding, "And I think you should wear the clothes I bought you in St. George, instead of that dowdy dress all the time."

"Maybe."

Her response prompted Hope to go one step further. "And have your hair styled and maybe wear a little bit of makeup, too."

This time Faith's eyes widened. "Oh, no. I couldn't."

"It would help you find that man you've been talking about."

"What man?"

"The man of your dreams."

Faith stared down at her slippers. "Mama wouldn't like it. She'd tell me I sold my soul to the devil."

"Arvin's the devil," Hope said. "And Mama's not around anymore."

LYDIA HADN'T ANTICIPATED seeing Hope again until after Faith's ultrasound appointment, so when Trish rapped softly on her open door, she was surprised to hear the receptionist say, "Hope Tanner's here. She wants to talk to you for a few minutes. Shall I send her back?"

The fact that Hope had returned so soon caused a nervous flutter in Lydia's stomach, reminding her she'd forgotten to eat lunch—again. She often became so engrossed in her work that the noon hour passed unnoticed. Especially since Devon was no longer working at the center, always nagging her to eat and bringing her sandwiches or salads from the popular cafés in town.

Devon…

"Lydia? Did you hear me?" Trish asked.

Lydia schooled her face into a calm mask. "Sorry."

"Do you want me to tell Hope you're too busy?"

"No, go ahead and send her back."

Trish disappeared, and Lydia pushed away from her desk, bracing for the next few minutes. She didn't relish staring into the face of the woman she'd wronged so many years ago. Seeing Hope again was like putting the imperfections of her own soul under a magnifying glass, the same imperfections that had chased away her beloved granddaughter.

Lydia had insisted on repaying Congressman Barlow the money he'd given her for Dalton, but it hadn't changed anything. She'd finally reconciled herself to the truth—that a simple exchange of funds was never going to redeem her. Not to Hope. Not to Devon. Not to herself. Her only consolation in the whole nasty affair was that she saw Dalton often and knew he was a healthy, happy boy, even without a mother.

At least Parker had been honest when he told her all those years ago that he'd give the child everything he had. He loved that boy more than life itself.

Lydia adjusted the wooden blinds on her window to look outside. A ray of sun cut through the branches of the surrounding pines, nearly blinding her. Ducking the harsh glare, she toyed with an idea she'd never considered before: what if she finally confessed, came clean and admitted the whole affair? She'd destroy her good reputation, which mattered more to her than almost anything else. But she was willing to sacrifice that to be as honest and forthright as she pretended to be. What she *wasn't* willing to sacrifice was what the truth would cost others—like Parker and Dalton and all those who worked at the center.

"Hi, Lydia."

Lydia swallowed, her throat suddenly dry, and turned. "Hello, dear. What brings you back to the clinic so soon?"

"I—I wanted to talk to you about some of the things my sister told you yesterday."

"Like…"

"That business about her…her husband and who he is."

"I won't tell anyone," Lydia said, immediately understanding her desire for privacy.

"I'd appreciate that. We're going to say she's from Salt Lake and she's divorced."

"Then from now on, I'll say the same, if it ever comes up."

"Great." Hope switched the manila envelope she was carrying to the other arm, obviously a little uncomfortable. "And there's something else."

"What's that, dear?"

"Well…I've been out all morning searching for a job. But everywhere I went, I kept thinking how much I'd rather work here, with you. The clinic's not far from the cabin, and it has such a wonderful atmosphere. So I thought I'd stop by to see if you could use a good obstetrics nurse. I updated my resumé before I left St. George and I have one here just in case," she said, withdrawing a sheet of paper from the envelope.

Lydia covered her mouth and coughed to hide her surprise. She typically shied away from people trained in childbirth by the medical profession. They tended to treat pregnancy as some sort of medical problem. But that aside...

"I know you think I'm crazy for coming back to Enchantment," Hope added quickly, handing it to her, "but I'm well. I'm much stronger than I was. I'm fine with everything."

Lydia gazed down at the resumé. She wasn't sure how anyone could be fine with what Hope had endured in her life, but she was too busy trying to come up with a way to let her down easy to focus on that. "I'm afraid working here at The Birth Place would be very different from the clinical atmosphere you're familiar with, Hope. We believe that childbirth is a natural, healthy process, and we encourage mothers to choose what they—"

"I understand all that," Hope interrupted enthusiastically. "And I'm completely supportive. I witnessed each of my sisters being born at home." She hesitated. "The only time I wouldn't be supportive is if a midwife refused to transfer a client to the hospital when and if problems arose."

Lydia walked back to her desk and perched on the edge of it. "I'm not supportive of that, either. But it's not only the difference in disciplines, Hope. Besides, I'm not sure we have anything that would be as temporary as you'd probably need."

"It doesn't have to be temporary," Hope replied. "I've decided that I'm willing to commit to a year."

Lydia had had a bad feeling ever since she'd heard Hope was in town. Now that feeling—an odd combination of dread mixed with inevitability—sank a little deeper, into her bones. "You're planning on staying for a whole year? But Faith mentioned there might be some danger of her husband finding the both of you. Do you think it's safe to put down roots?"

"I doubt he'll bother tracking us down once he realizes we've left the state. It would take entirely too much effort. And—" she folded her hands in front of her "—Enchantment is the closest thing I have to home."

The wistful note in Hope's voice made Lydia's chest tighten. Because of her own past, the baby *she'd* had to give up at a similar age, she'd always identified with this girl. She'd ached for her pain, felt a fierce anger against the father and uncle who'd wronged her so terribly. And she'd tried to help. Only, she'd ended up betraying her, instead, and by doing that, she'd failed herself and everyone who depended on her.

"We're...uh, pretty well staffed at the moment," she said. "I'm afraid—"

"Of course." Hope's interruption was an obvious effort to save them both the awkwardness of a rejection. "I completely understand. I just thought I'd ask." She plucked the resumé from her hand and smiled bravely, and Lydia felt as though she'd just stabbed the poor girl—young woman, now—in the back a second time. Hope needed her again, and instead of being there for her, Lydia was trying to cover up the sins of her past.

"Thanks for seeing me," Hope was saying, edging toward the door. "I'm sure I'll find a job soon. Nurses are in demand all over the place. And thanks for arranging for Faith to see Gina. I know—"

"Wait." Lydia knew she was going to regret this as soon as Hope walked out the door, but after what she'd done, she felt she owed the girl *something*. "Come to think of it, we're going into our busy time. What with the cold winters here, significantly more babies are born in the spring and summer. I could probably use someone with your experience, but your duties might be quite varied at first, until we work you into the system. Are you interested?"

Hope didn't look as though she trusted this sudden about-face. "Sure. I guess. What will I be doing?"

"You'll answer the phone if Trish, our receptionist, is busy. You'll escort clients to a room and get them started if whatever midwife they're seeing isn't available right away. You'll keep in touch with Dr. Ochoa's office. As you know, we transfer any high-risk patients to him and need to monitor their progress. You'll make new information charts, file or assist Parker with any special projects he's got going. Basically, you'll be a Jill-of-all-trades, at least initially. But if you're okay with being so flexible, why don't we see how things go?"

Hope blinked. "Are you sure you really—"

"I'm positive." Lydia smiled in spite of the knots in her stomach and the fact that she wasn't "positive" at all.

"I might want to become a midwife someday," Hope said. "Maybe I'll apprentice."

"That's always a possibility. You certainly have the training for it."

A brief knock sounded on the door, then Parker Reynolds breezed into the room. He was staring down at some papers he carried in one hand and didn't see Hope at first, but he forgot about whatever he was reading the moment he glanced up.

His gaze eventually settled on Lydia and not Hope, but she could tell it was not without significant effort. "I'm sorry. I didn't realize you were with someone."

Lydia motioned to Hope. "You know Hope Tanner."

He nodded in Hope's direction, almost imperceptibly, and his stilted movements told Lydia how difficult it was for him even to greet her. And she'd just hired her to work at The Birth Place!

"Is Faith okay?" he asked.

It was Hope who answered. "She's fine. I'm here about a job."

"A *job?*" His carefully blank expression slipped into surprise and dismay as he eyed the resumé she held out to him.

"Hope is an obstetrics nurse," Lydia explained, trying to draw Hope's attention so she wouldn't notice. "I think she'll be a valuable addition to our staff."

"No kidding." Parker shot her a look that said, *Are you crazy?*

"No kidding." Lydia straightened her spine to let him know she was still the owner of The Birth Place and would make whatever decisions she deemed fit. Two wrongs did not make a right.

His dark eyebrows lowered into a solid slash above his brown eyes. "Did you check with Kim? We have an operating budget, remember?"

"I remember very well, not that this is the time to remind me."

"Better now than later."

Hope's gaze shifted from Parker to Lydia. "If there's some sort of problem, I understand—"

"There's no problem, dear," Lydia broke in the same moment Parker said, "Why don't you leave your resumé with us, and we'll give you a call in a couple of days?"

"That won't be necessary," Lydia said, even though he'd already taken the resumé. "You'll start next Monday, Hope, if that's okay with you. We'll pay you what you were making at the hospital."

Hope hesitated, obviously unsure how to respond. "I didn't come back to cause trouble."

"You're not causing any trouble," Lydia assured her.

"Then, thank you." She reserved her gratitude for Lydia alone. "I'll be here." She tossed Parker a look of pure disdain, turned on her heel and marched out.

Lydia almost laughed despite the predicament she'd just landed them *both* in. Since his wife's death, Parker had grown quite accustomed to getting his way with women. He was always in control, usually right, and good at everything he attempted. Lydia liked him. She knew he was a real asset to the center, but just now, she felt like giving a little cheer for womanhood in general.

"Is this supposed to be funny?" Parker said.

The temptation to laugh quickly disappeared. "No." She reclaimed the seat behind her desk.

"Then what the hell did you just do?"

"She came here asking for a job, and I gave her one, okay?" Lydia raised her brows at him. "We owe her that much, don't you think?"

He scowled at Hope's resumé, then scrubbed a hand over his face as though he had so much surplus energy he didn't know what to do with it all. "We might owe her," he said, "but I'm pretty sure we can't afford to give her anything."

"I couldn't say no." Lydia went back to reading the mail Trish had brought in just before Hope arrived.

"Lydia…"

She carefully placed a letter from the Pediatric AIDS Foundation on the corner of her desk. "You're overreacting, Parker. She's only going to work here. That doesn't mean anything. We don't even know how long she'll stay." *I'm willing to commit to a year….*

"It means I'll have to see her every day."

"So will I."

"She could destroy this clinic, destroy you."

"I know."

"She could take Dalton away from me," he said, his voice gruff with emotion.

"She's not going to take Dalton away. She doesn't suspect anything. She just needs a break."

"You're a fool," he said angrily, and stalked out.

Lydia stared after him. "Tell me something I don't know."

CHAPTER ELEVEN

YOU'RE A FOOL. Parker's words echoed in his head long after he'd left Lydia's office. He'd never spoken to her like that before and felt bad for doing so, even though he was still upset. Probably because he considered himself much more of a fool. He'd been the one to start everything. He'd made a life-altering decision ten years ago, and now the consequences of that decision were coming home to roost.

What, did he think he could steal a woman's child and get away with it forever?

Resting his head on the back of his chair, he closed his eyes for a few seconds before opening them to gaze up at the ceiling. What the hell was he going to do? He couldn't let Hope waltz into his life at this late date, couldn't let her brush elbows with Dalton and run the risk that she might one day recognize the truth.

Standing, he locked his office door—something he rarely did—then sat down again. Maybe he was making too much of this. Maybe Hope wasn't what she appeared to be. If she wasn't, if there was some reason she wouldn't have been a good mother to Dalton, he'd be off the hook, right? He'd have something to fight for, a reason to feel good about what he'd done and what he was doing. He certainly wasn't going to condemn himself for separating Dalton from a woman who wouldn't have been able to provide a good life for him.

Feeling a quick infusion of hopeful energy, he picked up the phone and dialed the number for Valley View Hospital in St. George, which was listed on Hope's resumé. A moment later he was speaking to a woman named Sandra Cleary.

"*Who* are you?" Sandra said, sounding a bit cautious.

When Parker identified himself again and explained a little bit about The Birth Place, she relaxed considerably. "I'm calling regarding Hope Tanner," he said. "She's applied for a job with us and has you listed as a reference."

"Oh, of course. I hadn't realized she'd moved so far away."

Parker asked a couple of routine questions about the hospital in general and how long Hope had worked there. Then he went for the information he was most interested in knowing.

"So, what kind of woman would you say Hope Tanner is?" he asked.

To his chagrin, Ms. Cleary didn't even hesitate. "She's a wonderful person. I've known Hope for years. She can be somewhat withdrawn at times, but she's a hard worker. She's knowledgeable, reliable, honest and caring, all of which are prerequisites in this field, don't you think?"

"Definitely." He doodled on the yellow pad in front of him, wondering how to reach a little deeper. "And…let's see," he said as though reading from a form. "Does she have a stable personal life?"

"Personal life?"

"I know you might find that question a bit unusual," he explained, "but we're a tight-knit group and definitely need someone who doesn't let his or her personal life interfere with work."

"Oh, Hope would never do that," she said. "She never seemed to have much of a personal life, for one thing."

"Why do you think that is?" he asked.

"I can't say for sure. It certainly isn't because she's odd or difficult to get along with. She's just a bit aloof, a little hard to know."

"She must have a few bad habits," he said, hoping Ms. Cleary would elaborate. But again, he was disappointed by her response.

"Not that I know of."

"No drug or alcohol abuse? Anger-management problems? Difficulty remaining solvent?"

"Definitely not. Hope and I have gone out for a drink on occasion, but I've never seen her have more than a single glass of wine. To my knowledge she's never taken drugs, and... What else did you ask?"

"Never mind," he said. Instead of making him feel better, this call was making him feel significantly worse.

"Well, if I were you, I wouldn't worry about hiring her," she volunteered. "She's one of the finest people I know."

"Glad to hear it," he said, barely able to keep the sarcasm from his voice. "Thanks."

"No problem. I hope the information helps."

Parker swallowed a sigh. "You have no idea," he said, then he hung up and dropped his head into the palm of one hand. Just what he wanted to hear: Hope Tanner was a freakin' saint.

"I HATE HIM," Hope said.

"Who?" Faith asked, once again sitting across the table from her at the Sunflower Café.

Hope pushed aside the sprouts that had fallen out of her cucumber-and-tomato sandwich. "Parker Reynolds."

"That handsome guy we saw in here before? What brought him up?"

Hope had been thinking about Parker ever since she'd left the birthing center forty-five minutes earlier. "He was there when Lydia gave me the job."

"So? What'd he do that upset you?"

Hope couldn't really say. She couldn't point to some specific comment or action, because what he'd done had been so subtle. He'd once been her friend and yet, now that she was back, he would scarcely speak to her. When he saw her, he scowled as though he'd sooner see a cockroach. Obviously he was unhappy that she'd be joining the staff at the center.

"Nothing," she said, stirring the ice in her cup with her straw. She hated to admit she was upset because he didn't like her anymore. She didn't want to believe he could affect her so deeply.

"Then eat." Faith paused to take a sip of her drink. "You got the job you wanted. This is supposed to be a celebration, right?"

Hope fixed her with a steady gaze. "I'll celebrate when you get your hair cut and styled."

Faith rolled her eyes. "Jeez, Hope. Would it really mean that much to you?"

Hope shrugged. "There's not much point in dealing with the clothing issue until after the baby. But we could get started with your hair."

Fortunately, no one as far east as Enchantment was likely to recognize Faith for what she was—what she'd been, Hope corrected—so that was no longer much of a concern. Though there were pockets of polygamists all over the Western United States, even in parts of Canada and Mexico, nowhere were they more common or visible than in the state of Utah. To the people of New Mexico, Hope knew Faith simply looked old-fashioned and very plain. But it bothered her that every time *she* saw her sister, she was reminded of Arvin and Bonner and poor Oscar.

"I thought you wanted to shop for a crib," Faith said.

"Yes, but we've got the rest of the afternoon and nothing else to do. I think we can handle both." Hope fiddled with the ends of her own hair. Maybe it was time she changed styles, too. Maybe she should go really short, go for something *sexy*…

A thrill ran through her at the prospect of looking anything close to sexy, which surprised her almost as much as considering such a radical change in the first place. Her whole life, she'd gone to great lengths to be as plain and unnoticeable as possible. Why did her heart race at the thought of being more attractive now?

Instantly, she conjured up Parker Reynold's face in her mind.

Not for him, she decided. He'd become insufferable.

On the other hand, she didn't think it could hurt to start work next week feeling like a new woman—a bold, confident, *attractive* woman. She'd show Parker that she didn't need his friendship. And that she was as modern as any woman he'd met...

"Come on," she said, dumping the rest of her sandwich in the garbage, along with her plastic cup. "I'll get mine done, too."

"But..."

Hope propped her hands on her hips.

"Never mind," Faith grumbled, and followed her out.

"OMIGOSH! I LOOK SO...different," Faith said, staring at herself in the bathroom mirror.

Hope was standing behind her, watching her reaction. She thought Faith looked great—very fresh and appealing. Her sandy-colored hair feathered about her face in layers, giving her the same kind of trendy, fashionable appearance as the teenage girls Hope used to see at the mall in St. George.

It felt good to see her sister looking more like a normal girl than a haggard, middle-aged housewife. "Don't you like it?" she asked.

Faith scrunched up her nose. "I don't know. It makes me look really young."

"You're only eighteen."

"I don't feel that young."

Hope couldn't remember a time when she'd felt young, either. "Maybe we were born old. But we don't have to look it. I think it's a definite improvement," she said, but she wasn't so sure about her own short cut.

"You have beautiful eyes, very striking," the stylist had said before she started. "You're right to go short. It'll give you more dramatic impact."

Hope had been looking for sexy, but in that moment, dramatic had sounded pretty close. "If you think it'll look good," she'd said, and the stylist had smiled eagerly and whipped out her scissors.

"Oh, it's going to look good. Just wait until I'm finished with you."

And now she *was* finished.

"At least you didn't let her cut off as much as I did," Hope said.

Faith's eyes shifted to Hope's reflection. "I thought you were making a mistake when you did that, but now—" she cocked her head to one side "—now I think that stylist knew what she was talking about."

Hope gnawed on her lower lip as she weighed the changes. "It's not too bad, I guess."

"It's not bad at all. It makes you look…sophisticated."

Sophisticated was better than plain. Anything was better than plain. "At any rate, I'm not going to worry about it. It'll grow." She shrugged and turned away from the mirror. "Come on. I need help getting the crib out of the back seat. It might take us until the baby's born to figure out how to put the darn thing together."

"Are we still going to Taos tomorrow to buy fabric?" Faith asked as they headed down the hall.

"Since you wouldn't let me buy that darling baby quilt they had at Child's Play, we'll have to." Hope held the wooden screen door so it wouldn't hit her sister, and smiled as the scent of green growing things and rich earth immediately greeted her. They'd been right to come here, she decided. They could start over here. Eventually forget.

"That stuff was way too expensive," Faith said.

Hope walked across the wide, sloping lawn, which was

a little too shaded to grow much grass. "The shops here prey on tourists. But it was so darling with all those little rocking horses...."

"I'd rather make my baby's blanket."

Hope could certainly understand that sentiment. Her fingers itched to sew, cross-stitch, paint, *something*. She'd spent the past ten years making a home for herself, devoting her off-hours to improving it. Now that her belongings were all packed away in storage, she was completely out of her element. Quilting for the baby might help them both.

"Tomorrow's Saturday," she said. "Maybe after we visit the fabric store, we can find some good garage sales in Taos where we can..."

Her words fell away as two young girls riding bicycles passed by on the road. One was blond and had her hair pulled into a ponytail. The other was a brunette with long dark curls hanging in tangles about her face. They were around Autumn's age.

Hope could hear the high lilt of their voices as they talked and laughed together, and the sound brought back her dream of the night before...

Mommy! Mommy!

Hope's stomach lurched as she recognized her daughter's voice. She began searching what appeared to be a park, frantically looking, running everywhere until, finally, she found her dark-haired child on the swings. One hand tightly gripped the chain as her legs moved, pumping ever higher. The other hand waved to Hope. "Over here, Mommy! I'm over here!"

With a sense of awe, Hope hurried over to find that her child was a mirror image of herself. From a distance, Autumn seemed happy and loved. But as Hope drew closer, she could see that the pretty little girl who'd just called her Mommy was dirty and unkempt. Her hair was matted to her head, her dress torn. And she was so thin, too thin...

Obviously, her child wasn't being cared for as she'd always trusted. Autumn could have been living on the streets for the filth covering her spindly arms and legs.

An incredible anger surged through Hope, anger at whoever had neglected Autumn, and anger at herself for allowing others to raise her child. Yet there was relief, too, to think she'd found Autumn at last. Maybe they could put the past behind them. Autumn obviously needed her.

"Don't worry, Autumn," she called. "Mommy's here now. I'll take care of you, baby. You'll have everything you need from now on."

But Autumn just smiled in a mysterious way and wouldn't stop swinging. Hope stood at the base of the set of swings, pleading with her, but she just kept pumping and humming softly to herself—

"Hope? What is it?" Faith shook her shoulder, and Hope blinked to find her sister staring at her in concern.

"Nothing. I'm fine," she said, but it wasn't true. Her heart was hammering in her chest, and she felt the most overwhelming helplessness she'd ever known.

Eyebrows drawn together in confusion, Faith glanced at the girls on bicycles. "Was it those children? Did they say something to you?"

"No." Mentally shaking herself, Hope started toward the car again. She wouldn't let a dream bother her. A dream was just a dream; it wasn't real. Not like Arvin.

But the emotions behind that dream were real enough. And so were the doubts.

Please, keep her safe, she prayed.

PARKER WONDERED how he was going to get through the days now that he was working with Hope Tanner. It would've been bad enough having her come in periodically for Faith's prenatal checkups. But day-to-day contact was infinitely worse. It had been almost a week, yet every time he heard her or saw her pass his open door, he found himself clenching his jaw. He didn't want her here. He didn't want her anywhere near Enchantment—or Dalton.

"Mrs. Wilson, would you come with me?"

Hope's voice reached him again, and he got up and closed his door. As administrator, he handled the correspondence, arranged fund-raisers and private tours of their facility, okayed most expenditures, approved orders for supplies and negotiated new deals with vendors—amid myriad other tasks—and was rarely distracted. But he couldn't concentrate today.

"Do you miss Mom?" Dalton had wanted to know while Parker was helping him with his homework last night.

The question had caught Parker off guard. He still missed Vanessa in a vague sort of way, but it wasn't anything acute. "Not so much anymore," he'd said.

"That's good. I don't want you to be sad. All that talk about crying last week…" He made a face.

"It didn't have anything to do with your mom, okay?"

Parker had considered telling Dalton, right then and there, that he was adopted. He'd always wondered if the truth wouldn't be best. But Vanessa hadn't wanted him to say anything. She'd feared that knowledge of the adoption would destroy Dalton's self-esteem. Parker had gone along with her wishes, mostly because Dalton was too young to understand. Then when she died and Dalton grew older, there just hadn't been a good time to explain that he'd actually been born to someone else.

Now that he'd waited so long, Parker found himself in one heck of a pickle. At ten, Dalton was definitely old enough to understand his situation, but Parker doubted he'd look very kindly on the fact that his father and grandparents had let him live a lie for so long.

It was better not to say anything, he decided, coming to the same conclusion he reached every time he considered the situation. Especially in light of Hope's reappearance. He just needed to sit tight and wait for Faith to have her baby. Then maybe the two Tanner sisters would leave Enchantment, and he could deal with breaking the news— or not—to Dalton.

A light rap sounded on his door, interrupting his thoughts. "Mr. Reynolds?" The voice was soft, indistinct.

Mr. Reynolds? No one called him that at the center. "Come in."

Hope stuck her head through the opening, and Parker immediately felt a muscle begin to twitch in his cheek. "Yes?"

"Lydia asked me to see if you're ready for the staff meeting."

The staff meeting. He'd completely forgotten. Trish had scheduled it for the noon hour. They were ordering goat-cheese-and-veggie pizza and gathering in the waiting room.

He glanced at the work spread out on his desk—work he should've completed hours ago—and bit back a frustrated sigh. It was Hope's fault he couldn't concentrate. It was her fault he felt so damn guilty. And it was her fault his life could go down the toilet at any moment.

He jammed a hand through his hair. Okay, actually that last part was *his* fault. But at least the risk of having his life destroyed would be minimal if she wasn't around.

"I'll be there in a minute," he muttered, but she didn't leave it at that. She slipped inside, closed the door behind her and came to stand in front of his desk.

"I said I'll be there," he repeated, letting irritation mask his discomfort at having her so close.

"I know what you said," she replied, "but I think we should talk before the animosity between us gets any worse."

He stood and began shoving papers around as though he knew what he was doing. "What animosity?"

"Are you kidding? You don't like that I'm here, and I want to know why. I haven't done anything except return to a place I remember fondly. What's wrong with that? Surely Enchantment is big enough for both of us.''

He didn't want to look at her. Partly because she was so damn appealing, especially with that new haircut, and he didn't want to find Hope Tanner appealing. And partly because she was calling him on something he'd rather not face. He *was* being unfair. But the biggest irony of all was that he didn't dislike her—he disliked what he'd done to her and what that meant she could do to him.

''There's no problem between us,'' he said, but even that statement came out sounding terse.

''I thought we were friends when I left here.''

''We barely knew each other.'' To admit to anything beyond that would make what he'd done ten years ago that much more reprehensible.

''Okay.'' She turned her palms up. ''For whatever reason, you don't want to be my friend. I can live with that. But I'd like us to be comfortable around each other. Is that asking too much?''

He flipped through a folder on his desk.

''Are you going to answer me?''

''I told you, we don't have a problem. There's no reason you should feel uncomfortable.''

''I'm not the one who's uncomfortable.''

''What makes you think *I'm* uncomfortable?''

''You mean besides the fact that you scowl every time you see me? Or turn away?''

He glanced up and couldn't help noticing how much healthier she looked than when she'd left Enchantment. No longer a pale, skinny girl, this Hope had skin that glowed and curves in all the right places. She also had an impressive amount of confidence in her bearing, considering everything she'd been through.

Parker suddenly found himself softening. She seemed so earnest about making peace that he couldn't refuse her.

He didn't have to become her friend, he told himself.

He only had to treat her with the same courtesy he'd treat any other co-worker.

He just wished it didn't feel so...hypocritical.

"There you go, scowling again," she said.

"Sorry." He quickly cleared his face. "You're right."

She blinked in surprise. "What?"

"You're right. I've been a jerk."

A slight hesitation. "That's it?"

"Isn't that progress?"

"Well..." She looked over her shoulder at the closed door, as if she thought she had the wrong office. "Sort of, I guess. You could explain to me *why* you've been a jerk."

He gestured at the chaos on his desk. "Job stress?"

She gave him a smile that revealed dimples, and he couldn't help smiling back. She looked so much like Dalton. Though he doubted anyone else would ever notice, he saw it in the little things—the wide brow, the heart-shaped upper lip, the occasional expression in the eyes.

"Now that's the Parker Reynolds I remember. Hold that thought," she said, and walked out.

GOD, NOW THEY WERE friends.

As he watched her leave, Parker told himself he only had to treat her kindly, but he hadn't taken her sexy smile into account. Or the fact that he and Hope could so easily return to the natural friendly relationship they'd known ten years ago. He'd apologized and, just like that, they were back where they'd been before.

Which made him the worst kind of snake. Ten years ago he'd abused Hope's trust while pretending to be her friend. Now he was doing pretty much the same thing all over again.

He pinched the bridge of his nose, wishing she hadn't placed him in this situation. Why couldn't she just—

"Parker?" Lydia stuck her head in his office. "Are you coming or not?"

"Why did you let her come to work here?" he snapped.
She studied him for a moment. "What happened?"

"Nothing."

"Then you need to forget who she is and just go on with your life. It'll be much simpler that way."

"Are you joking?"

"Of course not."

"And when Dalton comes to the center?"

"You'll introduce him as your son."

Parker rounded his desk, closing the gap between them and lowered his voice. "You don't feel a little bad about that?"

"I feel terrible about the whole thing." She lifted her chin in that imperious way she had, forever the proud, arrogant woman who'd hired him nearly twelve years ago. "Would you rather we told her the truth?"

"God, no."

"Then what choice do we have?"

"We could lay her off, tell her we aren't going to be as busy as you anticipated. If she can't find work, she and Faith will be forced to move on."

"And you think *that's* kinder?" Lydia said, obviously appalled.

Parker felt buried by another avalanche of guilt. Of course it wasn't kinder. But it would mean he wouldn't have to face her nearly every day.

"As calm and controlled as she appears to be on the outside, she's been through more than we know," Lydia continued. "Are you going to make what we did even worse by refusing her?"

Parker sighed in resignation. "Not now, I guess."

"Good," she said, and turned on her heel.

Good? They couldn't tell Hope the truth and they couldn't send her away. They were stuck between a rock and a hard place.

With a curse, he followed Lydia to the meeting.

CHAPTER TWELVE

BEFORE THE STAFF MEETING actually began, Trish introduced Hope to almost everyone who worked at the center. Kim Sherman, the petite blond accountant, appeared to be in her mid-twenties—yet she seemed to hold herself apart from the others. Katherine Collins and Heidi Brandt, both full-time midwives, had been at the clinic when Hope delivered her baby. Dressed similarly in Birkenstock sandals, cap-sleeved T-shirts and flowing skirts, they'd obviously grown close over the years. They both welcomed her warmly.

The small, red-haired Gina Vaughn was new. Hope had already met her. Dawn Mitchell, the center's overflow midwife, had started nearly five years ago. She typically worked out of her house, Hope was told, so she'd come in specifically for the meeting. Tall and willowy, she was a mother of five who seemed, from her tight-fitting jeans and Western-style denim shirt, to be more conventional than her earthy, free-spirited counterparts. And Lenora Hernandez, a short, rather plump Hispanic woman, was the only nurse.

Hope was struck by how unpretentious and genuine everyone seemed. She was excited to be working with them—even Parker Reynolds. He stood off to one side, leaning against a wall with his arms folded, apparently brooding. But whenever she caught his eye, he made a concerted effort to smile. If it looked like more of a grimace, she wasn't going to worry about it. He'd apologized for his unfriendly manner; she'd accepted his apology and would go from there.

"Can we get started?" Lydia asked. She'd turned off the television and positioned herself next to the fireplace insert. Everyone else stood at the back, lounged on the chairs and couches or sat on the floor. "I know we all have work to do and appointments this afternoon, so go ahead and eat. I just want to discuss a few things while you have your lunch."

Lenora gently nudged Hope with a pizza box. Putting a slice on one of the paper plates that had circulated a few minutes earlier, Hope breathed in the delicious aromas and passed the pizza to Gina Vaughn, who stood to her right. Then they both settled on the floor.

"First, I hope you've all had a chance to meet our latest addition, Hope Tanner," Lydia said. "Hope, raise your hand."

Hope felt a moment's panic as all eyes turned her way, but she managed a small wave.

"We're happy she's joined the staff," Lydia went on. "She's an obstetrics nurse, so she brings a tremendous amount of knowledge with her. I'm sure she'll be a great asset to us. We've even talked about the possibility of her becoming a certified midwife. For someone with her background, it wouldn't be difficult. Until she decides what direction she wants to go, she'll be assisting wherever we need her." Lydia paused for a second. "Now, on to our agenda."

Lenora passed Hope a lemonade, which she accepted, grateful that everyone's attention had finally shifted away from her.

"First of all, I want to make sure we're spending enough time with our mothers. I know I'm a bit of a stickler on this issue, but I don't want anyone who comes here to feel as though we're simply herding her through a process that should be a beautiful and memorable experience. You need to ask yourselves—are you taking time to speak to your clients, and to really listen when they answer?''

Katherine Collins raised her hand.

''Katherine?''

''I've started doing something new. I record an interview with my ladies when they come in for their first visit,'' she said. ''I ask them for their favorite books, music and movies. We talk about parenting and what an ideal birth means to them. We even go into their background and family, if they're open to talking about that sort of stuff. It really helps me get in touch with them, you know? After they leave, I listen to the tape again and jot down the information in my binder.''

''I do the same thing,'' Heidi said. ''But I give my clients a crystal I've picked out especially for them, one that holds a personal value for me, so they know they're important to me. It really forges a bond between us.''

''Is every mother really interested in becoming *that* close to her midwife?'' Dawn asked, her voice slightly impatient. ''I mean, I believe in being friendly and supportive, but I don't have time to become everyone's best friend. I have a family of my own to raise, and my ladies have lives of their own, too.''

A discussion immediately ensued, weighing the pros and cons of establishing close, personal relationships with each client. Gina Vaughn and Lenora Hernandez seemed very interested in what was being said. Hope was, too. It was certainly a different approach from that at the hospital, which focused more on professionalism and meeting a mother's physical needs than nurturing her emotionally.

Curious about how Parker Reynolds was taking all this, Hope shot a glance his way, and found him staring right at her.

He shifted his gaze to Lydia the moment their eyes met, but he didn't look as though he was even following the conversation, let alone forming any opinions on it. Probably he ignored this kind of thing, Hope decided.

"Okay, that's enough," Lydia was saying. "We're going to have to move on. I won't tell you how to relate to your clients. You do what works for you, but be mindful of taking the proper amount of time and making the experience an enriching one." She double-checked the agenda Trish had passed out before the meeting. "Now, let's go over the procedures we should follow when a midwife feels a mother would be better served by a transfer to the Arroyo County Hospital...."

The meeting lasted about an hour. Hope was just getting a little restless, wanting a free minute to call and check on Faith, when Lydia waved Parker to the front.

"As you know, we've got our fund-raiser for SIDS research coming up," she said as he stepped through those sitting on the floor. "I've asked Parker to give us an update on how it's going, because I'm sure he can use our help on the promotion end."

Parker's eyes flicked over Hope before focusing on those closer to him. "We're planning to host another walk-a-thon, since that worked so well last year," he said. "But it's a campaign year, so my father-in-law is busy raising money for his own purposes and won't be able to help us. And we've lost our corporate sponsor. Without Congressman Barlow and Flying Diamond Oil Company, we're going to get stuck with a big advertising bill, not to mention some of the other promotional expenses. So what I need is for everyone to contact their friends, family and acquaintances to see if we can find a replacement. Last year we raised over $20,000 for SIDS research with this event. I'd like to surpass that this year. But if we have to start cutting corners, we might end up in the hole."

"What type of sponsor are we looking for?" Gina asked.

"Anyone willing to make a sizable donation in return for being listed on our promotion materials."

"What about gathering donations for the prizes, to entice more people to join the walk-a-thon?'' Heidi asked. ''Would that help?''

''We can always use more prizes.''

''Those camping, fishing and backpacking adventures Rusty Nunes offered last year were great,'' she said.

''They were.'' Despite the discussion, Parker seemed preoccupied. ''Rusty's just had major knee surgery, though, and can't participate this year,'' she said. ''But you've got the right idea. Things that appeal to the tourists generally work best.''

''Maybe we can get Red River Adventures to offer a free mountain bike as a drawing prize,'' Katherine said.

''What we need more than prize items is cash donors,'' Parker told them.

''Are you still going to Taos to see if you can drum up support, Parker?'' Lydia asked. ''I think that's a good idea.''

''I've already set several appointments with potential companies. But time is so short I need someone to help me fill them,'' he said.

''Do we have any volunteers?'' Lydia asked.

''I'd like to help,'' Katherine murmured, ''but Roger would kill me if I took on anything else right now. It's too hard to make arrangements for the kids.''

''I'd go, but one of my mothers is overdue,'' Heidi said. She and Katherine looked around, as though planning to handpick someone else, but the shy Trish quickly ducked her head and Lenora seemed to speak for both of them when she said, ''Oh, no, I'm no good at such things.''

Soon everyone was staring at Hope, and Hope knew they were thinking she was the perfect candidate. She had the time to go and no one depending on her except Faith. And she *had* been hired to help Parker with any special projects. Unless Hope missed her guess, *this* was a special project.

But she wasn't sure she wanted to spend an entire day

alone with Parker Reynolds. And she wasn't much of a salesperson.

"What, exactly, would it entail?" she asked.

"Parker?" Katherine prompted when he hesitated.

"We'd need to spend one, maybe two days in Taos," he said.

"Together?"

"Why drive separately?" Katherine said.

"Um…" Hope opened her mouth to refuse, but the weight of everyone's expectations made her hesitate. Lydia had been so good to her, and she wanted to be of some value to the center. Surely she could help out with the fund-raiser. One day with Parker couldn't be *that* big a deal. "I'll do it," she said.

Lydia and Parker exchanged a quick glance. "But you've barely arrived," Lydia said. "And Faith's getting close to the end of her term—"

"I don't think she's going to have the baby in the next week or so." Hope refused to look at Parker. She didn't want to see his reaction. "And Taos is only an hour away. It won't be a problem."

Silence ensued until a confused-sounding Heidi spoke up. "That's great, isn't it? Thanks, Hope. I'm sure Parker's grateful for the help."

If Parker was grateful, he didn't say so. Heidi, obviously catching the omission, hurried on. "This fund-raiser means a lot to all of us. It's our local contribution to worthy causes for the year."

"When do we go?" Hope asked.

"We'll talk about it," Parker said abruptly.

"Okay, that's it," Lydia said. "Trish, why don't you put the music back on and we'll all get to work."

Hope sat still as the room emptied. She'd just volunteered for a job that would essentially mean she'd be trying to talk various companies into donating thousands of dollars to a charity they might or might not care about, for some advertising value that was difficult to quantify.

Fund-raising wasn't something she'd ever pictured herself doing, and certainly not with Parker Reynolds.

She thought of telling him privately that it wasn't going to work out. Considering his lackluster reaction, she doubted he'd mind. But the way he stomped off gave her little opportunity to tell him anything and incited the stubborn streak she'd inherited from her father. She was going to accompany him for the good of the clinic, she told herself—and to show him that he had no reason in the world to dislike her.

THE SMELL OF CARROTS, potatoes, onions and some kind of meat greeted Hope the moment she opened the door to the cabin. She drew close to the fire Faith had built in the stove, enjoying its warmth. Even though it wasn't really cold enough for a fire, the crackle and flicker added to the homey ambiance, and she knew it would chase away the chill after the sun went down.

"Smells great in here. What's for dinner?" she asked.

"Just a meat loaf and some vegetables." Faith was bent over the fabric she had spread out on the kitchen table. "How was work?"

Hope thought about her commitment to help with the fund-raiser and frowned as she put her purse on the counter. "I've had better days. What about you?"

"It's been quiet around here, but I've made some real progress on the quilt." She snatched up several pieces of fabric she'd cut into various shapes for the old-fashioned baby quilt she was making and held them up.

The fact that Faith had been so happily occupied all day would normally have lightened Hope's mood. But she was still thinking about Parker Reynolds. "Any contractions or anything?"

"None."

She walked over to the answering machine she'd bought while they were shopping in Taos and pressed the message button, even though the light wasn't blinking. "No new messages," it said in its odd mechanical voice. She knew they weren't likely to get any messages, either, but old habits were hard to break. She remembered Jeff, the nurses with whom she'd worked and her neighbors in St. George. She hadn't exactly been close to any of them, but they'd all called her on occasion. Now she felt a sudden sense of loss.

Had she made the right choice in leaving everything she'd built over the past ten years? Was Arvin bluffing? Or was he truly dangerous?

She would have been stupid to take the chance.

"Were you expecting someone to call?" Faith asked, her scissors cutting smoothly through the fabric.

"No. No one has our number, except the people at the birthing center. I was just making sure this thing works. When you buy used electronics, you never know."

Fortunately, Hope didn't have to worry about Faith calling home again. The Loreys had canceled the long-distance service to the cabin to avoid any potential abuse by renters, and Hope had no plan to reinstate it.

"Have you felt the baby move?" Hope asked, changing the subject while she kicked off her shoes.

Faith dropped her scissors on the table and stretched. "More than I'd like. This baby is so strong it feels like she's going to break one of my ribs almost every time she kicks. You can even see her little foot if you watch closely."

Hope glanced at her sister over the back of the couch. "*Her?*"

"I think it's a girl."

"Will you be disappointed if it's not?"

"Of course not."

"Do you want to learn the baby's sex during your ultrasound appointment?"

Faith walked over to check on whatever she had cooking in the oven—the meat loaf, Hope supposed. "Can they really tell that easily?"

"Sometimes, depending on the baby's position. It's basically a picture of what's inside your womb."

"I'd rather be surprised," she said, her voice muffled now that she was turned away.

Hope remembered when she'd first heard she was having a girl. It had been a painful revelation, one that had made the decision to put the baby up for adoption that much more critical. At the time, she'd been so desperate, so terrified she'd wind up back in Superior or on the streets. She wasn't about to risk having her daughter raised the same way she'd been raised, wasn't about to give the Brethren control of yet another female life.

"Are you going to tell me what was so terrible about your day?" Faith asked.

"It wasn't terrible, exactly. I'm still learning my way around the center."

"What did you do today?"

"I helped the accountant, Kim Sherman, search through a bunch of files to prove the center had paid a certain vendor who claimed they hadn't received a check. And I helped Trish move a few things into the storage area upstairs."

"What about Parker Reynolds? How did he treat you?"

"Like I have the plague," Hope grumbled.

"You're kidding. Why?"

"Maybe I'll find out. We're going to be driving to Taos together sometime this week."

"For what?"

Hope explained, then asked, "You'll be okay while I'm gone?"

"Of course. I can always contact Gina if there's a problem. She called to check on me today, as a matter of fact."

"Already? That's a pleasant surprise."

When she realized Faith was taking dinner out of the

oven, Hope got up to help. "Maybe I'll have her swing by the day I'm in Taos."

"How long will you be gone?"

"Not much longer than the usual workday, I imagine."

Faith rolled her eyes as she set the meat loaf on the stove. "Then she doesn't have to come by. I'll be fine." She delved back into the oven for two large baked potatoes. "Oh, I almost forgot. We *did* get a call today," she said. "Mr. Deets called."

"My old landlord? How did he get this number?"

"From the leasing company, I guess."

"What did he want?"

"To see where he should send your security deposit."

Hope felt her blood run cold. "You didn't tell him, did you?"

Faith moved past her with the potatoes. "Of course not. I told him to send the money to the leasing company, and we'd pick it up there."

The leasing company wasn't far away. If Arvin learned even that address, it could still bring him to Enchantment....

"Hope?" Faith said. "Did I do okay? I had to give him something. Twelve hundred dollars is a lot of money. I thought you might need it."

"You did fine," Hope said, but she was imagining the worst. "Was he okay with your answer?"

"Sort of. He thought it was weird that I wouldn't give him our exact address. He said there'd been a lot of people asking about you and wondered if everything was okay."

Hope closed the oven door. "Did he mention who?"

"A guy named Jeff, for one."

Poor Jeff. She'd have to call him and let him know she wouldn't be coming back. "Is that all?"

Faith began to gather her patterns, fabric and scissors from the table. "No, there was some other guy, but he wouldn't leave his name."

"Did he say what he wanted?" Hope opened the silverware drawer to get them each a knife and fork.

"He just asked where you'd gone. Said your cat was getting into his trash again and he wanted to return him to you."

Hope's breath caught in her throat. "What?"

"I guess Oscar's been getting into the trash."

"That's what I thought you said. What did you tell Mr. Deets?"

"If whoever it was calls again to let him know Oscar belongs to Mr. Paris next door."

Faith headed into the living room with her sewing things, complaining about the fact that they should have brought Oscar with them, after all, but Hope didn't respond. Her mind was too busy sifting frantically through all the possibilities. Maybe someone had found a cat who looked like Oscar, thought it was hers and knew her well enough to track down Mr. Deets. But if that was true, why would he say her cat had been in his garbage *again?* No one had ever contacted Hope about a cat before. All the neighbors knew Oscar belonged to Mr. Paris.

And why didn't the caller leave his name?

CHAPTER THIRTEEN

PARKER STARED at the telephone and then at the slip of paper on which he'd scrawled Hope's number before leaving work. It was now almost a week after the staff meeting. He'd been planning to call her all evening but hadn't wanted to talk to her while Dalton was awake. He knew it would make him feel even guiltier for what he'd done—what he was still doing—to speak to Dalton's mother and risk his son asking, "Who is it, Dad?" Parker knew he could never let on that she was anything special to either of them.

Propping the phone against his shoulder, he began to dial. Before he could finish, however, he hung up and slumped back against the sofa cushion. He didn't want to talk to Hope, even though Dalton was now in bed. Seeing her, speaking to her, even *remembering* her raised questions he'd rather not answer. What if Hope became interested in knowing Dalton? What if Dalton became interested in knowing Hope? She seemed like a nice person, as though she'd held up pretty well, considering everything that had happened in her life. Was he wrong to keep them apart?

How could he be wrong when anything other than what he was doing put his son at risk? He didn't want Dalton mixed up in Hope's past. She had Faith with her and was once again on the run, which told him she still had contact with Superior and the strange people who lived there. Why would he want to introduce his son to all that?

He dialed her again and, this time, waited for the phone

to ring. Hope was just another employee at the center, he told himself. He had to believe that and act accordingly. "Hello?"

"Hope?"

"Yes?"

"This is Parker Reynolds."

"Oh."

His name met with scant enthusiasm, but after the way he'd behaved since she'd come to town, that didn't surprise him. "I'm not bothering you too late, am I?"

"No."

"I'm calling about our trip to Taos."

"Let me guess. You want to cancel."

Her bluntness took him off guard. He couldn't cancel. He needed her help too badly. But that didn't mean he wasn't tempted. "What makes you so sure?"

"You need to ask?" she said with a short laugh. "Even after we agreed to be friends, you haven't said two words to me."

Parker stared at the television he'd muted a few minutes earlier. "I've been busy."

"Right."

Somehow he was going to have to become a better actor. "It's nothing personal," he said.

He heard her sigh. "Would you mind telling me what's changed? We used to get along fine. I always believed you cared about me."

He had cared about her. He still did. That was part of the problem. "Nothing's changed."

"Have I grown horns on my forehead or something?"

"No. It's not you, okay?" He swallowed hard. "I'm having to make a few adjustments in my personal life. That's all."

"Somehow you're managing to like everyone else while you're making those adjustments."

"You're new. Maybe I'm shy."

"I don't believe that, but I can't force you to like me,

so I guess that excuse is as good as any. I just need to know where it leaves us with the SIDS project."

"It leaves us going to Taos tomorrow morning, if you can make it."

"That doesn't give me much notice," she said.

Because he'd put off calling her until the last possible moment. "I know, but I wasn't able to confirm all the appointments until this afternoon. If you can't get away, I'll have to take someone else." He held his breath, hoping for the best.

"I can probably make it. I just need to see if Faith can spend her day volunteering at the center or check if Gina can come by," she said. "I'd rather not leave her alone."

"Are you afraid she might go into labor?"

"No. The ultrasound indicated she has another two weeks, and I don't think she'll be early. She's not showing any of the usual signs."

He was about to ask her what she was worried about then, but Dalton came stumbling into the living room, yawning and rubbing his eyes. "Dad?"

Parker put a hand over the phone. "What is it, bud?"

"I just remembered that my manatee report is due tomorrow."

"Your what?"

"My manatee report. You know, those big mammals."

Parker frowned, glancing at the clock. "It's after ten, Dalton."

"I know."

"Why didn't you tell me this earlier?"

"I forgot."

"Is that your son?" Hope asked on the phone.

Parker couldn't answer her. He wanted to say, "Yes," as casually as any other father might claim his child, but the word stuck in his throat. "I've gotta go. I'll pick you up at your place at eight, unless I hear otherwise," he said, and ended the call.

HOPE DREAMED about Autumn again. This time they were in a grocery store, and Autumn kept peeking at her from one aisle after another. Hope raced frantically around the store, trying to locate her daughter, to make sure she was safe, but she never reached her. She only caught glimpses of a raggedy dress, a dirty tennis shoe or an impish grin.

When Parker arrived at eight, she felt as if she hadn't slept a wink. Her eyes were gritty, and she had a headache.

"You ready to go?" he asked. His gaze traveled over her white cardigan and the sleeveless dress she wore beneath, and for some strange reason Hope suddenly felt a little tingle go through her.

"Do you mind if we drop Faith at The Birth Place?" she asked. "She doesn't have a driver's license."

"No problem." He stood by the door and waited while she ducked inside, scooped her purse off the counter and called her sister.

Faith waddled out of her bedroom, pulling on a brown knitted shawl that was as hideous as her pioneer dress. "I'm all set."

Hope frowned at her. "You're not really going to wear that old thing, are you?"

"My shawl? What's wrong with it?" Her chin jutted out. "It's chilly in the mornings."

They'd argued about the shawl ever since Faith had draped it over her arm at the secondhand store they'd visited in town last weekend. Hope wanted her to modernize, but in Faith's mind, modern clothing was still a sin. The shawl had been her way of rebelling.

At least she'd gone along with the haircut.

"Never mind," Hope muttered, because she didn't want Parker to overhear.

She waited until Faith went outside, then locked the cabin up tight. They hadn't heard from Mr. Deets for more than a week, but Hope believed his mysterious caller had been Arvin. Who else would have mentioned a cat? Fortunately for them, Deets hadn't given them away, mostly because he couldn't. Arvin had called before the leasing company had contacted her old landlord for a reference, so Mr. Deets didn't know where they were at the time.

Had her uncle waited another day or two, Mr. Deets might have been more accommodating.

Shuddering at the thought, Hope dropped her keys in her purse and hurried down the steps to Parker's white Dodge Ram pickup.

Faith was standing near the open passenger door, and Parker was waiting next to her. "You first," Faith said. "I'll be getting out soon so I should be on the end."

Hope eyed the bench seat, knowing she had no chance of avoiding a short ride pressed against Parker's side.

Sighing, she hauled herself into the truck and slid to the center. Parker helped Faith into the cab before circling to the other side. Then his body warmed Hope as he sandwiched her between them.

A hint of his aftershave momentarily distracted Hope from her reluctance to sit so close to him. He smelled as fresh and homegrown as the forests surrounding Enchantment.

The doors slammed with a couple of resounding thuds, and Parker put the idling truck in gear.

"We shouldn't be back too late tonight," he said to no one in particular.

"I'm sure we can make quick work of it," Hope agreed, careful to keep her eyes on the road.

Faith rested her arms on her belly and spoke over an old Fleetwood Mac song playing on the radio. "Take as long as you need. When I called to see if I could help at the center today, Gina said her husband's on a trucking run and won't be home tonight. She invited me to have dinner with her and meet her kids. I really miss having kids around," she added, her voice a bit melancholy.

Hope remembered Sarah, the child who might have called them in St. George, and knew Faith was worried about her. She'd asked her parents to look after the little girl, but there was always the possibility that Arvin was abusing Sarah in a way she would never reveal. And Faith was so used to caring for siblings and cousins, the emptiness of the cabin probably made it feel like a tomb to her. Hope was glad she was going to be around people today.

"You'll soon have your own baby to take care of," she said, regretting her negative comments about the shawl. She needed to give Faith more time to adjust. She was doing well, considering.

They pulled up in front of The Birth Place, and Faith climbed out. "Thanks for the ride," she said. Bending to see around Hope, she smiled at Parker. "Try to have some fun while you're working, okay? I don't think Hope has nearly enough fun."

Hope felt her mouth drop open, but before she could respond, Faith closed the door. She glanced at Parker and found him arching a brow at her.

"She's wrong. I have fun all the time," she said, and scooted quickly away.

PARKER DROVE in silence until they started up the twisting canyon road that would eventually take them over the mountains and into the next valley. By then, his curiosity had gotten the better of him and he had to ask, "What do you think you'll do after Faith has her baby? Will you stay in Enchantment or move on?"

"I've given Lydia a year's commitment. After that, I don't know," Hope replied, staring out the window, as she'd done since they'd dropped off her sister.

A year's commitment? Somehow Lydia had neglected to mention that. "Lydia told me you're still dealing with the past. Is there any chance it might catch up with you here?"

"I guess there's always a chance," she said.

"Lydia also told me you went back to Superior for the

first time just a few weeks ago." He hoped he sounded as if he was just making casual conversation.

"That's true."

"How did you hold out so long?"

"Hold out?" she repeated. "It was harder to go back than to stay away."

Parker threw her a glance. "Why? Were you afraid you'd see Bonner again?"

Hope gaped at him and he instantly regretted bringing up Bonner's name. But ever since her return, he'd been dying to ask what had happened to the boy she'd talked about so much ten years ago. Bonner was, after all, Dalton's father. Parker tried to convince himself he was only interested in Bonner because Bonner could, at some point, have an impact on Dalton's life.

But Parker knew that wasn't the only reason. He was also curious to learn whether or not Hope was still carrying a torch for the father of her child. There had to be *some* reason she hadn't married and settled down. She was certainly attractive enough to have found a mate by now, regardless of her strange background.

"How do you remember Bonner's name?" she demanded.

Parker scowled and focused his attention on the road. "You were madly in love with him," he said. "You talked about him all the time."

"That was ten years ago! You couldn't even remember *my* name when you first saw me."

"Having you around again has jogged my memory."

The confusion on her face didn't clear, but he offered no further explanation.

"I don't understand you," she said, shaking her head.

He couldn't blame her. He hadn't been himself since her return. His concern for Dalton and his regret about what had happened were so inextricably mixed up with the tenderness he still felt toward her that he couldn't treat her consistently to save his life. Especially because that tenderness was somehow changing. Pity had formed the foundation of what he'd felt for Hope Tanner all those years ago. But pity played a much smaller part now.

"Forget I asked," he muttered.

He turned up the volume of the radio. He had no business asking Hope about anything, let alone something as personal as her relationship with Bonner. He needed to ignore her as much as possible until she and Faith eventually left and he could get on with his life. He'd already survived her first two weeks at the center. Certainly they *would* leave, even if it took a year.

"I did see him," she said, out of the blue.

He blinked in surprise. "What?"

"I saw Bonner, but not while I was in Superior. He came to my house afterward."

Parker tried to imagine Hope confronting the boy who'd gotten her pregnant. When she'd first come to Enchantment, she'd looked as if she was starving, and she probably had been—for food and for love. How could a guy who'd let a girl suffer like that live with himself, even if he had been only eighteen at the time?

"What for?" Parker couldn't help asking.

"He wanted me to marry him."

"You're joking! After all this time? After what he did? I hope you told him to go to hell."

"Actually, he told me *I'd* go to hell for refusing him." She chuckled, as if to laugh off his remark, but Parker could tell she didn't find it funny.

"Was it difficult?"

"Was what difficult?"

"Refusing him. Wasn't he offering you what you wanted so badly ten years ago?"

"What I wanted ten years ago isn't what I want now."

They drove in silence for the next few minutes as Parker tried to figure out what she might want now. Her entire family with her—or freedom from the past? A husband and family—or complete autonomy and a career?

"Do you believe that Bonner's right?" he finally asked.

"About what?"

"That refusing him means you'll go to hell?"

"It doesn't matter."

"Why not?"

She attempted to tuck a strand of hair behind her ear, but it was too short to be tamed. "Because I couldn't go back to him even if I wanted to. He's married to Charity, my middle sister. And two other women, besides."

Parker gritted his teeth against the disgust that nearly overwhelmed him. "So he'd have four wives?"

"Until he married his fifth."

"There's no limit?"

"Not really, no."

"Do the other wives have any say in who the man includes in the family?" Parker asked. "Any say in who he brings into his bed?"

"Each marriage supposedly comes as a calling from the church, so no one can argue with it. The Brethren bring in a certain man and tell him they've prayed about the situation and received an answer from God that he's required to take so-and-so to wife."

"What if he doesn't want to marry?"

"He's been taught, his whole life, that this is his duty. Most men go along with whomever the Brethren have chosen. They also make it clear which woman they'd *like* to have and, if they're in good standing with the church, she might become a second or third wife."

"Doesn't anybody care what the woman wants?"

"Not especially."

Parker couldn't imagine such a total lack of regard. His mother had always been his mainstay. "You weren't ever going to be Bonner's second or third wife," he said. "They were trying to force you into marrying someone else."

"What happened with me and Bonner was different."

Parker turned off the heat, which was beginning to feel stifling. "How?"

"A man's supposed to have a vocation before he marries. Bonner had just graduated from high school and was expected to go to a two-year college. The Brethren claimed they prayed about our situation, but God's answer was that we were not allowed to marry. They said God wanted to test my faith, to see if it was sufficient for my salvation, so they said I needed to marry Arvin."

"Your uncle."

She stared at him for several seconds. "You just happen to remember that, too?"

He grinned. "It's all coming back to me now."

She shook her head. "You're not an easy man to figure out."

"I'm not as difficult to understand as the men we've been talking about," he grumbled.

She didn't say anything.

"So Bonner's married to your sister?" he asked.

"Yes. They have three children together."

Parker wondered how badly that news had hurt Hope. She'd said she couldn't marry Bonner because he had other wives. She hadn't said she no longer had feelings for him. "So who did the Brethren choose for Faith?"

"Some old guy," she said vaguely.

Lydia had already told Parker that Faith was married to her uncle. He was willing to bet that uncle was the infamous Arvin of old. But he wasn't going to press Hope to admit or discuss it. He could certainly see why she'd rather keep that information to herself.

"Did you like St. George?" he asked, changing the subject.

She seemed to think long and hard before answering. "For the most part."

"What did you like?"

"I enjoyed being independent. I had a good job, a nice place to live."

"Did you meet anyone there? Ever consider getting married?"

She frowned. "I'm not cut out for marriage."

At this announcement, he sat up straighter and lowered the radio. "Why not? Don't you want kids?"

Something fleeting passed through her eyes, some small evidence of pain. Parker saw it, and then it was gone, and he didn't want to know where that flash had come from or why it was there. "It wouldn't be fair to marry just so I can have kids," she said.

"True. But you'll eventually find someone you want to share your life with, don't you think?"

"I'm afraid not." She shook her head as if completely convinced of her own words. "I'm not capable of falling in love."

"Of course you are. You loved Bonner, right?"

"I loved Bonner," she admitted. "But something in me broke after that." The smile she gave him was slightly crooked. "Now all I care about is Faith."

CHAPTER FOURTEEN

PARKER SAT BEHIND the wheel, his truck idling, as Hope went in to the gas station to use the rest room. After saying she'd never marry, she'd fallen asleep, only to wake up the moment they hit the outskirts of Taos and announce that she needed him to stop.

He watched her as she spoke to the attendant before trotting out with a key. Raising a finger to indicate she'd just be a minute, she crossed to the rest rooms beyond the pumps.

Now all I care about is Faith. Parker rubbed his chin, still smooth from his morning shave, as he contemplated those words. Maybe she cared about Faith, but she didn't have any *real* faith, he thought. Not in love, and certainly not in her future. She believed only in what she could see and touch and do for herself, and Parker couldn't say that he blamed her.

The unflinching way she dealt with such a bleak outlook had a strange effect on him, though. It made him want to shelter her, convince her that life wasn't as precarious as she thought, at least not when she was with him.

Maybe it was because she reminded him so much of Dalton. It certainly wasn't because she reminded him of any other woman he'd known, least of all Vanessa. Hope and the woman who'd been his wife weren't anything alike. Hope came off tough enough to conquer the world, like some kind of scrappy street fighter with a chip on the shoulder. Vanessa had been cultured and refined. Almost clingy. Her emotions had gone only as deep as the next whim. Except for her obsession with having a baby...

Parker wondered how Vanessa would have managed had she been given Hope's life. He couldn't imagine her surviving, let alone thriving the way Hope had. Hope's difficulties seemed to have strengthened her—so much so that he doubted she'd ever admit, even to herself, that she wanted anything more than what she had. And yet he sensed a hunger in her—

"Thanks for stopping," she said, climbing in. "I got us each a Slurpee."

She handed him one of the bright red-and-blue cups she'd been juggling when she opened the door, and out of nowhere, Parker decided Dalton would like her. Granted, she had the propensity to be a little too serious, but with time and the support of the right person—provided she ever met the right person—that could change. *If* she could learn to trust again. Unfortunately for Hope that was a big *if*.

He considered her love life as he put the truck in reverse and backed out of the parking space. Had she ever been with anyone other than Bonner? By twenty-seven, most women had accumulated plenty of sexual experience. But Hope wasn't like most women. She was friendly to a point, but beyond that, she was decidedly remote. He couldn't imagine her making love—at least not with any loss of control. She'd be guarded at best, he decided, and pitied the guy who fell in love with her.

"I should warn you that I'm no good with strangers," she was saying. She'd propped her drink between her knees and was fixing the damage her nap had done to her hair in the lighted mirror on the visor.

"You look fine," he said. "Just don't spill that."

"I'm not going to spill anything." She snapped the visor up. "You've turned into a real grump in those ten years since I left Enchantment, you know that? It's no wonder you haven't remarried."

Parker pretended to be fully absorbed as he approached the highway and waited for a break in traffic. "At least I plan to marry someday. Eventually," he added because he certainly hadn't made any concerted effort in that regard. After being hounded by Melody Rider and several other members of the PTA to get Dalton a mother, he'd had a few casual dates, but he had yet to meet anyone he considered a real possibility. Being married to Vanessa and having to put up with her controlling parents throughout the difficult years of her illness had taught him a few things. An important one being that there was a lot more to consider about a woman than the woman herself. Background, upbringing, family and associates were all part of the deal.

Which was another reason he felt sorry for whoever fell for Hope's pretty face and tempting body....

"Well, if you plan to remarry, good luck," she muttered.

"What's that supposed to mean?" he asked, forgetting about pulling onto the highway.

She didn't flinch as he turned to confront her. "You've changed. You used to be a nice guy, but now I don't think you'd be very easy to live with."

"I'm still a nice guy," he countered.

She didn't answer.

"Ask anyone."

She sipped her Slurpee and gazed out the windshield, obviously expecting him to get on with driving. "I don't need to ask anyone," she said. "I can tell for myself."

IT WAS AFTER FIVE when Hope checked her watch. She and Parker had taken a short break at noon to grab a sandwich at a small deli a few blocks away, but she was getting hungry again, and a little discouraged. She'd known she wasn't the best salesperson in the world, but she'd thought she could find at least *one* sponsor.

Maybe Parker was having better luck.

Shading her eyes, she gazed to the west, where she'd last seen him disappear into a tall office building. As far as she could tell, he hadn't come out of his last meeting yet.

Crossing the street, she headed toward Dino's Italian Eatery—and nearly bumped into him as he emerged from a small appliance store.

"Looking for me?"

"Tell me you've found the funding we need."

He frowned and shook his head. "I'm afraid not. I got the take-out pizza place to donate a coupon for a year's worth of free pizza, though. And the vacuum-repair guy here said he'd give me two completely reconditioned vacuums."

"We can't go back to the clinic with only this," she said.

He shoved his hands in his pockets. "We'll just have to come again tomorrow or the next day." He looked up at the sign above the restaurant closest to them. "But first, let's eat."

PARKER WATCHED HOPE sample her flan, feeling more relaxed than he'd been in her presence since she'd returned to Enchantment. They'd both called home and knew Faith and Dalton were fine. Dalton was with Bea, a grandmotherly type from his church; Parker paid her to baby-sit if he ever had to be away in the evening. And Faith was still at Gina's.

"How's the dessert?" he asked as the waitress brought his coffee. He'd ordered it as an afterthought—to keep him awake for the ride home. After plenty of chips and salsa, a margarita and a plateful of fajitas, he was just a little sleepy. The heat thrown off by the wood-burning stove in the corner of the hacienda-style restaurant probably wasn't helping.

"Excellent," she said. "Would you like to try it?"

"No, thanks." He added cream to his coffee. "I *would*

like to know what you think might happen if Faith's husband ever catches up with you, though.''

She tensed, and he almost regretted bringing up the subject now, when she seemed to be enjoying herself. But he doubted there'd be a better opportunity to ask. If he had his way, he wouldn't be spending a great deal of time with Hope Tanner in the future.

''I'm not sure what he'd do,'' she said, toying with her dessert.

''Is he violent?''

''I'd say so, yes.''

''How violent? He wouldn't try to drag you and Faith back to Enchantment or hurt you physically, would he?''

''Maybe.'' She took another bite of flan. ''He's done some things that definitely have me worried.''

''Like what?''

''Like...'' She grimaced ''Never mind. It doesn't matter.''

''I want to know.''

She set her spoon down and shoved her dessert away as though she suddenly found it distasteful. ''He came to St. George in the middle of the night and tried to break into my house. He cut the phone line, made a bunch of threats and the next morning I found my cat on the front doorstep, dead.''

Parker felt a surprising amount of anger. Hadn't Hope been through enough?

''Actually, Oscar was more than dead,'' she went on. ''He was mutilated almost beyond recognition.''

''Tell me you called the police.''

''I did. They told me I could file a restraining order, but I knew, with this guy, it wasn't going to do any good.''

Parker wished he could have a few minutes alone with Faith's husband. ''I'm sorry,'' he said and reached across the table to take her hand. He'd meant his touch to be casual yet comforting, but Hope's fingers were long, thin and definitely on the cool side. They felt almost...fragile. For a moment he was tempted to enfold them in his own, to warn them...

"I don't want you to be sorry for me. I'm fine," she said, pulling away.

Parker was grateful for her toughness. He couldn't sympathize with her problems without wanting to take some sort of responsibility for them. He couldn't take any responsibility without getting more deeply involved. And there was no way in hell he, of all people, could get more deeply involved with her. But that didn't stop him from asking if Bonner was dangerous, too.

Hope took longer to answer this question. "I don't think so," she said. "He's changed, but I'm sure he's not warped. Not like Faith's husband, at least."

Don't ask her anything else about Superior, a voice inside his head warned. He hadn't liked any of her answers so far. But he knew this could be his only chance to learn more about Dalton's biological father. "When Bonner visited you in St. George, did he ask about the baby?"

"No."

"You don't suppose he'd ever come here, do you?"

"Why would he? He doesn't know where I was when I gave birth. And he has a lot of other children to keep him busy. I don't think he cares about Autumn."

"Autumn?"

A blush infused her cheeks. "That's what I call her." She leaned back as the waitress came with their check and carried the rest of the plates away, and Parker suddenly wished they'd grabbed a take-out pizza and headed straight home. He did *not* want to know how she coped with her lost child. Things were bad enough already.

When the waitress left, Hope continued, "Even if he could find her, I doubt he'd meddle in her life. She's spent her most formative years in mainstream America, which means the concepts of the church would be so foreign to her she'd never convert. For the Brethren, raising a 'righteous' generation is the whole point of having children. They believe that those who don't belong to the church are cast out of God's kingdom forever. So to make a long story short, Bonner's too involved in his own life, and in the bliss he feels he's earned in the next one, to bother with Autumn.''

''But you're not.''

''I have no other children. And no church, either. But it wouldn't matter. I'd miss her just as much.''

Parker rubbed his chest because it felt as if his heart was knocking against his ribs. ''Have you ever thought about looking for…her?''

He held his breath as Hope's gaze settled on him, praying she wouldn't recognize the guilt in his eyes. ''All the time,'' she said with such heartfelt honesty that he suddenly understood—and couldn't help sympathizing with—the hunger he sensed in her. She was yearning for her child.

For his child.

For Dalton.

God, he *knew* he shouldn't have asked.

PARKER INSISTED on paying for dinner. Hope accepted as graciously as possible, but as soon as he disappeared in the direction of the rest room, she leaned back in the booth and closed her eyes. She'd almost told him about the dreams that had started since her return to Enchantment, the ones where she saw Autumn yet couldn't reach her. But the words had refused to leave her throat. That seemed to happen whenever she tried to share anything potentially painful.

Why couldn't she break through whatever barrier separated her from the rest of the world? She felt as though she was going through all the right motions but not really experiencing life. When had she shut off so much of herself?

She couldn't identify a time. It had occurred so gradually she'd never even realized it was happening. Burying her feelings helped her cope, and coping was all that had mattered—at first. As long as she could cope, she'd survive. But now...

She remembered the warmth she'd felt when Parker had covered her hand with his. Had she been capable, she would have given him some sort of welcoming sign—a smile, perhaps. Instead she'd sat there, wanting him to thread his fingers through hers, and simply because she was afraid of *wanting* such intimacy, she pulled away.

The cell phone Parker had left on the table rang, startling Hope. She could see that he'd bumped into someone he knew on his way back from the rest room, so she let it ring, assuming the call would transfer to voice-mail. The ringing finally stopped, but after a few seconds it started again, and the people in the next booth twisted around to scowl at her.

Glancing across the room, where Parker was still engrossed in conversation, Hope quickly picked up the phone and answered it.

A long pause greeted her hello. She nearly hung up before a young voice, obviously leery, said, "Who's this?"

"Hope Tanner. Who's this?"

"Dalton. Where's my dad?"

"He's here at a restaurant with me."

"Why are *you* answering his phone?"

"Because he's tied up right now. Would you like me to take a message?"

He didn't answer. He just said, "Oh," and then there was another silence before he added an accusatory, "I don't know you."

"Not yet. I've only been in town a couple of weeks."

"And my dad asked you out on a date *already?*"

Hope stiffened in surprise. "He didn't ask me out," she said. "We work together."

"He works with Lydia and Katherine, too, but he doesn't take them to dinner late at night," the boy pointed out.

Hope smiled at the suspicion in his voice. "You don't have anything to worry about," she said. "I can promise that your dad doesn't like me very much."

"Really?"

"Cross my heart."

"How do you know?"

"Well…" She reflected on it for a moment. "He didn't want to hire me at the center, but Lydia insisted. And even though he needed my help today, he didn't want to take me with him. And he frowns at me a lot. I don't think those are very good signs, do you?"

"No," Dalton agreed thoughtfully. "Especially the frowning part. He only does that when he's mad. What did you do to make him mad?"

"Nothing that I know of."

"Do you know Holt's mother?"

"No. Who's she?"

"She's my friend's mom. But I don't like her."

"Why not?"

"She keeps telling my dad I need stuff I really don't want."

"Like vegetables?" Hope asked. She somehow knew this conversation was deeper than peas and carrots, but she wanted Dalton to share only what he needed or wished to tell her.

"Yeah. And other stuff, *worse* stuff."

The drama in his voice nearly made Hope chuckle. Except that he was obviously very upset about this woman's interference in his life. "What could be worse than peas? Spinach?"

"No. Mrs. Rider wants me to cry. Over *homework*. Can you believe that?"

Hope moved the phone away from her ear and glanced

down at it. Had she heard him right? "Actually, I can't. Why's that?"

"She thinks I don't cry because I don't have a mother."

"Don't you sometimes want a mother?"

"Not if she's going to be like Mrs. Rider."

"I see your point. But surely Mrs. Rider has some good qualities."

"Not really. She wears her hair up on top of her head until it looks like a giant beehive." He said this with ample disgust, but it was more of an aside than anything.

"And?" Hope prompted.

"And she's always telling me to chew with my mouth closed and quit getting into the mud and to tuck in my shirt. She thinks I play too rough with Holt, and that I should sit still while he practices the piano. And she tells my dad things about me that I don't want her to."

Hope drew circles in the condensation from her water glass. "You mentioned that. But you didn't tell me *what* she tells your dad."

"She tells him lots of stuff. She's always coming up with something else that's wrong with me," he complained.

Hope was completely mystified by this. What could possibly be wrong with this endearing little boy? "What's her biggest complaint?"

"This week?"

"Yeah."

"She says I don't know how to express my emotions. Whatever that's supposed to mean."

"That's where the crying comes in," Hope said.

"I guess."

"Hmm, let me think." Hope wiped her wet fingers on a napkin. "How old are you, Dalton?"

"Ten."

Ten years old. Autumn's age. Hope felt her heart wrench but tried to ignore the pain. "I'd say ten years old is old enough."

"For what?"

"Well, sadness isn't the only emotion people have," Hope replied. "There's happiness and irritation and frustration and lots of others. Maybe you could show her that you can talk about your emotions by explaining that it bothers you when she speaks to your father about you, instead of talking to you directly."

"Really?" he said. "I could do that? I wouldn't get in trouble?"

Hope thought of how stern Parker could sometimes be and hoped she wasn't misleading his son. "Not if you handle it right. As long as you're respectful, I think she'll see you're much more capable than she realized." Out of the corner of her eye, Hope noticed Parker weaving through the tables and hurried to finish the conversation. "You sound very bright. You know how to be respectful, don't you?"

"Yeah," he said.

"Great. Give it a try."

"Okay. I'll talk to her." He hesitated. "What was your name again?"

"Hope."

"Hope, you want me to call you back after I'm through and tell you how it went?"

"If you'd like."

"What's your number?"

Hope smiled at his earnestness as she slowly recited her telephone number.

"Thanks," he said, sounding very relieved.

Parker reached her at that moment and gave her another of his many frowns. "Who is it?"

"Your son. Here's your dad," she said into the phone, and handed Parker his cell. "He sounds darling," she told him. "You must be very proud."

Parker hardly seemed grateful for her praise. Mumbling a terse thank-you, he turned away from her to talk.

"Who, Hope? No, you probably won't meet her," she

heard him say. He fell silent for a moment before lowering his voice even further. But Hope could still make out his next words. ''I don't care if you do, Dalton, she's just a business associate. There's no reason for the two of you ever to be together, okay?…I said no, and that's it.'' He glanced at Hope as though he feared she might've overheard, and she was suddenly glad she hadn't responded earlier when he'd touched her. She needed to figure out how to start caring again, instead of living like some kind of shade. But in order to do that, she had to find someone to whom she really mattered. And that definitely wasn't Parker Reynolds.

Grabbing her purse, she stalked out of the restaurant to give him the privacy he so obviously desired. She didn't need him. He might have been her friend ten years ago, but he wasn't her friend anymore.

CHAPTER FIFTEEN

THE HEATER hummed in the cab of the truck as they drove back to Enchantment. Parker had the radio playing, too, hoping to avoid conversation. But as it turned out, he had nothing to worry about. Ever since they'd left the restaurant, Hope sat with her arms folded, her eyes straight ahead. She hadn't so much as glanced his way, let alone opened her mouth to speak.

Parker shifted uncomfortably, feeling a little sheepish about his conversation with Dalton. He'd been so shocked to find Hope on the phone with his son, talking as though they were old friends, that he'd overreacted. Now they were both angry with him, and he knew he deserved it.

"Are you too hot?" he asked, breaking the silence with as neutral a question as possible.

"I'm fine," she answered tightly.

"Is Faith going to be waiting for you when you get home?"

"No." She averted her face even more when she spoke and twisted a lock of her hair between her fingers. "I told her to stay the night with Gina."

"Because you didn't want her home alone? Even for a few hours?"

She didn't answer.

"But you have no reason to believe Arvin knows where you are, right?"

She looked at him then, her eyes slightly narrowed, and he realized what he'd said wrong. He'd forgotten to pretend he didn't know that the man causing all the problems now was the same man causing all the problems ten years ago. "I'd appreciate it if you'd keep that information to yourself," she said. "Not for my sake, but for Faith's."

He would have done it for her, but he couldn't say that. She wouldn't believe it. "Of course I won't say anything."

Relieved when she didn't thank him, he drove for another few minutes, searching for some other way to draw her out. He hadn't meant to alienate her at the restaurant. Even though he knew a definite rift was probably best, he couldn't leave things as they stood. What he'd said to Dalton had been a knee-jerk reaction to the boy's instant affinity with Hope. They'd spoken for only a few minutes and already his son wanted to meet her—and this after a very cool reception for almost every woman Parker had dated.

"What about you?" he asked, ignoring her hostility.

"What about me?"

"Won't you be staying alone tonight?"

"I don't see how that concerns you," she said.

He sighed and tightened his grip on the wheel. "Look, I didn't mean to offend you by my conversation with Dalton. I just want him to understand that…"

"That what?" she asked, finally turning to face him.

"That he shouldn't become attached to you."

"Because…"

"Because getting attached to you could get him hurt. You're not even sure you're going to be sticking around."

She folded her arms and studied him for several seconds. "You know, until now, I thought all this was because you don't like me. But you liked me well enough ten years ago. Are you sure it's Dalton you're worried about?"

"If it wasn't?" He kept his eyes on the road.

"I'd tell you you're smart to play it safe," she said simply. "I'm not a good risk."

AS SOON AS Parker pulled into her driveway, Hope stared at the dark empty cabin, its windows gleaming in the moonlight, and tried to decide whether or not there'd been any activity in her absence. It certainly didn't look like it. But the glowing numerals on Parker's dashboard read 12:20 a.m., and a strong wind passed through the trees, sounding like rushing water and creating a sense of isolation even more intense than what she normally experienced. If Arvin *was* lurking in the shadows, after Parker left there'd be no one to help her.

Had her uncle managed to trace them?

The question loomed large in Hope's mind, as it had for the past twenty minutes. With every mile, her anxiety had grown. Thank goodness she'd had Faith stay with Gina or she'd be a nervous wreck. She couldn't bear it if anything happened to her sister or the baby. Logic told her that Arvin had little chance of finding them. But gut instinct seemed to whisper that, with sufficient motivation, anything was possible.

The shadows of the swaying branches overhead shifted on the ground as she climbed out of the truck. She probably wouldn't be able to tell if someone was trying to sneak up on her, she realized, and longed to dash into the house and lock the door behind her—if the house itself was safe.

Swallowing hard, she studied it again, but was determined not to let Parker know how frightened she was. Fear was good, she told herself. Fear was an emotion, and feeling any emotion these days reminded her that she was alive and not so very different from everyone else.

"Thanks for the ride," she said, choosing to remain as polite as possible.

He didn't respond. She shut the door and started for the cabin, and he surprised her by turning off the ignition and getting out.

Hope glanced back at him. "What are you doing?"

"Just checking the place. I want to make sure you're safe here."

"There's no need. I'm certain everything's fine." Despite her fear, she wanted to get rid of him as soon as possible. She didn't want to look at him. She couldn't get past the changes in him.

His boots made no sound on the thick layer of pine needles covering the ground, but she could hear the crinkle of his red parka as he walked. "Then you won't mind if I see for myself."

Hope hauled in a deep breath and led the way to her front door, resisting the gratitude that niggled at her mind. Parker was such a paradox. He didn't want her along today, and yet he'd bought her dinner. He didn't want her to meet his son, but he was concerned enough to check her cabin.

"How old is Arvin now?" he asked, waiting behind her as she unlocked the door.

"Fifty-six." She swung the door wide, flipped on the switch, and gazed inside.

"And how many wives does he have?"

Hope didn't really want to tell him. She knew how repulsive it was to the average person and how odd he'd found her answers to the questions he'd asked today. "A lot."

He shook his head, and she tried to ignore his unspoken disapproval as she crossed the threshold. The cabin was definitely on the cool side. Faith must have turned off the heat since they were going to be gone all day—her sister was so frugal. But Hope couldn't see anything out of place. "Looks like everything's fine."

Parker slipped past her and headed down the hall to pay a visit to the back rooms while she set her purse and keys on the kitchen counter. She could hear him moving through the cabin, but she didn't follow. She wanted to stay in the most comforting room in the house—the kitchen/dining/living room. Then a door slammed just as she was putting water in the microwave to make some tea, startling her so badly she nearly dropped the cup.

"Parker?"

"Come here a second," he called. His voice sounded normal enough, but there was an edge to it that made the hair on her arms stand up.

"What's wrong?" she asked, hurrying down the hall.

She could see for herself as soon as she opened the door to Faith's bedroom. Someone had thrown a rock through the window, creating a hole big enough to allow a strong draft to sweep through the room. The wind would have slammed the door shut again had Hope not kept one hand on it.

Parker picked up the rock lying amid the shattered glass that winked at her from the floor. "Have you seen any kids in the area?"

Hope shrugged, unease cramping her stomach. "Well…there were a couple of girls riding their bicycles on the street last week." She knew, even as she said it, that those girls hadn't thrown the rock. She just didn't want to face the possibility that Arvin had. Not only had she obtained a good job, one she thought she was really going to like, Faith would be able to have her baby at the center with Lydia's and Gina's help. She didn't want to face the changes that would need to take place if Arvin had followed them to Enchantment.

"Girls?" Parker echoed.

"It could be anyone," she said. "It's just a rock, right? A rock doesn't necessarily mean anything."

He crouched down, tossing the rock from hand to hand while peering up at the web of cracks in the broken window. "Do you have a flashlight?"

"The owners of the cabin left a few things in various cupboards and drawers," she said, "but if there's a flashlight, I haven't run across it yet."

"I'm sure they've got one somewhere. The electricity goes out too often in the winter for them not to. But to make things easy, I have one in the truck." He squeezed past her and she caught a whiff of warm male skin before he strode down the hall.

The front door opened and thudded shut, and she could hear his steps on the small porch. A few minutes later, she could see the beam of a flashlight combing the ground outside Faith's window.

She went outside with Parker because she didn't want to be inside alone, not knowing. "See anything?" she called, standing under the eaves.

"Not yet." He moved in a gridlike pattern, farther and farther away from her. After several minutes, he switched off the light and came back to the house.

"I don't see any evidence of children or anyone else having been here, but footprints don't show up well with all these pine needles on the ground."

"Of course," she said, trying to keep her teeth from chattering. The air was cool and crisp, but Hope suspected it was the adrenaline rushing through her that made her shiver.

"John Boyd lives about half a mile away," he said, speaking as though thinking aloud, "but he's a widower without any kids. The Knowles family rents out their cabin. It's on the other side of this place and closer to the lake. In the morning I'll go see who's staying there. In the meantime…"

She could barely make out his expression in the dark. His face seemed to be all planes and angles and shadowy whiskers, but she instinctively knew she wasn't going to like what he was about to say. "What?" she said suspiciously.

"I don't think you should stay here."

"It's past midnight! Where do you want me to go?"

He didn't answer. He gazed off to the side at the broken window. "Do you have a plastic garbage bag and some tape?"

She headed inside to get them, wondering what she and

Faith should do now. Move again? Her savings wouldn't last forever, and Faith was so close to term....

"Maybe we should call the police," he said.

She jumped at the sound of his voice because she hadn't realized he was so close behind her. "And tell them what?" she asked. "That I have a broken window? They'll advise me to wait until morning and call a glass company."

"Miguel will take you seriously."

"Miguel?"

"A sergeant on the Enchantment police force. He's a friend of mine. We went to school together."

"He's probably fast asleep right now." She held the front door for him as she stepped across the threshold. "I'll call in the morning, even though I doubt there's anything the police can do."

"They can keep an eye on the place."

"I guess," she said, but she was thinking that a lot could happen between occasional drive-bys.

"What are you going to do until morning?" he asked.

She started rummaging through a utility drawer in the kitchen, where she found a box of plastic trash bags, several screwdrivers, a hammer and some nails, some glue and a few other miscellaneous items, all left by the owners of the cabin. "I'll just have to stay on my guard."

"And how are you going to do that?" he asked, his voice skeptical. "Are you planning to stay up all night?"

Hope almost told him that she might as well. She hadn't slept much, anyway, ever since the dreams began. "Maybe."

"Do you have any weapons?"

She handed him the plastic bags and a roll of duct tape. "Just my brain."

"You're definitely not diabolical enough to handle Arvin." He walked down the hall. "If I have my guess, he's more than a little off balance, which has me worried," he said over his shoulder.

Why would anything about me worry you? she felt like asking. He didn't want her to meet his son. He didn't want her working at the center. Heck, he couldn't even remember her name when she first came back to Enchantment.

"This isn't your problem," she called after him. "You have a little boy at home. Go take care of him."

There was no answer for several minutes. Hope leaned against the counter as she waited for him to cover the broken window. She knew she'd have to vacuum up the glass before Faith came home, but she wasn't in any hurry to spend time in that room. Morning would be soon enough.

He returned and gave her the tape.

"Thanks," she said. "I appreciate what you've done."

"No problem."

"You'd better get going, huh?"

She read indecision and what looked like some kind of torment in his eyes. "I don't think so."

"What does that mean?"

Pivoting on one foot, he crossed the room to sit on the couch. "That I'm staying until morning."

Hope had never imagined he'd do anything of the sort. "But what about Dalton?"

"He was in bed last time I called. I'm sure Bea is, too, by now. She was planning on staying in the guest room, so it won't make any difference to her or Dalton whether I sleep here."

It would make a difference to Hope. After the window incident, she didn't want to be alone. But neither did she want the awkwardness of having Parker Reynolds in the house.

"That's not necessary," she insisted. "I'll be fine, really."

"And I'm not going anywhere, *really.*" He took the remote from the coffee table and switched on the television. *Nick at Night* came blaring into the room. Then he glanced at the stove, seemed to make a decision and began to build a fire.

Hope was speechless as she watched. When he tossed in a match, the newspaper he'd wadded up blackened and shrank beneath the devouring flame, and she finally found her voice. "I'm sorry, but I haven't invited you."

Straightening, he looked back at her. "What's the matter, Hope? Do I make you nervous?"

"Yes." She didn't do well with intimacy as a general rule. And being alone with Parker so late at night, the wind buffeting the trees outside, the fire crackling in the stove, felt very intimate. It wasn't as if he was anything like the nice, predictable men—or the not-so-nice but equally predictable men—she'd known since Bonner. She'd had no trouble letting each of them in and out of her life without a second thought.

For some reason, Parker was different. He was enigmatic and dark, at least with her. But he was also ruggedly handsome and extremely sexy.

"Why?" he asked.

"Because you can't seem to treat me decently, or at least consistently," she said, "and…" *And* was where she drew a blank. She couldn't tell him he was the first man she'd been attracted to since Bonner. The fact that she *was* attracted scared her. She wanted to feel desire, longed to know romantic love again. But this man was obviously another poor choice.

"And?" he prompted. His tone had softened and his expression had grown watchful, as though he'd somehow understood what she wasn't saying.

"It's time for bed," she said quickly. "I'll get you some blankets."

She made him a bed on the couch, then hurried up the ladder to her loft, where she lay awake listening to the television below and calling herself a fool. She wasn't idealistic or naive enough to think her life would have a fairy-tale ending. Especially with *her* beginning.

And yet, she seemed to be buying into Faith's dream— and wishing for a man of her own.

PARKER WATCHED television long after Hope went to bed, but he wasn't paying much attention to the movie he'd finally settled on. He could scarcely hear above the litany of words going through his mind: *You shouldn't be here. This is crazy. You can't afford to establish any kind of relationship with Hope Tanner.*

But he couldn't leave. Hope believed Arvin to be a viable threat, which meant he probably was a viable threat. And that rock incident definitely had him worried. It wasn't as though Hope lived in a large neighborhood with a lot of boisterous kids running around.

Parker propped his feet on the coffee table and told himself to stop worrying. Helping Hope out for one night hardly constituted a relationship. Certainly it didn't make his betrayal any worse.

Probably because it couldn't *get* any worse.

Grabbing the remote, he snapped off the television. It was nearly two in the morning. He needed to get some sleep; he still didn't have a sponsor for the SIDS fundraiser and would probably have to drive to Taos again in the morning. Maybe by then, he'd finally be able to put this night in perspective.

He tried to relax, tried to keep his mind carefully blank of Hope, and finally fell into a doze. But he hadn't been out long when a muffled cry yanked him awake.

"What is it?" he said, jumping to his feet, adrenaline pumping through his veins. "Hope?"

She didn't answer.

Had Arvin broken into the house and harmed her in some way? Parker couldn't tell. He couldn't hear anything now, but something had awoken him.

He stood very still and listened intently, waiting until the sound came again. This time he knew it originated from the loft. It wasn't a cry of pain so much as...a voice, he decided. Hope was speaking stridently, as though calling out to someone.

Who? Silently crossing the room, Parker climbed the ladder to find a small attic with sloping ceilings and a few simple Southwestern furnishings. He couldn't see any strangers, certainly no fiftyish man bent on dragging Hope back to Superior.

Hope was there, in bed. Alone. As he watched, she tossed and kicked and started talking again.

"But it's not safe! Come here!"

She kept muttering, most of it senseless, frantic jabber. Then she fell silent, only to start up again a few seconds later. "I said no! I'm coming…please, no…"

Her voice cracked and she seemed to be crying. Parker moved reluctantly to her bedside. Was she dreaming about Superior? Bonner? He knew she could be reliving a variety of unpleasant things.

"Hope? It's me." Sitting beside her on the mattress, he gently shook her awake.

At first she tried to bat his hands away. After a moment, she blinked and stared at him, wide-eyed, as though she wasn't quite sure where she was.

Parker gazed down at her and couldn't help thinking how beautiful she was, despite her alarm. "You were having a bad dream," he said, letting go of her because touching Hope seemed to trigger a weak-kneed sensation in him. "Are you okay?"

She nodded and scanned the room, apparently verifying the truth of what he told her.

"What were you dreaming about? Arvin?" He told himself not to look into her shiny eyes or admire her sweet face, but he did both. For a moment he thought he might drown in her gaze. If only he wasn't harboring such a terrible secret…

"No."

"Then what?"

"Nothing."

"Hope?" he persisted. Something had been going on in her dream. Something terrible.

"I can't remember," she said, but he felt fairly certain she could. Whatever she'd dreamed was simply too private or too painful to share.

"It was only a dream," he said, and wiped away the dampness on her cheeks. He'd told himself over and over how strong Hope had become, but she seemed pretty vulnerable now. And her pain touched him in some way, made him want to soothe her, shield her.

Hope was wearing a tank top, and in the moonlight slanting through the skylight above, her skin seemed to glow silver. He knew he shouldn't touch her again, but he let one finger slide lightly down the length of her arm. She shivered, perhaps feeling some of the same sexual awareness that was flooding through him, and the control he'd worked so hard to maintain began to unravel.

"You're beautiful, you know that?" he murmured.

She stared up as him as though she didn't know whether to trust his sincerity. But when his fingers reached her hand, she threaded her own fingers through his and actually hung on.

"How much longer until morning?" she asked.

"A few hours," he said, amazed at the breathless quality of his own voice. Since when had he become so...affected by her?

"That long?"

"Aren't you tired?"

"I don't want to go back to sleep."

His heart pounded a little harder as his mind presented him with suggestions of what they could do to make good use of that time. Dalton meant everything to him. But his son suddenly seemed so removed from the situation. Right now, it was just Hope and him and the promise of what she'd feel like in his arms....

"I could lie down with you for a while if that would help," he said. He was hoping she'd say no, that she'd put a decisive end to the madness inside him. But she didn't. She slid over.

"Do you want me to hold you?" he asked as he lay down. He knew he was drawing close to the one woman who could ruin him, but he couldn't seem to help himself. She needed him. He needed her. Somehow, they needed each other.

"I don't want to dream anymore," she whispered.

"I won't let you," he said. "I'll be right here."

She moved tentatively closer, and he pulled her into his arms.

The moment she came into contact with his chest, she stiffened. But she didn't push away or ask him to leave. "I...I don't want to make love with you," she said.

Parker definitely couldn't claim the same thing, but the sane part of him was at least partially grateful. "That's okay. I won't do anything you don't want me to."

"I'm not a good risk," she said.

"You've told me that."

"It's true."

"I'm forewarned, Hope. You have nothing to worry about. Just relax, okay?" He kneaded the tense muscles along her spine, but instead of feeling gratified when she began to relax against him, he felt even more aroused.

"Warm?" he asked.

She nodded.

"Good."

She pressed her cheek against his heart, and he closed his eyes and breathed in the clean scent of her hair, feeling pretty damn warm himself. "Everything will be fine in the morning," he said, but he knew that at least for him, morning was a long way off.

CHAPTER SIXTEEN

HOPE PROPPED HERSELF up on one elbow in the early-morning light and stared down into the face of the man who'd just spent the night in her bed. His hair was ruffled and dark whiskers covered his jaw and chin. She liked the faint lines bracketing his mouth—they said he laughed, at least sometimes—and the short scar on his forehead. These minor flaws added dimension to an already interesting face.

Her eyes lowered to his body, and the impulse to slip her hand beneath his T-shirt and touch his skin jolted through her. Maybe it was because she felt so strong and healthy this morning. Having Parker's arms around her had provided a barrier from her past, from her dreams, from her fear of the future, and she'd slept soundly for almost the first time since she'd gone back to Superior.

She wondered if she could get him to move and make it easier for her to touch him without being obvious, but he opened his eyes as soon as she shifted. "Is it morning?" he asked.

"Six o'clock."

"I gotta go," he said, but he didn't get up. He lifted one hand and caressed her arm as he had during the night, and Hope instinctively drew closer.

"You sleep okay?" he asked.

"I slept great."

"No more dreams?"

"No more dreams."

"That's good." He pulled her head down on his shoulder and she again felt the desire to slip her hand under his shirt.

"This is a nice room," he said, and she knew he was gazing up at the skylight. She could already feel the sun pouring through the glass, chasing away the cold and the shadows.

"It was nice of you to stay with me."

"We need to get that window fixed today."

"I'll call someone after eight."

He turned to look at her. "You ready to tell me about your dream?"

"No."

"Why?"

"I don't want to think about it." She rested a hand on his chest but refused to let herself explore. "You want to tell me about your wife?"

"My wife?" he asked, obviously surprised by her choice of topic.

"I never got to meet her. I've always wondered what she was like."

"Well—" he hesitated "—she was older than you, for one."

"No kidding," she said dryly, and his chuckle resonated through his chest.

"You were so young when we met," he said. "I'll never forget how skinny you were. I swear your eyes looked as big as saucers."

"I was almost eighteen. That's not so young."

"To a married man of twenty-six, it's very young."

She considered that for a moment curious whether his first impression of her affected what he thought of her now. "Do you still think of me as young?"

"I wish I did," he said.

Hope felt a tingle of excitement low in her belly, and wondered where that had come from. She didn't want Parker to see her as anything other than a friend, and age didn't matter when it came to friends. "What made you want to marry your wife?"

"She was fun, attractive, driven."

"She wasn't sick when you first met, was she?"

"She'd always had a bad heart, but her health didn't really start to go downhill until a few weeks after we got engaged."

"That must have been difficult."

"It was. We'd originally planned to be married in the spring, but once she got sick, her father started pushing for a fall wedding. He kept saying there wasn't any reason to wait, that they didn't have the time to plan a big wedding. But I've often suspected that was his way of making sure Vanessa got what she wanted. And he got my help and support in taking care of her."

"That's sad." Hope settled herself more comfortably on his shoulder. "And terribly unfair to you."

"Getting sick wasn't fair to Vanessa," he said. As he looked down at her, Hope was struck by the deep brown of his eyes and the long lashes that surrounded them.

"What did your parents feel about the situation?" she asked.

He blinked. "My mother died just after I graduated from high school, so she never knew Vanessa. It was only my dad. He thought I was crazy for going through with the whole thing, but he'd lost a lot of credibility with me by then. So I did what I felt I should."

"Do you think your relationship would have culminated in marriage if Vanessa hadn't gotten sick?" she asked.

"That's hard to say. A lot could've happened in nine months."

"Did you ever regret your decision?"

"Sometimes."

"It was probably tough taking care of someone so ill."

"It wasn't the actual care so much as putting up with the person her sickness caused her to become," he said.

"When I met her, she was bigger than life, outgoing and fun. But after she got sick, she was miserable. She just didn't feel well enough to be around anyone, and I couldn't make things any easier for her. Then she became obsessed with certain things, like germs and—"

"And having a baby?"

His eyebrows lifted as though the question surprised him. "How did you know?"

"I was here during that time, remember?"

"But you were dealing with your own problems. I didn't realize you knew anything about me."

"Are you kidding? The whole center celebrated the day you got word from the adoption agency that you'd been approved. I guess that's where you got Dalton, huh?"

"Yeah." His voice sounded gruffer than it had a moment earlier, but Hope ignored it.

"Do your in-laws help you out with Dalton?" she asked.

"They send him obscene amounts of money for nearly every holiday, insist we spend Christmas with them at their home in Taos and take him for two weeks each summer. But considering they live only an hour away, we don't see them often."

"And your father?"

"My father had already married the stereotypical bimbo and is still trying to recapture his youth."

"Wonderful," she said sarcastically. "I can tell you're proud."

"Yeah, well, we can't be held responsible for our parents."

"Thank God," she said.

She felt his hand slide up her shirt and rub her back. "Tell me about your family," he said. "What's your mother like?"

"Patient, self-sacrificing. Probably too self-sacrificing. If any of us needed anything while we were kids, she'd give up whatever she had to please us, but she never had much. I always wished my father would treat her better.''

''Was he abusive?''

''Most of the time not physically.'' She thought of the night he'd learned she was pregnant and tried not to wince. He'd been abusive that night, but then, he'd never had any of his children rebel the way she had. ''He'd just put her down, call her an idiot, things like that,'' she said.

''Did he treat his other wives the same way?''

''He treated some better than others.''

''Did he spend much time with you?''

''No, nor my mother, either. But he'd occasionally appear for dinner or for a conjugal visit.''

''Was your mother pleased when he turned up?''

Hope bit her bottom lip, remembering. ''She never said anything, but I always got the impression she wasn't. When he came over, she only had to work harder, and she was already working from dawn until dark.''

''Why'd she have to work extra-hard whenever he showed up?''

''Having him visit was like having company. The house had to be spotless, the meal perfect. In Superior, so much of a woman's worth is based on her piousness and her ability to cook, clean and bear children.''

''You must be a good cook.''

She shrugged. ''I'm okay, I guess.''

''Didn't your father help out with anything?''

''Jedidiah? Are you serious?'' Hope would have straightened so she could see Parker's face, but she was too comfortable to move. ''Housework was beneath him. He never did anything except lecture us about our faults and weaknesses and warn us against the temptations of the devil. My earliest recollection is of him reading the Bible, his voice thunderous, like one of those televangelists promising fiery punishment for the wicked.''

''How old were you?''

''Four or five.''

"It doesn't sound like you missed your father when he wasn't around."

"I didn't. I was terrified of him."

"Was your mother afraid of him, too?"

"She was more afraid of herself, of finally reaching the point where she couldn't put up with any more. Her battle seemed to be a private one and had very little to do with my father, except she believed that going against his word was like going against God Himself."

"I can't imagine that kind of life," Parker said. "Who took care of the cars and the yard and the stuff that husbands and fathers traditionally take care of?"

"Occasionally, when something around the house needed fixing, my mom asked for my father's help and he sent over one of my stepbrothers with a hammer or a screwdriver. But my father had no time for anything too domestic." She covered a yawn. "Heading such a large family is a lot like running a small company. Just trying to stifle the infighting and keep every son or daughter living by the strict tenets of the church absorbs a great deal of energy. Remember, my father has to juggle the demands of six wives, perform hours and hours of church service each week and work a full-time job."

"What's his job?"

"He manages the sand-and-gravel pit my grandfather deeded to the church before I was born."

"And that makes enough to support such a large family?"

"No. Church members share everything. The men work and contribute whatever they make to the church. Then the church grants each family so much money each month on which to live. The church owns all the property, too. The Brethren lend different homes to different members when they marry, or when a household gets too large for everyone to continue living together. There's even a sign in front of each lot or house that says, 'This Everlasting

Apostolic Property entrusted to Gilbert James Johnson' or whomever.''

Parker lay silent for several seconds. Hope wondered if he was falling asleep and felt her own eyelids grow heavy again. He was so solid and warm that she didn't fear anything right now, not even dreams.

''Why do they do it?'' he asked at length, letting her know he wasn't asleep, after all.

Hope considered her answer. There wasn't a simple explanation. How did any cult flourish? How did Jim Jones talk so many people into killing themselves? ''I think people like belonging to something, especially something that designates them as special or elite. I think they feel better about themselves if they sacrifice for what they consider a good cause. And I think the idea of going to a better place after this life appeals to them.'' She paused. ''It's probably a combination of motivations, I would guess.''

''I'm sure some of the men's motivation is a lot baser than all that psychological mumbo jumbo.''

''You're talking about sex.''

''That's exactly what I'm talking about.''

''For some, maybe. For my father, sex didn't seem to be a big part of things. He slept with my mother occasionally, but not often.''

''Obviously he was getting what he wanted other places. Didn't your mother ever get lonely for a real companion, a partner, a lover?''

''She probably did, but I think she learned how to fulfill her emotional needs through her friends and her children. Having to give my father sex only meant she'd get less time to herself that evening or none at all.''

''That's quite an attitude. Is that how you look at sex? As some sort of household chore?''

The tingling in Hope's stomach returned. She could smell the fabric softener on his T-shirt, and the muscular chest beneath her hand suddenly seemed far more tempting than any man's body had been to her since Bonner.

"I don't look at sex the way my mother does. I know it's different if you're with someone you love."

He played with a strand of her hair. "And how do you know that? Bonner?"

She nodded.

"You haven't loved anyone since?"

"Are you asking me if I've made love? Or been in love?"

"Both."

"I've made love to three other men. I felt nothing."

"That doesn't mean you'll never feel anything."

"Maybe not, but two of those were men I'd dated for several months. One had asked me to marry him. I should've felt *something*."

"And the third?"

"The third was definitely a mistake. He was just a guy I picked up, wishing I could *make* myself connect with someone. Of course it didn't work. That time was the worst, except I didn't have to feel any guilt for disappointing him."

Turning slightly, he lifted her chin and rubbed her bottom lip with the pad of his thumb. The tingle in her belly became something hot and liquid and seemed to swirl through her whole system. "I think you're wrong about your limitations."

"I don't," she said, but she was already experiencing more desire than she'd known in ten years.

"Maybe we should perform a little experiment." Bending closer, he covered her mouth with his, kissing her gently at first, and then with mounting pressure when she offered no resistance. By the time his tongue delved into her mouth, Hope was definitely ready to deepen the kiss.

She slipped her arms around his neck, angling her head, and for the first time in eleven years, felt a semblance of what she'd known in the barn with Bonner. Somehow the idea of allowing a man complete access to her body was exciting again, heady. She needed to feel vibrant and young and free, to cut herself loose for once from all the baggage she'd been carrying around. And Parker seemed to promise it all with only one kiss.

But then he broke away and got out of bed.

"I'm sorry. I have to go. I need to get Dalton to school," he said.

Hope didn't know what to say. She didn't want him to leave, but she knew better than to ask him to stay.

"I'll see you later," he said, but when he left, Hope felt more alone than ever before.

THE SOUND OF HAMMERING woke Hope with a start. After Parker left, she'd managed to doze off again. Now the sun sat higher in the sky and she wondered who'd be knocking on her door at…seven-thirty. Faith wouldn't have bothered knocking. She had a key. And…

The rock. The window. Was it Arvin? Getting out of bed, she jammed her arms into her robe, slid her feet into a pair of slippers and climbed down from the loft.

"Who is it?" she called when she reached the door.

"It's okay, Hope. It's me."

Parker. What was he doing back?

She unlocked the door and peeked out at him through the crack. It was obvious he hadn't been home, because he hadn't shaved. And his clothes were the ones he'd worn last night, so they were wrinkled. Still, he appeared fashionably unkempt, like a Calvin Klein model wearing nothing but a pair of threadbare jeans.

"What are you doing here?" she asked, opening the door a little farther and leaning against the jamb.

"It was just kids."

"What?"

"The rock. I went over to the Knowles cabin and found it occupied. There's a family staying there who fosters troubled teens. A fourteen-year-old boy threw the rock. But from the sounds of it, he's a bit of a pyromaniac, so we were probably lucky he only broke a window."

"You think he broke the window intending to set the place on fire?"

Parker rattled his keys, as though anxious to be on his way again. "It's possible. He didn't have a very good excuse for being here."

"Did he admit to doing it?"

"One of the other children, a girl just a year younger, ratted on him. She said she heard the breaking glass while she was trying to build a tree house in the woods and caught him near the window when she came to see what he'd done."

Hope shoved a self-conscious hand through her hair, sure her kind of unkempt wasn't nearly as sexy as his. "Did he get into trouble?"

"They put him on restriction and told him he had to work off the money to pay for the window, but they don't look like they have much, and they're only staying another few days. I wouldn't hold my breath about getting reimbursed."

"I'll pay for it," Hope said. "I'm just glad it wasn't Arvin coming to raise hell."

"So am I." His gaze fell to her lips, reminding her of his kiss, and Hope felt her cheeks flush. For someone who didn't like her, he'd given her a pretty thorough kiss. And for someone who didn't like him, she'd given him a pretty warm welcome. She wondered what Faith would say about the whole thing—and decided not to tell her. There wasn't any point in creating unrealistic expectations. Last night was a fluke. Nothing had changed.

"Well, thanks for your help," she said, breaking the awkward silence.

"No problem."

"Do you want me to go back to Taos with you today?"

"Actually—" he glanced at the truck as though it was his getaway vehicle, even took a step toward it "—I can handle it. I don't want to put Faith out of her house another day, and I know you'd only worry about her if she was here alone. I don't have any appointments set up, anyway. I thought I'd go into the clinic this morning, make some calls and see how many I could line up for this afternoon.''

''Okay.'' She knew they could both spend a week in Taos and not exhaust all the corporate and merchant possibilities. But after last night, she no longer felt so insulated from the world and, while it was exciting to think her heart might be thawing at long last, she realized the dangers of being vulnerable again.

''Gotta go.'' He thrust his hands in his pockets. ''Maybe I'll see you at work later.''

She said goodbye and went inside. But she watched him climb into his truck and noticed that he paused to look back—and shake his head.

CHAPTER SEVENTEEN

WHAT HAD HE BEEN thinking? Parker asked himself over and over the entire ride home. He'd kissed Hope. *Kissed* her. And it wasn't the obligatory peck he'd given the other women he'd dated in the past few years. This kiss had some real intent behind it. It was of the peel-your-clothes-off-as-fast-as-possible variety.

Thank God he'd stopped when he had. Maybe he had *some* scruples.

Or maybe not. He'd peeled her clothes off in his mind several times since then. And when she was standing at the door this morning, fresh from sleep, he'd wanted to slip his hands inside her robe and caress the soft skin that lay beneath....

Certainly *that* didn't reflect well on him. But last night hadn't been entirely his fault. He'd expected Hope to be unresponsive. He'd thought he was safe crawling into her bed to comfort her. She was a cold fish, right?

Wrong. She had enough heat to burn herself a place in all his future fantasies. Probably because it wasn't a wanton type of heat. It came from somewhere much deeper.

He pulled into his driveway and cut the engine, telling himself to forget Hope. He'd been obsessed with her ever since she'd returned. He needed to get back to life as usual, and Dalton was just the person to help him do that. Duty. Routine. Fatherhood. He'd lose himself in the sweet innocence of his child, he decided—until he hit the porch and his son came out of the house yelling, "Did you sleep with her, Dad? Huh? Do you have a girlfriend now?"

Parker glanced around to see if any of the neighbors were out and felt his face flush hot as sweet old Bea came up behind Dalton. "No," he said. "I don't have a girl-friend."

"Then where *were* you?"

"Someone's been bothering the woman you spoke to last night—"

"Hope," the boy supplied.

"Right, Hope. So I stayed with her to make sure she'd be safe."

Dalton rolled his eyes. "Maybe I would've believed that a couple of years ago, Dad, but I've seen enough television to know how it works."

"What television shows are you talking about?" Parker asked.

"*Friends. Seinfeld.* You name it."

Parker could hardly believe this was *his* son. "I thought girls were gross to you," he said. "I thought you had difficulty expressing your emotions."

"According to who? *Holt's* mother? I keep telling you not to listen to anything she says. She has—" he shook his head in frustration "—some sort of problem when it comes to me. And some girls *are* gross. Lisa Smith picks her nose."

"Thanks for the pleasant image," Parker said. Then, hoping to keep the focus of the conversation from return-ing to the fact that he'd been out all night, he added, "What about that cute little Melanie Ellis?"

Dalton scuffed one shoe against the other. "She's okay, I guess."

"Just okay?"

"Well, I'm never going to spend the night with her," he said, grimacing as if that would be the worst kind of torture. A split second later, his face cleared. "So, do I get to meet Hope now that you're sleeping with her? Hey, maybe I'll get a little brother or sister!"

The five-foot-tall, white-haired Bea fiddled with her

hearing aid. "What's that he said? You're sleeping with someone, trying to get him a little brother or sister?"

"No!" Parker cried.

"Oh. Too bad. The bridge club would've loved that one." She gave him a meaningful smile. "They think you're quite a hunk."

It would have been a compliment, except there wasn't a member of the group who still had twenty-twenty vision. "I appreciate that," Parker said, "but—"

"They're always asking me, 'Bea, when's that handsome Parker Reynolds going to settle down again?' And I tell them that your heart's plain broke."

"My heart's not broken," he said. "It's been eight years since—"

"Some hearts take longer to heal than others."

"Bea—"

"It's downright romantic."

"There's nothing romantic going on in my life."

"So when do I get to meet her, huh, Dad?" Dalton interjected. "Are you going to bring her over tonight? She sounded so cool on the phone. I bet she's nothing like Holt's mom. You think she's like Holt's mom?"

"She's definitely not like Holt's mom," Parker said.

"Not even a little bit?"

"Not even a little bit."

"Great," he said, his voice full of relief. "I'll take her."

WHEN HOPE HEARD a car in the drive an hour later, she moved quickly from the kitchen to the front window to see who it was. She thought it might be the family from closer to the lake coming to apologize about the window. But it was Gina, dropping off Faith. Only, Faith no longer looked like the sister Hope had said goodbye to yesterday. Gone was the ugly shawl and tattered pioneer dress. Faith was wearing a pair of crisp, white capris and a scoop neck T-shirt, with sandals. She looked stylish and modern. And she'd had her toes painted—bright red.

Hope opened the door before her sister could even reach the stoop. "Faith?" she said uncertainly.

"Hi! What's up?"

"That's what I want to ask you," Hope said.

Gina beeped the horn and waved, then rolled down her window. "I'll see you at the center in a few, huh?"

"Actually, I won't be there until around one," Hope told her. "I called Lydia to tell her I'd be late and she suggested I come in for the afternoon. I have a glass company coming out to fix a broken window."

"Okay. See you then." She drove off, and Hope turned back to Faith. "What happened?"

Faith shrugged, trying to play it down, but Hope could tell from the blush creeping up her neck that she wasn't as indifferent as she wanted to appear. "Nothing. What's with the window repair?"

"A kid in one of the other cabins broke the window in your room. Where did you get those clothes?"

"Someone gave Gina a bunch of maternity things. A few items happened to fit me, and Gina thought they looked nice, so she passed them along."

Hope's gaze fell to the sack her sister was carrying. "There's more?"

"There's more, but don't worry. I'm going to give them back after I deliver."

"How did Gina talk you into wearing something besides your dress?"

"She was so nice to me I didn't want to be rude."

"That's it?" The gravity in Hope's voice evoked a sheepish smile.

"Okay. There's a very handsome guy who lives next door to Gina. I only saw him from a distance. He was out washing his car. But in case we pass on the street sometime, I don't want him to think I'm homely."

A smile tugged at the corners of Hope's mouth. One

attractive man could do in a day what it would've taken Hope months to accomplish. "So, are you going to have Gina introduce you?"

"Maybe after the baby's born."

"He's single?"

"Of course! I wouldn't try to impress a married man." She set her sack on the table. "Gina said he grew up here but left for several years while he went to college. He just returned and is planning on opening a veterinary clinic." She clasped her hands in obvious excitement. "Isn't that great? I *love* animals."

Hope laughed at her sister's exuberance. She'd been right to take Faith away from Superior. At times she feared her sister would rather have the security and family she'd known than the freedom Hope offered. But already Faith was starting to embrace the joys of being a liberated woman.

"Sounds like a good match to me."

"You should see him, Hope. He has dark-blond hair and a fabulous smile. And his *body*—" She blushed more furiously now, but the gleam in her eye remained.

"His body?" Hope repeated.

"He took off his shirt because his dogs kept shaking water all over him, and—omigosh! I've never seen anything like his chest and arms. There were muscles everywhere. And his skin was golden-brown from the sun. He must jog outside with his dogs or something. He looks very athletic."

"And you were going to settle for Arvin."

Faith blanched. "I could never let Arvin touch me now. Leaving him and coming here, meeting Gina and Lydia and the others at the clinic and seeing this man has changed everything. He made me feel so warm inside." Her voice fell to a whisper. "I could actually picture myself *wanting* to take off my clothes for him. Isn't that terrible?"

"No," Hope said, "that's good. It means your experience with Arvin hasn't made you frigid. Just be careful not to get carried away now that you see the possibilities, okay? You don't want to get involved with the wrong guy. There're good and bad men in Superior, Faith, and there're good and bad men here. You have to be selective."

"Quit being such a worrier." Faith started laying out the clothing she'd brought in the bag. "I watched him from inside the house, for Pete's sake. He doesn't even know I'm alive, and even if he did, I'm sure he wouldn't be interested in a pregnant woman."

"You won't be pregnant much longer."

"I'll still have a new baby, which is probably more than enough to chase an exceptionally handsome guy like this away. I'm sure I won't be getting involved with anyone for a long while. But it's just so wonderful to realize that I have a whole new future available to me, that the star you told me about might someday be within my reach."

Hope chuckled as she admired the clothes. "I should've known you'd put it all in perspective. You might be eighteen, but you're going on thirty-eight, right?" Folding her arms, she relaxed against the table. "It's just that I want so much for you, Faith."

Faith flung the last pair of jeans over a chair and squeezed Hope's arm. "I know that," she said, growing serious. "And it's only possible because of you. I can't believe you came back for me, Hope. You're so brave." She smiled brightly. "And I can't thank you enough."

Shoving away from the table, Hope embraced her. The bulge of Faith's belly promised new life, a better future. Things would be different for this baby—she'd have the whole world at her feet—and Hope and Faith would be there to watch her excel.

Faith was right. The star they were both wishing on wasn't so far away.

"I love you," Hope said.

"Thank God." Faith clung to her even tighter. "Don't ever let go, okay, Hope?"

"I won't. I'll always be here for you."

"And I'll be here for you." Her sister pulled back and grinned as she wiped a tear from her face. "That's what sisters are for."

Hope wiped her own eyes. "That's what sisters are for."

WHEN HOPE ARRIVED at the clinic, the lobby was filled almost to overflowing.

"What's going on?" she asked Trish, who was looking anxious behind the reception counter. "Why are we so busy today?"

"Katherine and Heidi are both out, doing home deliveries. Lydia and Gina are trying to pick up the slack," she said, practically wringing her hands, "but they're falling behind."

Hope studied the day's calendar. "Do you want me to see if I can reschedule some of these appointments?"

Trish looked uncertain. "I've been waiting for Lydia to give me the word, but ever since Devon arrived, she—"

"Devon's here? From Albuquerque?" Hope interrupted. Today *was* a good day. She'd really missed Lydia's tall, blond granddaughter. Hope had been so uncertain of everything ten years ago that she hadn't allowed herself to trust very many people, but Devon had quickly become the closest thing she had to a friend.

"She arrived at lunch, and she and Lydia haven't been out of her office since," Trish said. "I just knocked to tell them how backlogged we are. I'm sure they'll be coming shortly. Lydia hates making any of our mothers wait."

Probably not as much as Trish hated making them wait, Hope thought, noticing that she glanced at the clock every few seconds.

"I'm sure you're right. Lydia wants the center to be

different from the average doctor's office, right?'' she said, and started on the filing that was waiting for her on some stacking trays.

When another fifteen minutes passed and Lydia and Devon still hadn't emerged, Hope thought she might have to insist on rescheduling the mothers who kept arriving. Everyone was getting restless.

''I think it would be better to…'' Trish began, but voices coming from the hall told Hope that Lydia and Devon were finally on their way.

''And you can forget it that easily?'' Devon was saying.

''Nothing about it's been easy,'' Lydia replied. ''You, of all people, should know that. Sometimes a person has to make a decision based on what's best for more than one individual, Devon. That's what I did, and that's what I'm doing now.''

''I don't see how this…''

Devon's words fell off the moment she saw Hope. ''Hope!'' she exclaimed, hurrying over to hug her. ''How wonderful to see you again! Lydia told me you were back, and I've been thrilled to think I might run into you while I'm here.''

''How are you?'' Hope asked.

''Good, since I got out of school. Those were long years, but I'm a certified nurse-midwife in Albuquerque now, and I like it.'' Hope detected a defiant tilt to Devon's chin as she looked at her grandmother, but if it bothered Lydia that Devon had pursued a master's degree in nursing science, instead of apprenticing with her, her stoic demeanor gave nothing away.

''So you're accredited?'' Hope said. ''That's wonderful.''

''If unnecessary,'' Lydia grumbled, and circumvented them without waiting for a response.

Devon ignored her. ''Lydia says you're in the same field.''

"I became an obstetrics nurse. I've always been drawn to babies."

"After what you went through, it's no wonder."

Lydia brushed past them again, escorting a woman to one of the examination rooms.

"What made you decide to leave here?" Hope asked. "I always thought you wanted to stay and—"

"Listen, I promised Lydia I'd help with the backlog here," Devon said, but Hope got the impression that it was the subject matter as much as the number of people waiting that made her cut the conversation short. "Any chance we can get together after work for coffee? It would be great to have a chance to catch up."

Hope thought of Faith, home working on her baby quilt and happily admiring her new clothes in the mirror. "Sure. I just need to check with my sister. If she's fine, I can go."

"Good, because I have to drive back to Albuquerque tomorrow."

"That soon? What brought you to town for such a quick trip?"

Devon's eyes cut toward the hall, where Lydia had gone. "My grandmother has some crazy notion that it's time to step down from the board of directors."

"But she loves the center, and working on the board gives her a lot of say in what happens here," Hope said, astonished that Lydia would even think of giving up her seat.

"I know, but she insists it's time for her to refocus on what really matters—the mothers. I think she wants to do more hands-on deliveries."

"Who would take her place?"

"That's just it," Devon said. "She wants me to."

"SO HOW LONG have you been having these dreams?" Devin asked, pushing her empty coffee cup away.

"Since my return to Enchantment." Hope finished her

mocha frappaccino and leaned back in the barstool-style chair. She was sitting across a small high table from Devon, in one corner of a trendy downtown coffee shop. Over the past forty-five minutes, they'd covered myriad topics. What had happened during the past ten years for each of them, the fact that Devon was seeing a doctor she'd met at college and Hope wasn't seeing anyone, the fact that Devon didn't want children, at least for another few years and that Hope longed for nothing more. They enjoyed their time together, despite the years they'd been apart.

But Hope couldn't leave well enough alone. She'd had to tell Devon about her dreams concerning Autumn, and now she had to face the sympathy in the other woman's eyes.

"That breaks my heart," Devon said.

Hope tried to shrug it off. "It's not a big deal. Everyone has bad dreams now and then, right?"

"Not everyone's lost a child."

"I didn't lose Autumn. I gave her away. I had to."

"I know."

"And anyway, the dreams will probably stop once I get used to being back."

Devon seemed to be watching her closely. "And if they don't?"

"I don't know. There's really nothing I can do."

"Have you told my grandmother about this?"

"Lydia? No. Why would I tell her?"

"I think she should know what you're going through."

"Why?"

Devon reshuffled the sugar packets in the middle of the table. "Would it make you feel any better if I told you I know your child went to a good home?"

Hope looked at her carefully. "Of course it would. But you don't know that, do you? Not for sure."

Her friend hesitated for several seconds. "Yes, I do," she said at last.

"But how?"

Devon closed her eyes. "I was there that night."

"What night?"

"The night you gave birth."

"But—"

Devon held up a hand. "When Lydia didn't come home, I wondered if maybe you'd gone into labor. I was worried about you both and drove over to the center. But because I was afraid to go around to the back lot—it's so much darker there with all those trees—I came through the front and ran into my grandmother. You'd just had the baby."

"Why didn't you come and see me?" Hope asked, remembering how bereft she'd felt at that moment. Having to say goodbye to the baby who'd been a part of her for nine months, without ever really seeing her, had been the most painful thing she'd ever done. She would have welcomed a friendly face in that hour. Lydia had left her alone for so long....

"Don't ask," Devon said. "I've got to go."

"Devon—"

The look on Devon's face made Hope pause. Her friend was obviously torn, but she seemed hurt in some way, too. "I'm sorry, Hope. I've already said more than I should have," she muttered, and hurried out the door.

LYDIA'S CAR was the only one in the small gravel lot at the back of the birthing center when Hope pulled the Impala around. Typically used for employees or mothers already in labor, the rear entrance led directly to the birthing rooms. The door was still unlocked, but that whole section of the center was dark. Lydia wasn't delivering babies; she was working late in her office.

Hope quietly made her way forward to the hall that branched off the waiting room, with the offices on one side and the small exam rooms on the other. Devon's cryptic words had set Hope's teeth on edge. All evening, while she'd helped Faith cut and sew, she'd been worrying about Devon's odd behavior in the coffee shop. But it wasn't until Faith had gone to bed that she'd decided to see if she could speak to Lydia about it—tonight. If anyone could tell her what was going on, Lydia could. As a pregnant runaway, Hope had believed Lydia knew everything and, to a certain extent, she still believed it.

But she was almost afraid to find out what the problem was. Something wasn't right. She could sense it. Especially around Devon. But she'd noticed it at other times, too, ever since she'd been back.

Staring at the light glowing beneath Lydia's closed door, Hope took a deep breath, raised her hand and knocked.

"Come in," Lydia said, obviously surprised to have a visitor.

Hope stepped into the office, feeling as though she'd just breached some holy inner sanctum.

"Hope!" Lydia rounded the desk and came toward her. "What brings you back here, and so late?" Her eyes darted to the clock, and Hope realized it was after eleven.

"I wanted a few minutes alone to talk," Hope said.

"About what?"

"I had coffee with Devon earlier."

Lydia's mouth tightened. "That's nice. She's always cared a great deal about you. As I have."

"You've both been very good to me, but—" Hope's palms grew moist "—Devon was acting a little strange."

If possible, Lydia seemed to hold herself more rigidly than before. "How so?"

"I don't know, exactly. Secretive, I guess. She told me she knew my baby went to a good home."

"He did. I told you that myself," Lydia replied, but her normally pointed, steady gaze faltered, and she glanced back at the clock.

"He?" Hope repeated. "I had a girl, remember?"

"Oh, yes. I'm sorry. I've delivered a lot of babies over the past ten years."

"Of course." Suddenly Hope didn't know what to ask. Lydia hadn't coerced her into giving up her baby. Hope had done it voluntarily. And the baby had gone to a good home. Both Lydia and Devon, people she trusted, confirmed that. So why was the hair still standing up on the back of Hope's neck? "Is everything okay, Lydia?"

"What do you mean?"

"Is there something else I should know?"

Lydia blinked several times, but her answer, when it finally came, was direct enough. "No."

Hope shook her head. "I think the stress of moving and dealing with Arvin again must be getting to me. I'm sorry to bother you."

Lydia walked to the door and held it open for her. "Seeing you is never any bother, but you're worrying about nothing, Hope. Everything's fine."

"Thanks," she said, but hesitated at the door. "Did you know that Devon came here the night I had Autumn? She was planning to visit me…."

"Autumn? You named her?" Lydia raised a disapproving brow. "That's always a mistake, Hope. You need to let her go, as I told you ten years ago."

"I understand. Did you know, about Devon, I mean?"

"Yes. I spoke to her that night."

"But she never came to see me."

"It was too late. I sent her home."

"Right. I should've thought of that. Good night."

"Good night," Lydia replied.

Hope started down the hall, but as soon as she heard Lydia's door close, she veered off to the receptionist's desk and retrieved the key she and Trish had once used to get inside the storage area upstairs. There was a small chance she could find her file buried in those old metal cabinets and possibly learn something about Autumn. She'd signed a contract the night Autumn was born, stating that she wouldn't try to contact her daughter until Autumn was of age, and she would have honored it despite her nightmares. But she couldn't forget Devon's words, *I've already told you more than I should have.*

What was there to hide?

CHAPTER EIGHTEEN

HOPE COULD HEAR Lydia speaking to someone on the phone, her voice a low murmur, as she slipped past the office and crept up the stairs. She had no idea whether or not there'd be anything in her file about Autumn, beyond basic birth statistics, but she had no better place to start looking. She'd gone ten long years without knowing anything about her child. Ten years too long.

Suddenly the piece of paper she'd signed didn't seem important at all. The only thing that seemed important was making sure Autumn was safe and well.

The stairs creaked as she moved, sounding abnormally loud in the otherwise quiet building, but Hope remembered that Lydia was on the phone and forced herself to continue. She respected Lydia and owed her a great deal. She didn't want to wind up in an ugly confrontation about privacy laws and ethics violations that could cost her her job—and their friendship. But she had to do this. She cared more about Autumn than anything else.

Fortunately, light filtered through the windows of the spare offices off the second-story landing, and Hope could see well enough to open the wooden door to the storage area.

A much deeper darkness than that in the hall, along with a musty odor, immediately enveloped her as she stepped inside. She paused, pressing her back against the wall as she tried to gain her bearings.

From her earlier visit, Hope knew the basic layout. The storage area consisted of three small rooms and a bit of attic space that had also been converted to storage. But she had no idea which files were stored where, and the darkness made the place feel completely foreign. There were a couple of small windows, but none very close and only a little moonlight showed through.

She breathed shallowly for several seconds, listening for any noise before deciding she had to take advantage of the time she had. She could always try to steal a key to the center and come back in the middle of the night when no one was around, but she'd never stolen anything in her life and felt that would be going too far. She was just taking a quick peek at her own file. Certainly there wasn't any harm in that.

Patting the wall, she finally encountered a switch and flooded the room with light so bright she felt sure the whole world would see it—and Lydia would come stomping up the stairs to stop her.

But that was unrealistic, and she knew it. The windows overlooked the woods in back.

Calmer now, Hope wandered from room to room, reading the labels on the various filing cabinets.

Trish was well organized, which was going to make her search easy. Every drawer was marked by year, and the charts and files inside were alphabetical.

Hope found the year she'd given birth to Autumn in the middle room and yanked open the file drawer.

Sharp, Smith, Sutter, Taggert, Tanner... Hope thought her heart might jump out of her chest when she came upon her own name. She quickly pulled the file from its place. Inside she found a record of her visits to the birth center, her height and weight through those last two months, a few notes from Lydia about her general health and progress, and a record of her delivery, but nothing on Autumn. Checking the drawer again, she found another file labeled, "Tanner, Hope (baby)," but it was empty.

Hope stared at the empty manila folder, wondering why someone would make a file for nothing. She couldn't imagine Devon, who'd been the receptionist the summer she'd had Autumn, doing it. She couldn't see Trish doing it, either. Lydia had always demanded an efficient staff. Which meant there had once been *something* in the file. But what? Her baby's adoption records? If so, where had they gone? And why?

Turning the folder in her hands, Hope noticed a telephone number written in pencil on the front flap. It had no area code, which made her think it might be local.

Was it connected to Autumn? More than likely, the file had simply been used as a message pad. But it was the only thing there, so she tore it off, stuffed it in the back pocket of her jeans and was just returning both files to their rightful place when something she'd seen in her delivery record made her turn back to it.

Lydia had written about Autumn's birth, but part of what she'd recorded didn't match Hope's memory of the event. For starters, Lydia made no mention of having induced labor. According to her notes, Hope had called her at ten o'clock that night, saying her contractions were only a few minutes apart.

Hope had never called Lydia. Lydia had contacted *her* and told her it was time to deliver the baby. She'd said she was worried that Hope's placenta was starting to deteriorate. But there was no mention of that, either. And they'd been alone, yet Lydia claimed Rita, another midwife who'd been working at the center back then, had assisted her with the delivery.

Hope studied Lydia's flowing script, wondering what it all meant. Had Lydia confused her with someone else? Had she waited so long to record the details of Autumn's birth that she'd forgotten? Or had there been some other reason to…

Hope was so engrossed in her thoughts that she almost didn't hear the sound of a car on the gravel circular drive out front. When she did, she snapped her head up and listened more closely, immediately recognizing the hum of an engine…and then silence.

Someone else was here. Jamming the folders back where they belonged, she closed the file drawer as quietly as possible and rushed for the lightswitch. The light could easily go unnoticed to someone approaching from the front, but she wasn't about to push her luck. She'd seen all she was going to see, anyway. Now she needed to get out.

Dashing down the stairs, she heard a car door slam and stopped abruptly. She knew she couldn't beat whoever it was past the front entrance. She was trapped. She'd have to wait until—''

"Hope?"

Parker Reynolds's voice shattered the silence she'd tried so hard not to destroy, making Hope's knees go weak.

"Hope? It's Parker," he hollered. "Where are you?"

PARKER TOLD HIMSELF not to worry. He'd cleaned out the files and burned everything that could possibly be problematic. Hope could search through every piece of paper the center possessed, and she still wouldn't find anything. But being safe in his web of lies didn't make him feel any better for spinning them. Especially when he remembered the trust she'd finally given him by letting him hold her the night before.

If he told her about Dalton, he could finally feel right with her and with the world. The temptation to do so had zipped through his mind at intervals all day, every time he thought of her. But at what cost? Dalton stood to lose the very foundation of his life. Lydia stood to lose her good reputation and the center. His fellow employees stood to lose their jobs. There were probably other ramifications, as well, consequences Parker hadn't even considered yet.

And still he was tempted to tell her.

He hated a liar. He hated being a liar even more.

"Hope? Are you coming?" he called again, wondering if she was going to make him search for her.

"How did you know I was here?" she asked, surprising him by her closeness when she finally appeared at the bottom of the stairs. She glanced at Lydia's closed door almost as if she expected Lydia to come out and confront her, but Parker already knew Lydia wouldn't. That was why she'd called him. So she wouldn't be forced to play the offended party, and Hope could continue to work at the center as though she'd never broken into the storage area.

"Your car's around back," he said.

"You came in the front." She folded her arms and tilted her head to one side, studying him. "Lydia called you, didn't she."

"Yes."

"Why?"

Because she didn't want to deal with Hope. She felt too guilty. But he couldn't tell her that. "Because it's getting late and she wanted me to see you safely home."

"I can find my own way home."

He couldn't help admiring her indomitable spirit. Dalton possessed her strength and fortitude, he realized, and suddenly saw her background in a whole new light. Hope might have come from a polygamist cult, but she'd escaped her past and done something with her life. *She's a wonderful person*, the woman he'd spoken to at Valley View Hospital had said, and he knew she was right. Hope had a good character. He could think of a lot worse legacies to give a child. "She's worried about you."

A look of confusion replaced the belligerence on her face. "I don't get it. I don't get any of this."

"That's because there's nothing to get," he said. "Let's go."

He waited for her to pull around from the back, then followed her car to the cabin, grateful that Faith would be home this time. He wasn't sure he could trust himself alone with Hope Tanner again, despite everything he stood to lose.

"Thanks," she said with a wave as soon as they arrived, and jogged up the front steps, her keys at the ready. She obviously didn't plan on having him come in to check things out.

He felt a moment's relief and started to back up when something caught his eye. What was it? Hesitating, he squinted to see beyond the beam of his headlights and noticed that several limbs of the pine tree closest to the drive had recently been torn off. They hung at an odd angle, limp and lifeless, and some red paint marked the trunk.

Had there been an accident in the past twenty-four hours? He was just getting out to investigate when Hope came running from the cabin.

"Parker! She's gone! Faith's gone!"

He thought she was coming to him, but she veered off at the last second and went to her own car. She had her purse and her keys, but she was shaking so badly she could scarcely unlock the door.

Parker hurried over to her. "What do you mean? Where has she gone?"

"Superior, of course." She jerked away when he tried to catch her hand. "But I'm not going to let him hurt her. I p-promised her I'd be there for her."

"Are you sure she's not staying with Gina?"

She nodded, still fumbling with her keys. "She was here asleep when I left. And just look at the cabin! Everything's turned over and smashed. And—" she managed to get her door open "—and Arvin wrote a few choice words about her and me on the wall."

"You can't go there alone," Parker said.

"I go everywhere alone," she replied, and tried to slam the door, but he stood in the way.

"I'm going with you."

"You can't. It's hours and hours away. And you have to take care of your son."

"He knew I'd be getting back late from Taos today, so Bea's there. I'll call Dalton's grandparents and insist they step in and help for a while. I've never asked anything of them before. They can do that much. Dalton will be fine."

"But what about the clinic? And the fund-raiser?"

Parker thought of Lydia and how bad she felt about the past—so bad she'd risked hiring Hope at the clinic. *We owe her that much.* "This is where she'd want me to be," he said. "She'll just have to take over on the fund-raiser, maybe call in a few favors from Devon and the other midwives."

"But I don't know what's going to happen or how long I'll be gone," Hope argued. "I don't know if—" she blinked, obviously fighting tears "—if Faith's going to be okay. I gotta go. Get out of my way."

"Hope." He said her name forcefully to get her to calm down. "You can't take off like this. Give me a minute, and I'll drive you to Superior. We'll find Faith together, okay? We'll make sure she's safe, I promise."

Her eyes turned toward him, and he read her pain and doubt. "This isn't your problem," she whispered.

Cupping her chin, he tilted her face and felt his heart lurch at the same time. "It is now. Let's go inside so you can pack a small suitcase. We might be gone a while."

HOPE DIDN'T SPEAK for the first few hours. She sat rigidly in the passenger seat of the truck, staring out the windshield as though she could will her way to Superior at the speed of light if only she concentrated hard enough.

"How long were you gone tonight when you went to the birth center?" Parker asked.

Hope's posture relaxed a little, but he could tell by the strain in her face that she was extremely fatigued. "Not long. A couple of hours at the most."

"Okay, and it took a while for us to pack and make

arrangements. Still, they can't be very far ahead of us. Are you sure they'd go back right away?''

She bit her lip while she considered his question. ''I can't imagine Arvin doing anything else. He doesn't have much money. The church only gives him enough to pay his bills and meet the most basic needs of his families. He wouldn't want to squander money on a motel. Besides, I think he'd want to go where he feels powerful, and that's definitely Superior. He's like a fish out of water anywhere else.''

''What if he was too tired to drive? He might already have spent the day in a car, trying to reach Enchantment.''

''I hope he's going to Superior,'' she said. ''I have no idea where else to look.''

Parker didn't comment. He knew she had to be imagining her beautiful young sister in a motel room with her uncle. The image that flashed through his mind turned his stomach. ''If they are going back to Superior, where do you think he'll take her?''

''I don't know. He could take her to any of his wives' homes.''

''And they'd cover for him, even if Faith didn't want to be there?''

''I think Ila Jane would help her if she could, but I'm sure Arvin realizes that, too, so he won't go there until he feels he has Faith under his control again.''

''Maybe we should call this Ila Jane. Or your parents or someone, explain what's happened and tell them to look out for Faith.''

''I thought of that. But…''

''But?''

''I tried to talk to them before I left St. George. They're too blind to Arvin's faults. They won't believe Faith's in any real danger, so they won't interfere.'' Her words came out as almost a whisper, and Parker felt a strong desire to step in and protect her. She'd been fighting this battle on her own for long enough, dammit. It was time these so-called religious men quit abusing women and faced someone their own size.

"What about the police?"

"Who would we call? The Enchantment Police? The Superior Police?"

Parker rolled down his window to get some fresh air and to help him stay awake. They were already entering Arizona, which meant the air was much warmer than it had been in the high wilderness of New Mexico. "If they've left Enchantment, the Enchantment police couldn't do anything. It would have to be the Superior police."

"Good luck. They try to ignore the polygamist population as much as possible. They won't do anything unless we can prove that a crime has occurred. And by the time we do and they respond—" she shrugged "—it's a gamble whether they'll be any help at all."

"I still think we should call them. Maybe we can talk them into keeping an eye on Arvin's residences. Do you know where all his wives live?"

"Not all of them, no. Most houses, once they become the property of the church, stay that way for years and years, but families can be shuffled around because of overcrowding or whatever."

"But it's a tight-knit community, right? With a little help, we can find her."

"You have to understand that these people won't be on our side."

And she was going to drive into that, knowing she had no support from the police or anyone else. "You're an unusual woman," he said, shaking his head.

"I know. That's what you don't like about me."

He sent another glance her way, remembering her kiss, and realized she couldn't be more wrong. "I like everything about you," he said. "That's what has me worried."

"I've thought of someone I want to call," Hope announced just after they crossed the Utah border. The sun was coming up, but she hadn't given in and slept at all, so she looked as tired as Parker felt. They'd both been awake for close to twenty-four hours.

"Who's that?" he asked.

"Bonner."

Parker's brows shot up in surprise. "Why Bonner? He won't help us, will he?"

"I don't know, but after what he put me through, I think he owes me," she said.

"Do you have his number?" Parker asked, feeling an unexpected twinge of jealousy.

"It's listed."

"What if he already knows Arvin came after Faith and supports him in it?"

"I don't think he'd agree with any type of violence. He's pompous and full of himself, but he's not crazy like Arvin." She sighed. "In any case, it's worth a try."

Parker had to agree. They needed some kind of ally or, once they arrived in Superior, Arvin could hide Faith almost indefinitely.

Pulling over at the first gas station he could find, he stood next to the telephone booth, staring off toward the highway, as Hope called information for Bonner Thatcher. His cell phone battery had died, and in his hurry to start after Arvin, he'd left his charger behind.

"You want me to make the call?" he asked when she rested her forehead on the metal face of the phone, instead of dialing the number he'd jotted down for her.

Closing her eyes, she rubbed both temples. "No, I have to do it."

Parker found the proper change in his pocket and handed it to her. She dropped the money in the slot and dialed.

"Hello? Charity?…It's me… Have you heard from Faith? Do you know where Arvin might be?" She shook her head at Parker to indicate Charity didn't know anything about Faith or Arvin. "Can I speak to Bonner, then?…What?…Charity, that's not true. You don't have anything to worry about. Listen to me, I—"

Suddenly she pulled the receiver away from her ear and stared down at it as though it had bitten her. "She hung up on me," she said, her eyes lifting to his.

Parker set the receiver back on its hook. "She's not willing to cross your father?"

"She told me to stay away from Bonner."

"But she's already sharing him with three other women."

"She said she's not willing to share him with me."

CHAPTER NINETEEN

IT WASN'T MUCH of a motel, but they'd been on the road for fourteen hours. They were exhausted, and the Old West Inn was the best they were going to find in a town so small it wasn't even marked on the map Parker had purchased at the gas station.

Loaded with the duffel bags that held what they'd brought of their belongings, Parker held the door for Hope, frowning at the drab orange bedspreads, the laminated furniture, the brown shag carpet, the faint smell of mold.

"Nice," she said dryly.

"It's not the Hilton," he replied. But he wasn't about to suggest they change their plans. He'd spent two whole hours convincing Hope they'd be better off stopping for a few hours' rest.

"Which bed do you want?" he asked.

She shook her head. "It doesn't matter to me."

He carried her bag to the bathroom so she'd have her toiletries, kicked off his shoes and called information for the police department in Superior. A Sergeant Peters answered the phone and said he'd have someone drive by the list of addresses Hope had given Parker while they were on the road. He also said they'd look for a red car with some paint damage. But there was no real conviction in his voice, and Parker knew Hope was right. The police felt little need to get involved when the only crime that had occurred, so far, had happened in New Mexico. "How do you know she was abducted against her will?"

Peters had wanted to know. "People wander off every day, especially women that age."

Parker had finally gotten so frustrated he'd hung up.

"Do you want to try calling Bonner again?" he asked after giving himself a few moments to cool off.

Hope glanced at the phone, and Parker could tell that calling Bonner was the last thing she wanted to do. But she got up from the other bed and came over.

"No one's answering," she said after a few minutes.

"We'll try again later."

"Maybe I should call my mother, see if she's heard anything."

One of her younger sisters answered, judging by Hope's end of the conversation. "Hi, LaRee, this is Hope. Do you remember me?...It's been a long time, honey...I know. Yes, that was me in the park. Listen, have you seen Faith?...It's really important that I find her...Are you sure?"

She shot a look at Parker; something was obviously wrong.

"What is it?" he asked.

"My father's there. He wants to speak to me."

"Good. See if you can get him to help us."

"You don't understand. I'm the last person he'd— Hello," she said into the phone. "I don't care whether you like it or not, we need to find Faith. Arvin's lost his mind. You know he killed our cat...He said he was going to make us pay...No, I'm not lying. You can ask Bonner...I won't leave Superior until I've talked to Faith, Jed. Only when she tells me she wants to stay will I go... Because that's your name. I certainly don't claim you as my father...No, *you* listen, I—"

Parker gently nudged her. "Let me talk to him, okay?"

Hope blinked up at him. "What?"

"Let me talk to him."

Without saying anything further, she handed him the phone. He lifted it to his ear to hear a gruff male voice yelling something about what an ungrateful child she'd always been.

"Excuse me," Parker said, cutting him off.

"What? Who is this?"

Hope moved to the bed, sat cross-legged on top of it and stared at him. "My name is Parker Reynolds. I'm a friend of Hope's, and we're on our way to Superior."

"Well, you might as well turn around because there's nothing here for either one of you," came the answer.

"I'm afraid we can't do that," Parker replied. "Faith's about to have her baby. She could go into labor at any time. We need to find her and make sure both she and the baby are safe."

"We take care of our own around here. There're plenty of women who can deliver that baby. You don't need to involve yourself."

"I'm already involved…Jed, is it? And I'm going to stay involved until we find Faith. If you want us to leave, you can make it real simple. Have Faith call us, okay?"

"I won't have her do anything of the sort. I don't know who the hell you think you are, but—"

"I've told you who I am," Parker interrupted. "Now you need to know one more thing. I won't stand by and see you or your crazy brother abuse Hope or Faith any longer, do you understand? And if Arvin hurts Faith, there's going to be some serious trouble. You need to tell him that. You need to tell him that he's going to be sorry he ever met me." He hung up because he wasn't willing to give audience to the explosion of temper that met this announcement.

"That probably calmed him right down," Hope said, and for the first time since they'd left Enchantment, she seemed to be on the verge of smiling.

Parker chuckled because there wasn't anything else he could do and walked over to her. "Are you going to be okay?" he asked, sitting beside her and taking her hand. "You have me really worried, you know that?"

She stared down at their entwined fingers. "You didn't even want me to work at the center. Why are you doing this?" she asked. "Why are you helping me?"

Parker ran the knuckles of his free hand down the side of her face, so tempted to tell her the truth that the words nearly formed on his tongue. But then he thought of Dalton's boyish, endearing smile, pictured his son throwing a football or talking about some girl who sat next to him at school and got him in trouble because she talked too much.

Dalton had become his life. He didn't know what he'd do if Hope decided to fight him for her son. He couldn't tell her. But he owed Dalton's birth mother. He'd help her find her sister.

"I need to check on Dalton," he said, and moved back to the phone to avoid answering her.

Bea picked up on the third ring. "Hi, Bea, how's Dalton?" Parker had asked her to stay at the house until Dalton's grandmother arrived. It hadn't been easy talking Amanda Barlow into baby-sitting, but she'd finally agreed and was due to arrive that evening.

"He's fine," she said. "I got him from Holt's house just a few minutes ago, and he's just now finishing his homework and having a snack. Amanda called to say she'll be a little late tonight, but she's still coming."

"Good."

"It's your father," he heard her tell Dalton.

"I want to talk to him," Dalton said.

The phone changed hands. "Hi, Dad. Why haven't you been answering your cell?"

"My battery's dead, and I left my charger in the other car. But I'll buy a new one as soon as I can find a place that sells them, so you should be able to reach me by tomorrow."

"Tomorrow! Where are you?"

"I'm in Utah, and it looks like I'm going to be here

for a few days. Will you be okay with Grandma taking care of you in the evenings?"

"Yeah. She told Bea she's bringing me a pitching machine. That's why she's gonna be late. She needs Grandpa to load it for her. And we'll be going back to her place for the weekend."

"Do you mind?"

"I guess not."

"How did school go today?"

"I got an A on my spelling test."

"That's great. Put your paper on the refrigerator so I can see it when I get home."

"Okay. So why are you in Utah?"

"A friend of mine needed me to bring her here."

"Hope?"

"That's her."

"Oh, good. She's with you, then? Can I talk to her?"

Parker glanced over at Hope and sucked in a quick breath as he caught a glimpse of her bare back. "She's busy right now," he said, forcing himself to turn away while she finished changing her shirt.

"Aw, Dad," Dalton complained. "Come on. I just want to talk to her for a minute."

Parker sighed and waited for Hope to finish righting her sweatshirt. "He wants to talk to you," he said, and passed her the phone.

MILDLY SURPRISED, Hope put the phone to her ear. Parker was so protective of Dalton, she couldn't believe he was letting her speak to him.

"Hi, Dalton," she said somewhat hesitantly. "What's up?"

"I talked to Mrs. Holt today."

"You did? What happened?"

"I told her I appreciate that she's concerned about me, but I'm doing fine."

"Perfect. And? What did she say?"

"She said she was glad to hear it, but that I still need a mother to help me smooth the rough edges."

"What rough edges?"

"I don't know. I guess watching too much TV and getting in the mud and all that."

"And your response was?"

"My dad's met someone, and I think he's going to marry her soon, so you don't have to worry about me anymore."

Hope's jaw sagged. "You didn't."

"Yup. And being respectful worked great, just like you said," he replied.

"But who has your dad met?" she asked.

"Are you kidding?" he laughed. "You!"

ONCE IN THE BATHROOM, Hope cast her jeans aside and pulled on the sweat bottoms she'd brought to sleep in, still feeling a little shell-shocked from her conversation with Dalton. Where could he have gotten the idea that she and Parker might get married?

"Hope?" Parker knocked on the door. "I'm going out for some ice. Would you like anything?"

"No, thanks."

"You wouldn't eat when we stopped. How about a cup of soup?"

"I'm really not hungry."

"You should eat something."

"Okay," she said. It was easier to give in than to fight him. "Just get me a sandwich or whatever's easiest."

"Great. I'll be right back."

She didn't step out of the bathroom until she heard the door close behind him. Maybe if she fell asleep before he returned, he wouldn't pose any more questions about her conversation with Dalton. He'd already asked her, three times, what Dalton had wanted to tell her. She'd glossed over their attempt to get Mrs. Rider to butt out of Dalton's life and didn't mention the part about her. But she knew

Parker was still curious. She'd reacted too oddly there at the end.

Unfortunately, she was too worried about Faith to go straight to bed. She thought maybe she should try calling Bonner one more time.

She dialed his number and hoped Charity didn't answer. What her sister had said hurt, especially now, when there was so much else going on in her life.

The phone rang and rang without answer. Hope hung up and dialed again. After six rings, someone finally picked up.

"Hello?" A male voice.

"Bonner?"

"Who is it?"

Hope would have breathed a sigh of relief, except speaking to Bonner wasn't a whole lot easier than talking to Charity. "It's Hope."

No response.

"Aren't you going to say anything?"

"What can I say? Your father said you're with a man. I'm not going to lie and say that doesn't bother me."

"How can it bother you?" she asked. "It's been ten years."

"It could be fifty. It wouldn't change anything."

"Well, he's...he's just a friend," she said.

"You're sure about that?"

Hope remembered Dalton saying, *You!* and shook her head. Could the world get any more confusing? "I'm sure. Listen, I really need to find Faith."

"You're not the only one."

Hope stiffened in surprise. "What do you mean by that? Don't *you* know where she is?"

"No."

"You'd tell me if you did, wouldn't you, Bonner?"

"Hope, if I knew where she was, I'd go get her myself. Jed's going crazy. Arvin disappeared three days ago, and we haven't heard from him. We've been in meetings all day, trying to figure out what we should do."

"So you're telling me Arvin hasn't come back to Superior."

"That's what I'm telling you."

"He will," she said. He had to, or they might never find Faith....

"What makes you so sure?"

"Where else could he go?"

"I don't know," Bonner said. He sounded tired and far less pompous than he had in her living room in St. George. "Everything's in a bit of an uproar here. We're handling the situation as best we can."

"Just do me one favor, okay?"

"What's that?"

"Call me if you hear anything."

"Why would I do that?" he asked.

She hesitated. "For old times' sake?"

She thought she heard him sigh. "Fine," he said, and she gave him the number at the motel, as well as Parker's cell-phone number.

"WHO WAS THAT?" Parker asked, letting himself in just as she was hanging up. When they'd checked in, he'd asked if she'd like a separate room, and Hope had told him she saw no point in renting two rooms when they were only going to be sleeping for a few hours. But her motivation hadn't been nearly so practical. She'd wanted to keep Parker with her. She was still afraid to depend on his support, but she couldn't deny that having him there made everything more bearable.

"I finally got hold of Bonner," she said.

Parker stopped digging in the sack of takeout food he'd brought in with him. "Charity let you through?"

"I don't know if she was there. He answered the phone."

"What did he say?"

"Faith and Arvin aren't back in Superior yet." She decided not to tell him that the entire church was frantic, wondering where Arvin had gone and what he was doing, and that even her father, the great Jedidiah Tanner, was worried. She was afraid Parker would insist they turn the whole thing over to the police and go home, and she couldn't do that. She wouldn't go back to Enchantment without Faith.

"That's good," Parker said. "That gives you time to get some rest."

Hope nodded and accepted the burger he handed her, trying not to grimace. She stared at it for several seconds, wondering how she was going to get anything down when she was so tense. But Parker was watching her, so she unwrapped it and took a small bite—a bite she had to wash down with soda.

"Was Bonner friendlier than your sister?" he asked, motioning her to take another bite.

"He wasn't *un*friendly," she said when she'd managed to swallow a second time.

He gave her the sack. "That doesn't tell me much."

Hope shrugged, glumly eyeing her burger, knowing from the smell of the sack that Parker had bought fries, too. "He didn't say a whole lot. He agreed to call us if he hears anything, though."

"That's big of him."

"I guess." Hope took another bite of burger and commanded herself to chew, but the moment Parker turned his attention to the television, she quickly dumped her entire dinner in the garbage. She couldn't eat any more, not without being sick.

"You ready to—" He turned and saw that her burger was suddenly gone and frowned. "Hope, you have to eat. If you don't keep up your strength, how will you help Faith?"

"I ate all I could," she said truthfully. How was she going to help Faith, anyway? All Hope could think about were the true-crime shows she'd seen on television—the ones where dead bodies were buried in the woods or thrown in a river. The victim was almost always a woman. And the murderer was almost always the woman's husband.

Damn Arvin! Why couldn't he just leave them alone? He and the other Brethren had destroyed enough lives.

If only Hope hadn't left the cabin… Suddenly remembering the telephone number she'd found written on her baby's empty file, she went back into the bathroom for her duffel bag, dug the scrap of folder out of her jeans and put it inside her purse. She didn't want to lose it. Logic told her that chances were good it had nothing to do with Autumn.

Emotion told her it might be her only link.

PARKER'S TIRED EYES burned as he sat on the foot of his bed and watched television, waiting for Hope to fall asleep on the other bed. He thought the noise of the TV might help them block out the sound of the ice machine a few doors down, and the folks in the room next door, who had two very noisy children. He needed something to distract him from the memory of seeing Hope's bare back. He'd never considered a woman's back as particularly erotic, but that one glimpse of Hope had had a powerful effect on him. Maybe it was because he remembered so clearly the feel of her smooth skin.

"Aren't *you* going to sleep?" Hope asked.

Parker glanced back at her. She was still wearing the baggy sweatshirt she'd changed into, and her hair was mussed, but it only made her seem more accessible….

He didn't need accessible. He needed to find Faith and get home where he was safe with Dalton.

"I'll relax eventually," he muttered.

"Don't you want to lie down?"

"In a minute."

He returned his attention to the television, but she

propped herself up on her pillow and gazed at him in the mirror. "I mean with me," she said when she caught his eye.

Her words hit him like a strong right hook and left him reeling, unable to respond. So much of what was happening made no sense. Somehow he was in a motel room with the one woman he should avoid at all costs—and he wanted to make love to her more than he'd ever wanted to make love with anyone before.

It had to be fate's revenge for what he'd done.

"I don't think that would be a very good idea," he said.

"Why not?"

"You said you didn't want to make love with me. I don't think you should trust me to—"

"I didn't say that tonight," she interrupted.

He swallowed hard as he stared at her. The promising swell of her breasts beneath the soft cotton of her sweatshirt was almost too tempting to refuse. But he knew, if he made love to her, his conscience would eventually get the best of him and he'd end up telling her about Dalton. He wouldn't be able to lie to her at that point—at least he wouldn't be able to lie to her and continue living with himself.

"You don't really want something that intimate right now," he said. "You're frightened for Faith and you're hurt and confused and—"

"I know what I want," she replied. "I want to feel alive again. I want to know there are still good things in my life. I'm tired of playing it safe and living in the background of other people's worlds—like…like some sort of character actor with a part too small and insignificant to be fulfilling."

Her eyes seemed to ask him not to refuse her and the torture he saw in their depths was nearly his undoing. "Hope, I'm sorry…."

"Forget it," she said, and rolled over.

CHAPTER TWENTY

PARKER TURNED DOWN the volume on the television and studied the lump in the other bed. Then he pulled off his shirt and socks, donned the basketball trunks he generally wore to bed during the spring and summer and tossed his clothes into the corner.

The sound of his jeans hitting the floor made Hope turn. He motioned for her to move over.

"Forget it. I'm fine," she said.

"Move."

"I said—"

"Just move."

A confused look crossed her face, but she made room for him, and he climbed into bed with her.

"I thought you—"

"Shh." Wrapping his arms tightly around her, he pulled her backside into the curve of his body.

"I don't understand, Parker," she said once she came into contact with evidence of his arousal. "You obviously want—"

"I don't want anything," he said. "Just go to sleep."

"I can't," she replied, but he held perfectly still for several minutes, doing his best to keep her warm and secure, and she finally relaxed in his arms.

When he knew she was sleeping, Parker pressed his lips to her hair. "There're a lot of things I'd trade to be able to have you, Hope," he whispered.

But Dalton wasn't one of them.

THE TELEPHONE woke Hope. She lay blinking in bed, Parker's arm heavy across her middle. The sun had gone down, leaving them in total darkness except for the flicker of the television, which Parker had left on to mask the other noises in the motel so they could sleep. Because everything was so dark, she felt disoriented. She didn't know if it was the middle of the night or just past dinnertime.

Checking the digital numbers on the alarm clock as she got out of bed and hurried to grab the phone, she saw that it was far later than she wanted it to be—1:15 a.m.

"Hello?"

Parker had started to stir when she did. Now he propped himself up on one elbow. "Who is it?" he asked.

Hope wasn't sure yet. No one had responded. "Hello?" she said again.

There was a click, then a dial tone. She hung up as terrible feeling of foreboding crept over her.

"You okay?" Parker asked.

Hope didn't know what to say. Faith was in trouble. She knew it in her heart and in her bones.

"Hope?" Parker sounded worried.

"I'm afraid," she said, but the telephone rang again before she could say what she was afraid of, and she snatched it up. "Hello?"

"We've found Arvin and Faith."

Bonner. "You have?"

"Yes, but you'd better get over here, fast."

"Where?" she cried. "Where's here?"

"Remember the barn?"

How could she ever forget? "Is this some kind of cruel joke?" she asked.

"It's no joke. If you want to help Faith, you'll get over to the barn as soon as possible."

"But I'm probably two hours away. Can you wait there until I arrive? Make sure nothing happens to Faith?"

"No. I've got to go."

He hung up, leaving Hope staring at the phone in her hand, breathing hard and fast.

"What is it?" Parker asked.

"Bonner's found Faith."

"Where?"

"In the barn." Hope closed her eyes, feeling sick at the mere mention of the place where she and Bonner used to meet.

"The barn?" Parker queried. "What's she doing in a barn?"

"I don't know," she said. "But something isn't right. Let's go."

IT WAS RAINING when they finally arrived in Superior. Tiny droplets beaded on the side windows of the truck and rolled down the glass as the wipers beat steadily across the windshield. Hope watched their methodical movement as if Faith's life depended on every sweep, and willed the miles to pass faster.

I'm coming Faith, she thought. *Hang on, I'm coming.*

"Make a left two blocks down, at 200 West," she said when the light in the center of town finally turned green.

So far, Parker had shown little regard for the speed limit. He punched the gas pedal and they rocketed through the intersection. At this point, Hope knew Parker didn't care if they got pulled over. They'd lead the police to whatever scene was awaiting them at the barn.

But there probably wasn't enough activity to warrant a speed trap at three-thirty in the morning. Hope saw no flashing lights coming up from behind, heard no sirens. The whole town looked dead asleep.

"Why the barn?" Parker asked as they started into the surrounding farmland. He'd asked before but she'd put him off.

"What do you mean?" she responded, hoping to avoid the issue again.

"Why would Arvin take her to a barn?"

"I'm not positive," Hope said, "but I think it might have something to do with me."

"How?"

"Bonner's family lived on the farm. That was where Bonner and I used to…spend time together away from the prying eyes of the others."

A slight pause. "Would Arvin know that?"

"When the truth of my pregnancy came out, my father called an emergency council and I had to confess the entire affair before all the Brethren."

"Including Arvin."

"Yes, Arvin heard it all. Dates. Times. Places."

"Does Bonner still live there?"

"He's probably living in the main house with Charity. Maybe more of his wives live there, too. I'm not sure. My guess would be that his parents have moved into the smaller caretaker's house in back."

"A real family affair," he said sarcastically, and Hope knew he was as tense as she was. They didn't really know what they were getting into. Bonner could easily have set her up for an ambush.

Evidently Parker was thinking along the same lines because he asked, "How much do you trust Bonner?"

"I don't trust anyone," she answered simply.

He looked as though he wanted to say something, but the set of his jaw remained grim and he didn't speak.

"Slow down," she said. "You have to turn soon, but it's difficult to see in the dark."

The truck slowed and she leaned forward to spot the road sign. "This is it," she said.

Parker took the corner going fast enough that the tires squealed. He gunned the engine again as they came out of the turn, but Hope wasn't frightened by the speed. It gave her a measure of relief to know they were traveling as fast as possible. It wouldn't be long now. They were less than a mile away.

"Parker?" she said when she glimpsed a light in the farmhouse, indicating that someone was up.

"What?" His eyes were watchful, his body taut with expectation.

"I don't know how bad this is going to be."

He didn't take his eyes from the road. "It'll be okay."

She rubbed her hands together to ward off the cold that seemed to be coming from somewhere inside her. It was warm in the cab of the truck. The defroster had been on for miles to keep the windows from fogging up. "It might not be," she said. "We'd be foolish not to realize that. And you have a little boy at home. If…if something's up, if Bonner is actually in there with Arvin and they have a little surprise planned for us, I don't want you to do anything stupid. Just get out right away and go for the police."

"Don't worry about me," he said.

The dirt road leading to the farm came up on their right more quickly than Hope had anticipated. "Turn here," she said, and braced herself against the dash when he hit the brakes.

They swung around the corner and began to bounce in and out of potholes, splashing mud onto the windshield as they went.

The farmhouse was a large white wooden structure built more than sixty years earlier. It sat at the end of the drive, with a sad little porch and a cherry tree in front. The barn was beyond and to the left. In the darkness, it looked larger than Hope remembered, more imposing.

A flash of lightning lit the sky, and thunder boomed and rolled in the distance. "Should we stop at the house?" Parker asked.

The rain began to fall noticeably harder. "No. I don't want Charity to know I'm here. There's no reason to involve her if we can help it. Bonner was very specific about Faith being in the barn."

"It doesn't look like anyone's in the barn."

Hope could make out the barest hint of light seeping through the crack of the old double doors. "There's someone there. I just don't know who it is."

Parker navigated around a couple of old cars that had probably been broken down for years, past an overturned wheelbarrow and some obsolete farm equipment. He parked next to a tractor and a van, and what was left of last year's hay, which was stacked in bundles and covered with white plastic.

A dog, chained up in the yard, began barking wildly the moment Hope climbed out.

Parker grimaced at the noise. "If they didn't know we were here before, they do now," he said, and told her to wait while he grabbed a tire iron from the toolbox in the back of his truck.

Hope considered the iron and the strength of purpose revealed in his face. She didn't want to believe a weapon would be necessary. But she wasn't about to insist he put it down. He had the right to protect himself. They'd be stupid not to consider the possibility that things could get violent.

"Stay behind me," he said, but Hope immediately started jogging for the barn, too anxious to play it safe. All she could see in her mind's eye was Oscar, lying mutilated and dead on her doormat. She wasn't going to let anything like that happen to Faith.

Parker caught up with her after only a few steps and jerked her behind him. The dog's barking became a futile whine as he turned in circles and finally sat on the wet ground.

The murmur of voices came from inside the barn. But the sound shifted on the wind, rising and falling, so she couldn't catch enough of it to make out any words.

Parker insisted she stay behind him while he peeked through the crack in the doors.

"Can you see anything?" she asked.

He shook his head. "We're going to have to go in blind."

Holding the tire iron ready, he threw open the door. The heavy wooden panel slammed against the outside wall, sounding like a shotgun blast, and the five men inside looked startled.

Hope immediately recognized her father, her uncle Rulon, and Bonner's father, Elton Thatcher. She also noticed another man, a friend of the family. The leader of the church, R.J. Grissom, was there, too. They were clustered in a corner, sheltering something or someone behind them: Faith.

"Oh, my God." Hope shoved past her father and the others to find her sister lying on the ground in a pile of straw. "Faith? Are you okay?"

"Hope?" Faith's voice was weak, and she was shivering, despite several coats piled underneath and on top of her. The only light was from a fluorescent bulb hanging from one of the rafters near the door, but Hope could see that Faith was hurt. She had a black eye, a swollen lip and God knew what else.

"What happened?" Hope asked, kneeling at her side.

"Arvin. He...he beat me and—" she licked her fat upper lip "—tried to rape me right here...where he said you gave yourself to Bonner. But—" Hope thought she detected a slight smile on her sister's face "—he couldn't get hard enough. It...it made him so angry." She tried to laugh.

"What are you doing here? How did you find us?" her father demanded.

Hope didn't bother to answer him. "Where's Arvin?"

"He left," someone else supplied.

"Where'd he go?" she asked, appealing to the others. "Where's Arvin?"

"We don't know," her father said. He had a stern set to his mouth and his eyes were unfathomable, but she could tell he was agitated.

"Bonner's looking for him," Bonner's father, Elton, piped up. "He called me as soon as Arvin showed up here."

"This would never have happened if you'd done the right thing," R.J. put in behind her.

She was busy checking Faith's injuries. "And you think the right thing was to marry Arvin?" she challenged.

A quick glance told her a muscle twitched in her father's cheek. "I'd told him he could have you when you were old enough."

"*Have* me? We're not living in biblical times." Faith moaned when Hope's fingers brushed a particularly sensitive spot. "That wasn't your decision to make," Hope added.

"God hasn't changed," R.J. said. "It was His decision."

Hope thought Faith's injuries would heal, but she wasn't sure what damage Arvin might have caused the baby. "Listen to you!" she said to the men gathered behind her. "And you think it's *my* fault we're here right now?"

No one answered.

"How did Arvin get away?" she asked, taking Faith's hand and giving it a reassuring squeeze. "We're going to get you out of here," she murmured to her sister.

"Bonner heard the ruckus in here. As soon as he came to investigate, Arvin got in his car and drove away," Rulon volunteered.

Parker had dropped the tire iron and was kneeling across from her. "Has anyone called an ambulance?"

R.J. nudged her father out of the way so he could step closer. "I don't know who you are," he said, eyeing Parker with significant distrust, "but this has nothing to do with outsiders. It's our problem, and we'll take care of it. We don't need any help from you or Hope or anyone else."

"You mean you don't need any trouble," Hope said, wondering how she and Parker were going to manage moving Faith without hurting her further.

"Arvin's going to pay for this," Parker said. "He's not getting away with it."

"He'll pay," R.J. agreed, "but he'll pay our way. We'll cut him off from all church support and leave him to flounder on his own for a while. That will teach him to cross us."

Hope nudged Parker to gain his attention. "We'll have to carry her out."

"No problem." Parker slipped an arm beneath Faith, but Rulon put a restraining hand on his shoulder.

"Don't," he said. "You might not care about this church, Hope, but we do. Faith's just a little beat-up. She'll heal. And running away like that…she was asking for it."

"*Asking* for it?" Hope echoed, incredulous. "You're as crazy as Arvin is." She pulled the hair away from Faith's cheek to reveal a nasty bruise. "You call that a little beat-up? Who knows what else Arvin's done to her. He might have kicked her, hurt the baby. You heard her say he tried to rape her."

"She's his wife," R.J. said. "You can't rape your own wife."

"That's bullshit," Parker said.

"Jed—" Hope's eyes were riveted on her father, who was hovering over them "—she could lose the baby. I know she doesn't mean that much to you. I know none of us do. But you don't want a baby's blood on your hands, do you?"

He straightened as though she'd just insulted him. "You're wrong," he said, but Faith moaned at that moment and tried to get up on her own.

Hope turned her attention to her sister. "Relax," she whispered.

"Help me," Faith murmured. "The baby…"

Hope fought the anger that threatened to consume her. She had to remain cool and calm. She had to think. "I'm here now, Faith," she said, taking her hand. "And I'm so sorry, honey. Arvin will never hurt you again. I promise. It's over. Everything's going to be okay."

Faith started to cry, and Hope felt as though someone was tearing her heart right out of her chest. How could she have let this happen? "My baby," Faith sobbed. "I think he hurt my baby…" Suddenly she stiffened and groaned and grabbed her middle.

"What is it?" Hope said, but she didn't need to ask. Faith was obviously in labor. "How long as this been going on?" she asked the men as Faith's face contorted with pain.

They glanced uncomfortably at each other. "We…we don't know," Elton finally conceded. "We found her like this after Bonner called. She was having pains then, too, but…but we gave her a blessing."

"That's *it?* You didn't get one of the midwives to help her?"

"We can't let word of this get out," R.J. said. "It could damage the church. Besides, she doesn't need a midwife. In the old days, women had babies by themselves all the time. This is God's punishment for rebelling against Him. This is the natural consequence of sin. We first learn of it in the Bible, with Eve. Right, Jed? She's no better than Eve."

Her father didn't answer, and for the first time, he didn't look so sure of himself.

"It's a perfectly natural phenomenon," Rulon chimed in, lending his support to R.J. as usual. But his expression was grave, and Hope could tell he was worried, too. "She'll have the baby in a while. Then everything will be fine."

Hope found their ignorance so appalling she couldn't even respond to it, especially while Faith was suffering. But Parker responded. She saw his hands curl into fists as he gazed up at them, heard the scorn in his voice. "If you think God is behind this, you don't know anything about God," he said. "And if she or the baby dies, you're all going to jail."

"We didn't hurt her!" Bonner's father cried.

"You didn't help her, either," Parker replied.

Another pain racked Faith and Hope helped her breathe through it. When it was over, Faith lay back, limp, obviously exhausted, and Hope wished for the inside of a hospital room as she'd never wished for anything else. She'd delivered a few babies in her tenure at Valley View, but she'd had the support of other nurses, an emergency doctor downstairs, all the emergency equipment she could need, an ample supply of blood and a sterile environment. Here she had nothing, only a dirty stall and a few coats.

She thought of the farmhouse and the beds that would be available there. "Where's Charity? Why isn't she here?"

"Bonner packed her and the kids up and took them to Marianne's the moment he figured there might be trouble," her father said.

"But I'm sure the house is unlocked," Hope said. "No one ever locks any doors here, right?" Unless things had changed, the members of the Everlasting Apostolic Church didn't have anything worth stealing. "Maybe we can move her into the—"

Faith's gut-wrenching cry interrupted her. "No," she said. "It's too late. It's coming. The baby's coming."

"Tell me what to do and I'll do it," Parker said, his expression intense. "Do you want me to take her out of here? Find a phone and call an ambulance?"

Hope pulled up the sleeves of her sweater, fighting the panic that edged closer with every minute. "There's no ambulance service. And the closest medical center is in Richfield. Once she has the baby, we'll have to take her there ourselves."

"Once she has the baby?" he echoed.

Hope nodded. "Just hold her hand and keep telling her everything's going to be okay while I check her so I know what I'm dealing with."

"And then what?" Parker asked.

"Pray the baby isn't breach."

PARKER HAD NEVER SEEN a woman give birth before, which was surprising, considering he'd worked at The Birth Place for nearly twelve years. It was a part of the business in which he didn't involve himself. The midwives handled all of that. Vanessa had had a couple of miscarriages, but he'd gotten her to the hospital in plenty of time and the doctors had taken care of everything. Those were sad, disappointing occasions, especially for his poor wife. But this...this was something else entirely. Anger, fear and hope flooded through him in equal proportions, leaving him so agitated he didn't know what to do with himself.

"One more push," Hope said. "Come on, Faith, you can do it."

"I can't," she groaned. Sweat matted her hair to her forehead, despite the cool temperature and, beneath the purple bruises Arvin had left, her face was so pale it was almost translucent. She looked utterly spent.

"Is she okay?" Jed called, poking his head inside the barn. At Hope's request, her father had sent the men to the house to gather a few items, then shooed everyone out, except her and Parker. But she could tell he was having difficulty waiting.

Hope didn't have the time or the energy to respond. "I saw the baby's head during the last contraction," she told Faith. "One more good push should be all it takes."

Another contraction came, but Faith didn't even try to push. She started to twist and moan, and Hope's fear-filled eyes turned Parker's way. "If the baby doesn't come soon, I don't know what we're going to do."

"It'll come," he told her. Then he squeezed Faith's

hand. "One more push, Faith. You can do it. You're a strong girl. Show me how strong you are."

Parker heard the barn door close again, but he knew Jed and the others hadn't left. They were hovering close by, waiting.

"Here comes another contraction," Hope said.

"Let's go, Faith," Parker said, and she finally bore down. He could feel her shaking as she squeezed his arm and wished he could lend her some of his strength. *Come on,* he prayed, *let the baby come now. Come on.*

"That's it, honey," Hope said. "Here she is... Here she is..."

Parker caught a glimpse of the baby's head, and relief almost overwhelmed him. But when the contraction ended, Faith collapsed and the head disappeared back inside her womb.

Tears began to stream down Hope's face. "Parker, if she loses this baby..."

"She's not going to lose it," he said.

"Come on, Faith." Hope's voice was angry, impatient this time. "Arvin's not going to cost us this baby, dammit. You can do it. Come on!"

"What's wrong?" Hope's father called, opening the door again.

"Keep the door shut," Parker hollered. He feared the panic was starting to get to Hope. She was losing the calm she'd had throughout the delivery, and he needed her. Faith needed her. "Hope, it's okay," he said, his voice low. "Don't let her down."

Hope gritted her teeth and lifted her chin, defiance flashing in her eyes. "I will *never* let her down," she said. "She's my sister. She's having this baby, and she and the baby are both going to be fine."

Parker nodded. "That's the truth. Believe it," he said with absolute confidence.

Another contraction hit and Faith moaned.

"Now," Hope said. "Now, Faith."

Faith seemed to gather her remaining strength and pushed. It was a feeble effort at first, but with Hope's encouragement, she fought harder.

"Do you want this baby?" Hope asked.

"I want this baby," she panted.

"Then show me, Faith. How badly do you want this baby? How badly?"

"I…want…this…baby!" The words sounded torn from her throat, but the determination behind them worked. The baby's head finally slid out just before the contraction ended, and Hope immediately began clearing its breathing passages with the clean sheet Elton had brought from the house. With the next contraction, the baby's body emerged.

Feeling a little light-headed, Parker drew a deep breath and blinked at the tiny, red body.

It was a boy.

CHAPTER TWENTY-ONE

"YOU DID IT," Hope whispered the moment Faith's baby let out its first cry. "Listen to those lungs. You did it, Faith! What a brave woman you are."

Parker covered Faith to keep her warm, then smoothed the hair from her forehead as Hope tied the umbilical cord off with a shoelace.

"Is that going to be okay?" Jed asked. He'd come into the barn the second he heard the baby, and the others were beginning to file in and cluster around, too.

"I think so," Hope said. "The afterbirth delivered just fine, and I'm pretty sure the placental blood has already gone into the baby, where it's supposed to be. This should ensure that it stays there." She double-checked her knot. "I could probably cut the cord, but I'd rather not risk infection. It'd be better to take the baby to the hospital still connected to Faith and let them handle it there."

"Congratulations," Parker said to Faith. "You have a beautiful baby boy."

Faith's eyes were closed. Her breathing was shallow, but she wasn't losing a lot of blood. Hope thought she was recovering. "Did you hear, honey?" she asked.

Faith opened her eyes and attempted a smile, but Hope could tell she was almost too exhausted to move. "Look at him." Hope held the crying baby up for her to see. "He's perfect. I bet he weighs almost seven pounds."

A real smile curved Faith's lips at that, and she reached out for him. "He's beautiful. Let me hold him."

Hope wrapped the baby in a blanket and settled him in

the crook of Faith's arm, so that supporting him wouldn't take any effort. "We're going to transport you to the hospital now, okay, honey?" she said. "You just rest and we'll take care of everything. We'll let the baby suckle while we drive. That should help your uterus contract and slow the bleeding. It'll be good for both of you."

Hope felt shaky after the infusion of so much adrenaline, but she managed to stand and face the men of Superior. Parker came up behind her. She felt his presence and would have reached back to take his hand, except that hers were still sticky with blood. "We're leaving now," she said. "We're going far away and never coming back, so you have no reason to stop us."

R.J.'s eyes narrowed and he stepped forward. "I don't think so. You've got to understand that we didn't want this. We didn't want any of this. It was Arvin's doing."

"I know that," she said. "But if you keep his sins a secret, you're as guilty as he is."

R.J. gaped at her, obviously not used to hearing such damning words, especially from a woman.

"How dare you try to tell me—"

"You'd be surprised by what I dare to tell you," she said as Parker handed her the baby. He shot R.J. a warning glance that seemed to stifle his reply, because the man stepped back.

"Let's go," Parker said, scooping Faith into his arms.

They started out, but R.J. barred their way. "Are you just going to let them walk away without a word?" he said to Jed. "What kind of man are you that you can't take care of your own family? They could go straight to the police and cause all kinds of trouble."

Jed's gaze settled on Faith, and to her astonishment, Hope noticed tear tracks on his cheeks. "You were wrong when you said I don't care, Hope," he said. "I love her. I've always loved all my children." He looked at her, then, and his eyes seemed to add, "Even you."

"If you love her, let us go," Hope said softly, holding

the baby close. "And make sure Arvin doesn't come after us."

Jed looked at the others as if hoping for their support.

"This doesn't set a good example for your other children, Jed," Elton said. "If you let Hope and Faith get away with this, your other daughters will defy you at every turn."

"Arvin's our brother," Rulon chimed in. "He's made a mistake, but shouldn't we stand by him and help him repent?"

"Faith will lose her eternal reward if she leaves God's church," R.J. added. "She'll become a child of hell."

"But forcing her to do what I want…" Jed tugged on his beard. "Somehow, that isn't the answer," he said, sounding weary. "I've learned that the hard way."

"Jed—" R.J. began.

Her father waved Parker toward the door. "Take her."

"You're doing the right thing," Hope said, and for the first time she felt a flicker of respect for the man who'd sired her. But the door flew open before they reached it, and Bonner dragged Arvin inside.

"I found him," he announced, his hair plastered to his head from the rain.

"Where?" R.J. wanted to know.

"In bed with Rachel."

"Trying to prove you're still a man, Arvin? Since you couldn't get it up with Faith?" Hope said.

"You want to see if I can still get it up, Hope?" Arvin replied, his dark eyes glinting with that touch of madness that had always frightened her. "You're the one who's caused all this, you know. I hope you're happy. Look what she's done, Jed. I don't know why I ever wanted her in the first place. She was never any good."

Jed turned to face him, and Hope could tell that any brotherly love he'd felt for Arvin had finally died out. "She's always been better than you, Arvin. Now get in my car. I'm taking you down to the police station."

"What?" Arvin cried. "You can't take me to the police. You're my *brother,* for God's sake."

"You're no brother of mine," Jed said. "You almost killed my daughter and could have killed her baby. As far as I'm concerned, you can rot in jail the rest of your life. I'll certainly do nothing to help you."

"R.J., think of the scandal this will cause, the negative attention it will bring the church," Arvin said, his voice rising in panic.

R.J. stared at the ground for several seconds, shaking his head. Finally he said, "Jed's right. You've gone too far this time, Arvin. There's nothing we can do."

Arvin turned frantic eyes on Rulon. "Wait, I'm sorry. I'll repent. I'm one of you. I have wives to take care of, children. Rulon? Can you believe Jed would turn on me like this?"

Rulon looked from R.J. to Jed, and Hope saw his shoulders slump. He obviously felt more loyalty to Arvin than he did to her or Faith, but he wasn't about to cross R.J. "You've really done it now, Arvin," he said.

"Judas!" Arvin screamed, struggling as Elton Thatcher took hold of him. "You're all going to hell! I had a vision last night that you'd betray me. Hope has poisoned all of you, just like she poisoned Faith."

Elton moved to grab Arvin's feet because he was thrashing around so much that Elton couldn't get him outside.

"You'll be sorry," Arvin said as they wrestled him through the door.

A car door slammed a few seconds later. Hope could no longer hear Arvin's shouts above the patter of the rain, but she could feel Bonner's eyes on her. She glanced at him, then let her gaze slowly circle the barn. This place held so many bittersweet memories—Bonner telling her he loved her, Bonner touching her for the first time. They'd planned their lives here, lying in the hay on a lazy summer afternoon, the smell of animals and warm earth all around. Hope had thought that once she married Bonner, she'd live here forever.

None of that had happened, but it didn't hurt anymore. Faith and the baby were safe. Even the men who used to hold so much power over her didn't seem as daunting as they used to. Merely old. And Parker was with her. Somehow that was most significant of all.

"Thanks for calling me, Bonner," she said.

"You're welcome."

Parker hesitated at the door. Seeing him standing there, Hope finally knew where she belonged. And it wasn't in Superior. She might have come from these people, but the last tie had been severed.

"I'll be in the truck," he said, and stepped outside.

Bonner jerked his head in the direction Parker had gone. "You sure that guy's just a friend?"

Hope didn't know what to say. Did Parker mean more to her than a friend? She'd thought she could never love again, that she'd never get over Bonner. But when she looked at Bonner, she felt only a touch of nostalgia. When she looked at Parker, she felt good and safe, as if nothing bad had ever happened.

"I'm not sure," she said.

Bonner studied her. "Well, if he ends up with you, he's one lucky son of a gun."

Hope smiled, grateful for her heart's release, and briefly hugged him with her free arm before facing her father.

"I guess we're on our way. Will you give Mama our goodbyes?"

Jed nodded. "It's late. You four be careful."

"Thanks…Dad," she said, then she covered the baby's head to protect him from the rain and the cold, and hurried outside.

"HOW DO YOU FEEL?" Hope asked Faith, sitting at her bedside eight hours later.

"Better." She was nursing her baby, and even though

it had only been a few hours since they'd checked in to the Richfield Community Medical Center, she already seemed much stronger. Arvin had broken one of her ribs and caused a lot of bruising, which would take a while to heal, but it was a small miracle that neither Faith nor the baby had sustained any serious internal injuries.

"He's so perfect," she said about her baby. "Isn't he?"

Hope nodded and leaned back to close her eyes. She had to rest, just for a minute. She'd had very little sleep over the past week, and the stress of the delivery had depleted her energy.

Parker knocked on the open door before poking his head into the room. He hadn't had a chance to shave during the past couple of days and had purchased a baseball cap somewhere. He looked a little rough around the edges, but Hope felt her pulse leap just the same. He seemed to be having that effect on her more and more.

"Come in," Faith said, pulling her covers a little higher.

Parker strode into the room. When Hope saw he was carrying a tray of food, she groaned. "Oh, no. He's going to make me eat again," she said. "I knew when he said he was going down to the cafeteria I was in trouble."

He managed a wounded expression. "Come on, now. Don't have a bad attitude."

"I'm not hungry," Hope complained.

"You should be starving. It's just a bowl of vegetable soup and some crackers. Eat, and then we'll go and get some sleep. I think Faith's in good hands now."

"Of course she's in good hands," a nurse said, sweeping into the room. "I'm in charge of her while she's here." She took a few minutes to show Faith how to use a syringe to clear the baby's breathing passages, if necessary, checked Faith's blood pressure and collected the tray from Faith's lunch.

"Everything's looking good," she said, pausing at the

foot of the bed. "You ready for me to take your little guy to the nursery so you can get some sleep?"

"Not yet," Faith said.

"Okay. I'll check back with you in half an hour." She started to leave, but paused at the door. "Oh, have you thought of a name for the baby yet? You have three days, of course, but the lady from our records department called. They're waiting to finish the birth certificate."

Faith looked questioningly at Hope. "What do you think? I thought I was going to have a girl."

Hope considered the tiny bundle in her sister's arms. "Do you want to name him after someone in the family?" she asked, crossing her fingers that her sister's answer would be no.

"The men's names are all so old-fashioned," Faith said.

Hope hid a smile at the changes that had taken place in her sister and relaxed. "Then what about Brady? I read about a Brady in a book once and always thought that would be a good boy's name."

Parker set the tray of food he'd brought on the rolling table and pushed it in front of Hope.

Faith lightly patted her baby's bottom. "Brady Tanner…" she said, trying it on for size. "What if I add Mama's maiden name and make it Brady Preston Tanner?"

"That's nice," Parker said.

The nurse nodded. "I agree."

"What do *you* think?" Hope asked Faith.

Her sister smiled. "I think that name is just about as perfect as he is."

HOPE SAT STARING at the number written on the scrap of file folder she'd taken from The Birth Place. Every time she thought about dialing that number, her palms grew moist and her heart began to race. She wasn't sure if she was more afraid that it *would* lead to her daughter or that it wouldn't. The future was so uncertain either way. If she happened to find Autumn, what then? At this point, she had no way of knowing whether the adoptive parents would look kindly on letting her have any type of association with her child. Chances were very good that they wouldn't. But maybe she'd be able to let go of Autumn, if only she could assure herself of her daughter's safety and happiness. After seeing Faith with her baby in the hospital, after holding little Brady in her arms, the need to find Autumn felt even more immediate.

Glancing toward the bathroom, where Parker was taking a shower, she lifted the receiver. The number on the file didn't have an area code, but she was pretty sure that meant it was local to Enchantment. Of course, it would be long-distance from their motel in Richfield, but Hope didn't care about the cost. She'd gladly reimburse Parker as soon as they checked out, since he'd insisted on charging the room to his credit card.

Hope's hand shook as she dialed the number. She wanted to learn *something* about Autumn....

The phone rang several times. Finally an answering machine picked up. "Hello, this is the Barlow residence. We're away from the phone right now, so please leave your name and number and we'll call you back as soon as possible," a woman's voice said.

Hope caught her breath, debated leaving a message, then lost her courage and hung up. It would be better to state her name and her purpose when she could speak to a real person, right?

Barlow. She wrote the name next to the number on the piece of file folder and made little doodles around it as she contemplated this tiny bit of new information. She didn't recognize the name—except for Congressman Barlow—but at least now she could check the records at The Birth Place to see if any Barlows had ever delivered a baby there. If this number belonged to the congressman or one of the center's mothers, it probably wasn't connected to Autumn.

The shower went off and Hope grabbed her purse. She was about to put the number away, but a vision of Faith holding her baby gave her the motivation to dial one more time. She *would* leave a message, she decided. If no one returned her call, she'd try again later.

The answering machine picked up and, gathering her nerve, Hope waited for the beep. "Hello, my name is Hope Tanner," she said when it began to record. "I—I'm not sure I'm calling the right house, but if you have any information regarding a baby girl who was adopted in August of 1993 from The Birth Place in Enchantment, New Mexico, could you please give me a call? Please? I'd really appreciate it."

She left her number in Enchantment and was just hanging up when the bathroom door opened. A wave of steam rolled out, carrying the scent of soap and shampoo. Parker emerged a few seconds later, his hair wet and dripping onto his bare shoulders and chest, a towel wrapped around his lean hips.

"That felt great," he said, pausing at the sink to brush his teeth and comb his hair.

Hope shoved the number back into her purse. "I think I'm ready for a shower, too."

"I thought you were going to take a nap first."

"I've changed my mind." She hurried into the bathroom and closed the door, hoping Parker would be asleep when she got out. Bonner's words went through her mind whenever she looked at him now—*Are you sure he's just a friend?* She was pretty certain the answer to that question was no. She felt an admiration and appreciation for him she'd never felt for anyone else. And she yearned to touch him, to feel his hands on her. Certainly, after years of feeling nothing, that served as *some* indication.

But every time things started drifting that way, he

pulled back. She wasn't about to set herself up for more rejection. Faith and the baby were safe and happy.

She couldn't ask the world for anything more.

HOPE TOOK a long shower to give Parker plenty of time to fall asleep, but when she'd finished, she found him sitting on the edge of the bed watching television. And he was still wearing only a towel.

His eyes turned to her the second she opened the door, and she saw that he looked troubled. "What is it?" she asked.

"I should get a separate room," he said.

"Why?"

"Because I can't sleep when you're so damn close and completely naked."

She blinked in surprise. "I'm wearing a towel!"

"It doesn't matter."

"I thought you had no interest in me."

"I've never said that," he responded.

"Then what?"

"Nothing."

She stepped between his knees and put her arms around his neck. "Tell me what's wrong."

He closed his eyes. "I can't."

"Why?"

"There's nothing wrong."

She didn't believe him, but it was difficult to concentrate because he was starting to tug on her towel. She could feel it loosen and begin to fall away.

"Parker," she said, catching it just in time.

His eyes met hers, then slowly lowered to what he'd almost revealed. "I want you. I want you so badly I can't stop myself, no matter how hard I try."

"What's wrong with that?" she whispered.

"A lot," he said, but he tugged a little harder on her towel, and in the next instant, Hope let it fall away.

He stared at her, then raised a finger to circle the nipple of one breast.

Hope's stomach leaped at the sensation. This was desire, she realized. This was *feeling*. She'd definitely come out of hibernation.

Clenching her hands in his hair, she tilted his face up to receive her kiss. "I want you, too," she said, and touched her lips to his.

He moaned low in his throat as she began to explore his mouth. She'd never been so bold with a man before. But after ten years of being unable to muster much of a response—to anyone—she was drowning in desire. She wanted to make love to Parker Reynolds, here and now, in a glorious celebration of the good things in life. She knew those things existed. She believed in them again.

He pulled her down onto the bed. He still had the towel wrapped around his waist, but he slipped his hands beneath her and rocked her hips so that the pressure of his arousal hit her where she wanted him most.

"You smell so good," he muttered as he kissed her mouth, her neck, her ear.

Hope knew they should probably talk about whatever it was that had been bothering him. But she didn't want to talk. The warmth and wetness of his tongue moving over her nipple was sending euphoria humming through her like a drug, exciting her and relaxing her at the same time.

"Take off the towel," she said.

He leaned up on one elbow and gazed down at her, and that troubled look entered his eyes again. "Hope—"

"Don't tell me," she said. "You don't have any birth control."

"I have birth control."

"Then what?"

He hesitated, as though groping for the right words.

"Parker?" she prompted.

"Nothing." Closing his eyes, he swore under his

breath. Then he got up to get his wallet and pulled the towel away. And when he took her in his arms again, it felt as if every star Hope had ever wished on suddenly came rushing toward her.

CHAPTER TWENTY-TWO

PARKER DIDN'T WANT to get out of bed. But somebody had to answer the phone. The incessant ringing had to be stopped.

"That might be Faith. You'd better get it," he mumbled to Hope.

Hope buried her head under one of their pillows. "No, I think it's Dalton. You wouldn't want to miss his call."

Parker chuckled at how easily she'd sidestepped him and rolled over, running a hand down her bare back. Whoever it was could wait, he thought at first, kissing her shoulder. But then he considered the fact that his son might be missing him or might need him for something, and shoved himself out of bed.

Scratching his chest as he stumbled across the room to reach his cell phone, he squinted against the bright sunlight stabbing through a crack in the draperies. According to the clock, it was ten twenty. They'd slept for nearly fifteen hours.

"Hello?" he said, still reluctant to come to full awareness.

"Parker?" It was Amanda.

"Is Dalton okay?" he asked, growing more alert.

"He's fine. He's in school, where he's supposed to be. But I'm afraid we have a problem. A serious problem."

Parker sat on the foot of the bed across from where Hope was sleeping.

"What kind of problem."

"I just called home to pick up my messages. Some

woman, Hope Something-or-other, left a message asking me to call her if I have any information about a baby girl adopted from The Birth Place in Enchantment ten years ago."

Now Parker was completely lucid and his heart was hammering in his chest. "Say that again?"

"You heard me. Someone called the house, fishing for information about Dalton's adoption. I think it was about his adoption, anyway. The woman mentioned a baby girl, but she had the date and place of Dalton's birth."

"Oh, God." Parker leaned his elbows on his knees and dropped his head into his hands. He'd known he'd have to pay the piper for last night. But he hadn't expected the piper to come collecting quite so soon. He didn't even get to wake up with Hope....

"Parker?" Amanda said.

"What?"

"What should we do?"

That was the million-dollar question. He'd fallen in love with Hope, but that didn't make telling her any safer. It gave him that much more to lose. She was going to hate him when she learned what he'd done. And if she hated him *and* took her son...

How the hell had she tracked down his in-laws?

"I don't know," he admitted.

"What do you mean, you don't know? We need to talk about this and make some careful decisions. If this is Dalton's birth mother nosing around, we have to get rid of her right away. I won't have her coming in at this late date and ruining his life."

Parker glanced at Hope, remembering the way it had felt to make love to her, wanting to make love to her again...and again... "Don't talk about her that way," he said.

"What way?" Amanda asked.

"In that tone of voice."

"Are you experimenting with drugs?"

"Of course not."

"Then what's wrong with you? I tell you Dalton's birth mother might be back, and you tell me to watch my tone of voice when I talk about her? What I want to know is how she got our phone number."

"That's what I want to know, too," he said on a sigh.

"She's obviously after her baby. And I can promise you this—if you let her get anywhere close, you'll be sorry. You have to protect your interests, Parker, or you'll lose Dalton."

He pinched the bridge of his nose. What about Hope's interests? He didn't want to lose Dalton. Dalton meant everything to him. But Hope was quickly coming to mean as much.

"I'll phone you back," he said.

"Parker—"

"I said I'd phone you back, Amanda," he told her, and ended the call.

WHILE HOPE CONTINUED to sleep, Parker stood at the window in nothing but a pair of jeans. He stared through the crack in the draperies at the mostly empty parking lot, going over his conversation with his mother-in-law.

I can promise you this—if you let her get anywhere close, you'll be sorry....

What should he do? Last night, somewhere in the back of his mind, he'd decided to let things develop with Hope and see where they went before he told her anything about Dalton. That plan wasn't quite honest or fair, but it allowed him to pursue his feelings for Hope while keeping Dalton safe.

Now he knew she was tracking down her lost baby and had actually found the right door—which left him with only two choices. He could unite with John and Amanda and continue to lie. If the truth was ever publicized, it would blemish, if not ruin, his father-in-law's career, and John was a powerful, determined man who would stop at almost nothing to preserve his reputation. Parker knew they could safeguard their secret. He saw Hope every day—hell, he was *sleeping* with her. He could easily manipulate the situation to his advantage, keep her guessing, monitor her discoveries, even plant false information to throw her completely off the track.

But did he really want to do that to her when he could give her the one thing she wanted more than anything else? How could he be so callous and selfish?

He folded his arms and leaned against the wall as a man brought a baby in a carrier out of another motel room. The man's wife called to him, and he waited for her. Then they walked to the car together and kissed after tucking their baby inside.

It was a common-enough scene, but it made Parker realize that he wanted to have that same kind of togetherness and trust with Hope. And he wasn't going to achieve that by lying to her. They'd both given their hearts when they'd made love last night. There'd been nothing mechanical about what they'd shared. He couldn't betray something that special, or her, and still respect himself. Not even for Dalton.

He closed his eyes and bumped his head softly against the wall. He had to tell her the truth.

HOPE AWOKE to find Parker standing near the door, looking out the window. When she stirred, he glanced over, but he didn't come back to bed like she wanted him to.

"Hi," she said, feeling a little shy and embarrassed now that she was facing him in the middle of the day. She'd never experienced a night like the one they'd just shared, even with Bonner, and had never felt more fulfilled or complete.

"Hi," he said. "You sleep well?"

She nodded, wondering about his mood. Did he regret what had happened?

Hope drew the blankets up to cover herself and hugged

her knees to her chest, anxiety sweeping through her as she waited to see what he'd say next.

He crossed the room and sat on the bed, loosely clasping his hands between his knees. "You got a call this morning," he announced.

"I did? From Faith?"

"No, from Amanda Barlow."

"Barlow." She felt a rush of excitement. "She called me back?"

He nodded.

"What did she say?" Hope curled her fingernails into her palms and said a silent prayer that he wouldn't tell her she'd bothered some poor woman who'd happened to have a baby at the center at the same time she did. "Does she know anything about my baby?"

He didn't answer right away.

"Parker?"

"She does," he admitted at last, his gaze watchful.

Hope felt her pulse kick up. "And? What does she know? Did she say?"

He cleared his throat. "Well, for starters, she knows the ultrasound technician made a mistake when you were pregnant. Your baby was never a girl."

Hope sucked in her breath and held it as she stared at him. Her baby wasn't a girl? There was no Autumn, no long-lost daughter like the one she'd been dreaming about? "But…that can't be true."

"It's true."

She blinked several times. "You mean I had a son?"

He nodded, and Hope began to suspect there was more going on here than a simple call from the Barlows. She remembered Lydia saying, *He did go to a good home. I told you that*…. She remembered reading about things that had never occurred but were recorded in her file, and Devon, acting so strange when Hope told her about the nightmares, asking if she'd ever mentioned them to her grandmother.

I just think she should know what you're going through....

What had Lydia done?

Whatever it was, Hope had the sudden suspicion that Parker had been in on it. But she didn't want to believe that. She was falling in love with Parker. Lydia and Parker were about the only two people she'd ever trusted.

"Tell me," she said. "Tell me everything."

He raked his fingers through his hair, looking miserable, but Hope couldn't care less about *his* misery. She was too shocked and confused herself.

"Your son didn't go through the normal adoption channels, Hope," he said.

"He didn't?" Nausea threatened, but Hope fought it back. She had to face this. She had to know. "Where did he go?" she asked, her voice barely a whisper.

"To my house," he said.

"MRS. BARLOW is your mother-in-law?" Hope said, the color draining from her face. "And Dalton's my *son?*"

Parker nodded, so terrified he could scarcely breathe. What would she say next? Would she tell him never to touch her again? To expect a court battle for custody of Dalton?

"*You* wanted my baby?"

Parker tried to explain about Vanessa, but everything he said sounded like such a weak excuse for what he'd done. He'd basically guaranteed that Dalton would grow up without a mother. He could see that now. But at the time, he'd truly believed Vanessa might make it.

"I'm sorry," he said. "I know you probably can't forgive me. But I've done my best to take care of him, Hope. I've loved him as my own son, as much as I'm capable of loving another human being. And he's such a good boy." He paused, trying to gain control of his emotions. "I think you'd be proud of him."

She sat staring blankly for several seconds and didn'
respond.

"After last night, I know you probably won't want to
see me again," he continued. "But I—" he took a bol
stering breath and fought to keep his voice steady "—bu
I'd really like to go on seeing you if you can ever forgive
me."

She blinked and focused on him. "And Dalton?"

"I'd like us both to be part of his life. I know he'
love you. It would be good for him to have a mother—
his mother."

Parker was sure he could hear his own heartbeat in the
silence that followed.

"Why did you finally tell me?" Hope asked.

He thought about how much he'd agonized over the
decision and realized there was only one answer. "Be
cause I love you."

Her eyes widened and she pressed a hand to her ches
as though she was having difficulty breathing. "I don'
know what to say. I don't even know what to think."

Parker could imagine a few things he'd like her to say
"I forgive you...I love you...I can't wait to be part o
Dalton's life." Anything along those lines would be nice
but he knew it was too much to hope for.

"Hope—" He intended to tell her it might take time
to sort out her feelings, that he was sure they could work
through this, that he'd prove himself to her eventually
But she cut him off as though she'd already heard more
than enough.

"I mean, I can't even imagine that Dalton is..." He
words faltered, but she tried again. "I can't believe there'
no Autumn." She shook her head helplessly. "And
you...you knew all along and you didn't tell me."

"I couldn't risk Dalton, Hope. I know that sounds lame
but..." It did sound lame, so lame he couldn't continue
How could a man justify what he'd done? He couldn't
"I'm sorry," he muttered again.

Suddenly she sprang to her feet. "I have to go. I have to get out of here and…and go."

A fresh wave of fear assaulted him. "Where?"

"I don't know. I can't deal with this right here, with you, with…what happened last night. I need some time to think."

"Take my truck," he said, standing to dig the keys out of his pocket. He hated to let her go anywhere without him, but he definitely didn't want her on foot.

"I can't," she said, tears gathering in her eyes. "I…I don't know if I'm coming back." She grabbed her purse and left, and Parker knew better than to stop her. But letting her go was the second-hardest thing he'd ever done.

Telling her had been the first.

FAITH SQUEEZED Hope's hand, effectively gaining her attention. "You going to be okay?"

"I don't know," Hope said. "I—I trusted Parker. Now I feel so numb and…and—"

"But he has your child, Hope." Faith's voice was filled with awe and excitement. "And he's willing to share him. Doesn't that count for something?"

"It counts for a lot. That's what I keep telling myself, too. But he's had my child for ten years. He and Lydia *lied* to me, they betrayed the only trust I had to give…"

"They were wrong," Faith said. "There's no question about that. But Parker didn't *have* to tell you, even now. He could've let you go right on believing you'd had a girl."

"I might have found out," Hope said, because she didn't want to see any good in Parker. She couldn't love him and hate him at the same time, but that was exactly what she seemed to be doing. "I was starting to search for her."

"You might not have found anything. Parker risked his heart and the son he adores—"

"I don't want to talk about it anymore," Hope interrupted.

"I think we should," Faith replied, her assertiveness surprising Hope. When had her sister matured so much?

"What good can possibly come from rehashing such a—"

"Such a miracle?" Faith inserted.

A miracle? "Learning that the only two people I've trusted since leaving Superior betrayed me—that's a miracle?"

"It's not a miracle to find your child? To know that Dalton's always been safe and loved, that he's had a wonderful father like Parker? Isn't your child's health and happiness the one thing you've always prayed for?"

Hope stared at her sister, feeling a tingle go through her whole body. "Of course it is."

"Then think of this—if your baby had been adopted by another family, chances are you'd never have had the opportunity to know him. When you look at the situation like that, Parker did you a huge favor—when he took Dalton, when he kept him there in Enchantment where you could find him again, when he cared for him so well." She hesitated, then added softly, "And when he offered to love you, too."

Hope felt the warmth of tears on her face. For the first time in ages, she couldn't hold them back. It *was* a miracle. She already had Faith and Brady. Now, if she could only find a little forgiveness in her heart, she'd have Dalton and Parker. No more nightmares. No more living alone without love. No more not knowing.

Maybe someday they could be a family....

"Can't you forgive him?" Faith pressed.

Hope sniffed and smiled through her tears. She certainly wasn't living in the background anymore. Everything she felt was so acute, so poignant. But she was grateful to be alive again. That was a small miracle in itself.

"I can forgive him," she said at last, and picked up the phone.

Parker answered on the first ring. "Hope?"

"It's me," she said.

Silence fell, and she knew he was waiting. "I—I'm at the hospital. Will you come get me?"

HOPE SAT ACROSS from Parker at the International House of Pancakes. Because it was midafternoon, the place wasn't busy, which meant their waitress had a little too much time on her hands. She kept swinging by their booth with the coffeepot to see if they needed a refill.

"Are you okay?" Parker asked as the waitress filled their cups for the third time in about fifteen minutes.

Hope felt better than she'd felt in years. And yet she was almost afraid to embrace the optimism that had enveloped her at the hospital. Was Faith right? Was she looking at a miracle? Or would Parker turn out to be more of a mirage?

"I'm fine." She poured some more sugar into her coffee, being careful to keep her attention on what she was doing. She and Parker had so much to discuss, but she was almost afraid to hear what he had to say, and he seemed just as tentative.

"What are you thinking?" he prompted.

She finally raised her eyes to meet his. He looked good, she thought. He wasn't wearing anything special, just a faded pair of jeans and a T-shirt, but he'd showered and shaved and she couldn't help admiring the strong line of his jaw. She remembered lying with her head on his chest last night listening to his heartbeat after they'd made love, and wondered where their relationship would go from here.

"I'm thinking about you," she admitted.

"I was afraid of that." His hands circled his coffee cup, but he didn't lift it to his mouth. "Tell me they're good thoughts."

"Last night was…good," she said, and felt herself blush.

He chuckled, looking slightly relieved. "That's a great place to start. I was hoping you'd feel that way."

She set her spoon aside. "What should we do about Dalton?"

He rubbed his chin in what appeared to be a casual motion, but his eyes were watchful, and she knew that risking Dalton hadn't been easy for him. "For his sake, I'd like you to give him time. I'd like to introduce you and let you develop a relationship with him. I know he'll love you. But I don't think we should spring any big surprises on him until he's familiar with you and… attached."

Hope could see the logic in what Parker suggested. She didn't want to upset Dalton, either. She thought he could only benefit from full cooperation between the two of them and wanted to slip into his life as seamlessly as possible. "Okay. So where does that leave us?"

He reached across the table to take her hand. "That's what I'm waiting to hear."

"What type of relationship are you looking for?"

"A close one," he said. He stroked her fingers, but his gaze never strayed from her face. "I'm in love with you, Hope."

Those words made Hope feel as though she'd just barreled down the first tall hill of a roller coaster.

"Do you think you could ever love me back?" he asked.

She folded her arms in an attempt to control the flutter in her stomach, and he frowned as she pulled away. "Is that a no?"

"It's not a no. It's just…it's just that things are happening so fast. I don't know what to believe."

"We can work through the past, Hope," he said.

"We'll make up for everything you've missed. Will you at least give us a chance?"

Hope took another sip of her coffee, then nodded.

HOPE WATCHED Parker load the truck. Faith wasn't out of the hospital yet, but he needed to drive Hope back to Enchantment so she could pick up her own car. It might be Friday afternoon, the beginning of the weekend for most people, but after heading home to see Dalton, he planned to start getting caught up on all the work he'd missed.

When he noticed her standing at the door watching him, he turned. "You all set?" he asked.

She glanced back into the room, amazed by everything that had happened in such a short time. She'd lost her heart. She'd found her son.

"What's up?" he asked. "You've been so quiet."

"I've been thinking."

"About…"

"You—again."

"Uh-oh." He gave her a devilish grin and came over to wrap his arms around her. "That always worries me," he said, nipping at her neck. "Tell me you're thinking about last night, because that's about all *I* can think about."

She laughed. This man had brought her to Faith's side. He'd supported her through her darkest hour—twice now, if she counted ten years ago when he'd befriended her. "Actually I'm thinking about tonight, and tomorrow night, and the night after."

He cocked an eyebrow at her. "That sounds promising."

"I just realized something."

"What's that?"

"I don't want to sleep without you."

He brushed a kiss across her lips. "I can make arrangements to ensure that if you want," he said, his voice going slightly husky.

She let her fingers delve into his thick hair and kissed

him again, this time more deeply. God, he felt good to her. He felt better than anything she'd ever experienced. Surely *that* was something she could trust. "You can?" she said.

"Mm-hm. But there's only one thing."

"What's that?"

"We have a ten-year-old boy."

"Which means…"

"We'd better get married first, don't you think?"

Married… The roller-coaster sensation returned.

Hope took Parker's face between her hands so she could look him in the eye. "Are you serious, Parker? Marriage, already?"

"How long does it take to know you want to spend your life with someone?" he asked. "That you've finally found the one person you were meant to be with from the beginning?"

Not long, she decided. Because, when she closed her eyes, she could already see herself wearing Parker's ring, bearing his children, helping him raise Dalton. "I can picture us together," she said.

"Then picture this. You, me and Dalton in Vegas as soon as possible."

"Vegas?" Hope thought of the wedding she'd always envisioned for herself, but that type of ceremony suddenly seemed very hollow. "No," she said. "I want to wait until Dalton gets to know me. And then when he's okay with the changes in his life—" she felt a smile coming on and knew Faith, at least, would appreciate what she was about to say "—I want to be married in a church."

HOPE TOOK a deep breath to calm her nerves. "Do I look okay?" she asked Parker.

He smiled and squeezed her hand before ringing the doorbell to his in-laws' large rambler in Taos. "You look great," he said. "You have nothing to worry about, any way. Holt's mother is short and plump with curly black hair.''

''*Holt's* mother?''

''Never mind,'' he said as an older woman with a long, rather pointed nose and pure white hair swept up off her face answered the door. She was wearing a tasteful amount of cosmetics, a few expensive-looking diamond rings and conservative designer clothes—a pair of black slacks, a white silk blouse, expensive Italian shoes and a red jacket. She looked like the type of woman who'd always belonged to a country club.

''Parker!'' she said, stepping back in surprise. ''You told us not to expect you until after the weekend.'' Her cool, gray eyes cut immediately to Hope. ''Who's this?''

Parker let go of Hope's hand and put his arm around her, instead. Hope knew it was more than a gesture of affection—it was a show of support. ''Amanda, this is Hope Tanner.''

Amanda pressed one of her bejeweled hands to her chest, and her mouth opened and closed twice before she found her voice. ''Hope *Tanner?*''

''That's right. You remember. She left a message on your answering machine the day before last. And now I've brought her to meet her son.''

Amanda stepped out of the house, carefully closing the door behind her. ''Have you lost your mind, Parker?'' she said, keeping her voice low. ''Think of the shock this is going to be for Dalton. He doesn't even know he was adopted, for God's sake.''

''Relax,'' Parker said, his voice calm and smooth. ''Nothing's going to change right away. He knows I've been seeing quite a lot of Hope and he wants to meet her—that's all. We won't tell him anything until we both agree he's ready.''

''And how will you know when he's ready?'' she asked.

''It probably won't be until after we're married,'' Parker said. "By then he'll probably be calling her Mom, anyway."

"M-married?" Amanda echoed. She looked as if she'd just been struck, but she didn't have time to say anything else because the door swung open behind her, and a young boy with dark hair and hazel eyes poked his head outside.

"Dad!" he said, flinging himself at Parker the moment he spotted them. "I'm so glad you're back. Look what Grandma's been making me wear." He pulled away to show his father the creased khakis, loafers and stiff white shirt that had been forced on him. "I look like Grandpa," he said with disgust.

Hope had felt her knees go weak at the first sight of her child. He was thin, like her father, but he had her mother's thick, unruly hair, with a Dennis the Menace cowlick. And his eyes seemed so...bright.

She'd dreamed of this moment ever since she'd given birth.

"Dalton, this is Hope," Parker said, turning him by the shoulders.

"Hi, Dalton," Hope said, her heart in her throat. She wanted to put her arms around him and hold him close, but she knew it was too soon. There'd be time for that, she promised herself. She and Parker were going to be married in a few months. Then they'd be living together as a family in Parker's house, along with Faith and Brady, and she'd be caring for Dalton as if she'd never lost him.

"Hi," he replied, smiling shyly.

"Your father and I were planning to take you out for ice cream, if it's okay with your grandmother," Hope said.

His eyes brightened even more. "Can I change my clothes first?"

"As far as I'm concerned, a pair of jeans is good enough," Hope told him.

"Great." He released a dramatic sigh and grinned up at Parker. "I *told* you I'd like her."

He dashed into the house to change, leaving them with Amanda once again.

Hope tried not to squirm as Dalton's grandmother frowned at her. ''A scandal won't bode well for anyone,'' she said as soon as Dalton was out of earshot.

''There won't be a scandal,'' Hope said. ''The past is the past. We're going to leave it where it is.''

''We're just not going to let the past rob us of a future,'' Parker added. Then he smiled the smile Hope had come to love.

*   *   *   *   *

Please turn the page to read an excerpt from the next book in THE BIRTH PLACE *series from Superromance Join us for a Christmas in Enchantment! Meet Dr. Joanna Weston (and her entourage!) as she comes to Enchantment to create a new beginning...* CHRISTMAS AT SHADOW CREEK *by Roxanne Rustand is available in November wherever Harlequin books are sold.*

CHAPTER ONE

DR. JOANNA WESTON had finally arrived in Enchantment, New Mexico.

The trip had been anything but easy. A thousand miles of driving, a flat tire and a two-day layover to replace a carburetor. And she'd been so careful, taking the steep, hairpin turns at a crawl, coasting to stops, and taking rest breaks every three hours so her latest acquisition—an old, lame paint gelding—could clamber out of his trailer to stretch his tired muscles.

He should have been grateful for finding himself in New Mexico, instead of a glue factory.

Instead, five minutes ago, he'd taken one look at the split-rail fence surrounding his new pasture, broken into a lope and cleared it with ease. His tail raised like a banner of victory, he gave a few hard bucks before disappearing into the aspen-and-pine studded foothills surrounding Joanna's cabin. Hills that steadily climbed higher into the Sangre de Cristo Mountains. Uninhabited, unfenced and endless, from what she could see.

Snagging the halter and rope she'd just hung on a nail by the door, Joanna scooped up a small bucket of feed and hurried through the pasture gate by the barn.

She crossed the parched grass at a jog, muttering under her breath. The same impulsive behavior that had led her to attend that San Diego horse sale in late Augsut had also made her step on the brakes while passing an animals shelter a few days afterward. Moose, her large Great Pyrenees puppy was the result of that stop. ''Buying a family?'' her ex-husband, Allen, had chided coolly at the last county medical meeting she'd attended. "You really ought to consider therapy, Jo."

Something she'd seriously considered after he left their marriage last year for a twenty-two-year-old charm with a Victoria's Secret body and the giddy smile of a teenager. But moving here for a few months to fill in for a local pediatrician was probably the best therapy she could have found. And a gentle old horse and faithful dog would surely be better company and more dependable than Allen.

As she climbed through the gnarled fence rails at the far side of the pasture and entered government land, she bent to break off a wiry stem of sagebrush. The peppery, pungent scent of the tiny silver-green leaves tickled her nose.

After another fifteen minutes, she stopped in the shade of a massive boulder and decided she hadn't been particularly wise. A water bottle would have been a good idea, given the arid climate and heavy dust that rose with her every step.

Unaccustomed to Enchantment's altitude—over eight thousand feet in town and even higher here—she felt breathless and a little nauseous. A headache started throbbing behind her eyes. The sun was already settling low on the horizon.

Calling Galahad's name one last time, she listened for distant hoofbeats, but heard nothing beyond the crisp rattling of aspen leaves overhead. With a heavy heart, she turned to go home. When she reached the cabin, she would call the sheriff and report her lost horse. With luck, maybe someone would see him and at least report his general location.

An unexpected splash of red caught her eye as she started back down a different path.

Through the shadows, she could make out the form of someone slumped against a boulder a few dozen yards away. She stilled as dozens of old news reports rushed through her thoughts. Serial killers. Escaped convicts, gone missing in remote areas.

The city girl in her sent urgent warnings. *Time to get home. Now.*

But the splash of red wasn't moving.

What if this was an innocent hiker, bleeding to death after a fall? Or an older person who was confused and lost?

Wishing she had her cell phone—though the reception had been poor even back at the cabin—she edged a few feet closer.

She could see the guy better now, though he was facing in the opposite direction and didn't seem aware of her. Western hat, dark hair, a flannel shirt of red plaid. Spurs glinted at the heels of his boots, so he hadn't been hiking.

He slowly rose to his feet, using the rocks at his side for leverage, and settled his hat lower on his head. He began hobbling in the opposite direction.

She hesitated, then noticed the gash on the side of his jaw and the ragged tear along the thigh of his jeans. "Hey!" she called out. "Are you okay?"

His head jerked around and he stared at her in obvious surprise. Beneath the shadow of his hat brim she saw a strong, square jaw, narrow nose and warm brown eyes. He was in his mid-thirties, maybe.

"Lose your horse?" she asked, approaching slowly.

When his gaze fell to the halter slung over her shoulder and the bucket of grain in her hand, his mouth twitched. "Apparently you've lost yours. Let me guess—a big, skinny, black-and-white paint gelding."

"You saw him?" Relief flooded her. "Really? Was he okay?"

"Oh, yeah. Well enough to barrel around those boulders at roughly the speed of light and knock my filly right off her feet. I don't know which animal was more surprised."

Remorse slid through Joanna as she imagined how badly this man could have been hurt. Killed, maybe. "Gosh, my gelding is really so gentle. I'm sure he didn't mean any harm."

She thought she saw the guy roll his eyes at that one. "No harm done. Except that now both horses are probably hightailing it up into the hills or heading towards my ranch. Together."

"You think Galahad followed? Really?"

"Galahad?"

She felt her cheeks warm. "I...um...visited my first horse auction on a lark a few weeks ago. I told the guy next to me that I thought Galahad was pretty, and he said that only the kill buyers would bid on the horse, because he was lame."

"You bought a *lame gelding?*" His voice was filled with disbelief. "At a *sale?*"

"They would have killed him! I know I can't ride him—there was just something about him that I couldn't ignore." She lifted her shoulders. "Anyway, he's a sweet old guy."

"Well, ma'am, I'm sure he is." Given the lift of one corner of the man's mouth and the patient expression in his eyes, he probably considered her a foolish city slicker.

Not that it mattered. After Allen, she had absolutely no use for any man with a superiority complex—and that pretty much took care of every man she knew. If this guy thought she was inept, so be it.

"It's gonna be dark in less than an hour, ma'am. You'd better get home." He reached for his back pocket, wincing as he retrieved a worn leather wallet. From inside he withdrew a business card. "I'd sure be glad to help you get home, but my transportation left without me."

"I'm so—"

He waved away her second apology. "Don't worry about it. Call tomorrow and I'll let you know if your horse turns up at my place. Or,'' he added, ''you can let me know if my filly shows up at yours.''

''You should let me take a look at your injuries,'' she murmured as she accepted the card. *Ben Carson, Shadow Creek Ranch. Quarter horses and Charolais cattle.* ''Do you feel dizzy? Did you hit your head?''

He raised a brow.

The laceration on his cheek was still bleeding a little, and when he didn't answer, her concern deepened. ''I'm a doctor, for heaven's sake. Consider this free roadside service. Your lucky day.''

''Lucky,'' he echoed dryly. ''But no thanks.''

''I don't live all that far from here. At least let me give you a lift home.''

''No, ma'am.'' He started limping away, but the slick leather sole of one of his boots slipped on the rocks once again, sending a volley of pebbles ricocheting down the rocky slope. Swearing under his breath, he leaned over, his hands braced on his thighs.

Men. If there was a gene for bullheadedness, it surely had to be linked to the Y chromosone.

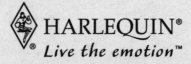